Chicago Crime Story

A true-crime novel inspired by actual events

By

Frank Goff

Published by SuburbanBuzz.com, LLC

ISBN: 978-1-7360820-8-9

DEDICATION

This book is dedicated to my brother, retired Chicago Police Officer Gerry Goff #8481, born November 16, 1957. He died on April 7, 2022, and was highly decorated during his twenty-one years with the CPD, including The Award Of Valor.

Gerry was assigned to the 8th District and the Mass Transit Unit. He served on active duty in the United States Marine Corps for six years. He earned a bachelor's degree in criminology and was the proud father of five.

My brother was the funniest man I've ever known, and I'll always cherish his sense of humor. He had a big heart and always looked out for others. I wish he had done the same for himself.

Officers, please reach out for help when you are faced with your demons. You have people who love you and are willing to help. You owe it to your loved ones, but most of all, you owe it to yourself.

Rest In Peace, my dear brother.

TABLE OF CONTENTS

Introduction: I Never Thought I'd Carry a Badge

As a kid, I loved to play cops and robbers, like all the other guys in the neighborhood. It was a game, and it was fun. The difference is that a game is over at the end of the day. I found out later in life that when you aren't playing, life is real and sometimes hits you hard…nightmares follow. Not just for me but for any cop that's worked the street and has come face to face with the devil. Each case impacts you as both a cop and a human being. This is my story, but it could very well be the story of any number of cops who took the time to put pen to paper.

If things didn't happen the way they did, my life would have taken a different path, and that wouldn't have been a desirable one. Thankfully, I was arrested at the age of thirteen for being in possession of a sawed-off shotgun, and that contact with law enforcement changed my life.

Every single chapter in this book is true. I use the real names of cops and judges involved. I do not use the victim or the witnesses' real names. Instead you will see a # once in front of the alias I gave them. I did the same with some officers at their request.

After writing my first book *The Guardian*, officers often asked why I hadn't included some of the more dangerous parts of the job, like officer involved shootings, especially by the officers I teach through Pat McCarthy's Street Crimes Program. I was reluctant for a number of reasons, but since there has been so much interest generated, I've included some of these stories in this book.

I hope that by sharing the life-threatening experiences, officers and the general public will better understand what the cop on the street faces on a daily basis and hopefully open the eyes of newer officers about the inherent dangers they may face and how they might avoid them. Most of all, I want cops to learn from my mistakes.

CAUTION

Note that conversations in quotes are real and always taken directly from case reports, GPRs, personal notes on the scene, memory, and conversations with officers involved in every chapter of this book.

With that said, there is rough language ahead and real-life portrayals of what happens on the mean streets of Chicago. Don't even attempt to read this book if the harsh reality of what goes on in the real world, coupled with accurate descriptions of the criminals involved; and the verbiage they use is too intense for you, stop right here. Grab a box of crayons and a coloring book and seek out a safe space for yourself. That space is not between the front and back covers of this book. It exists only in the bubble of the politically correct, paper doll world you believe exists.

Chapter 1: First Blood

It was like someone had just popped the cork on a bottle of champagne. The smell and flavor were not of an alcoholic brew but one of iron. That's what blood tastes like.

I was kneeling over him, doing my best to stem the crimson flow pulsating from his neck with each beat of his young heart. Even though I tried, I knew it wasn't enough. The warm slather of thickened blood quickly found its way down my uniform shirt. The top three buttons were opened to help ward off the heat on this muggy summer afternoon in Chicago.

My heart pounded so hard that I thought the growing crowd of neighbors could hear it as well. My head was pounding too. I was scared, not for me but for him. His situation looked as bad as it could be.

Bright blue eyes focused on mine, and an already weakened voice was fading fast. "I want Momma."

Pink foam oozed through his orange tee-shirt, and he coughed up more blood. This time it graced his chin. His injuries were serious — a sucking chest wound and massive blood loss. Even with my lack of any special lifesaving skills, it was clear he wasn't going to survive. I knew it, and so did my partner, who was talking on the radio as I looked up at him, hoping for some guidance.

In a voice barely above a whisper, the boy tried to say something. I leaned closer, intent on not missing what I knew would be his last words.

"Policeman, am I gonna die?"

I hadn't realized it, but he held my finger on his chest while his eyes searched mine for an answer. All the loud voices, chatter, and traffic sounds around me vanished. I focused every bit of attention I could muster on this little guy. This was going to be the most important next few minutes of both of our lives. The last moments of his life were as valuable to me as they were to him. I didn't want him to die feeling alone or without that spark of hope I would give him. So I lied.

"No. I'm gonna take care of you. What's your name?"

The blood was no longer forcing its way out of his body. It was down to a trickle, so I moved my hand away from his chest. He was struggling to breathe, and this gave him a few last breaths. He coughed, and through the gurgling sounds, I managed to make out the name Billy…before he closed his eyes for the last time. I estimate no more than thirty seconds had passed since I came in contact with him and when he died. I didn't know what to do. I didn't want to stand up and leave him, so I stayed on my knees and let him hold on for a little while longer. His grip had faded, but the warmth in his hand had not. I squeezed his finger, hoping that somehow he knew he was not alone. I realized how intimate the moment of death was, even though it was shared with a stranger. We were connected forever…

A woman was screaming over the howling sounds of responding units, including the fire department.

"Where's my son? Where's Billy?"

Her neighbors tried to hold her back as she made her way through the crowd. I'm sure they meant well, probably having seen that on TV. But this was real life.

"Let her through." My words were wasted; it was obvious that nothing would stop this mom.

The look on her face said it all. Pure heartbreak, shock, and disbelief all rolled into a snapshot. Even today, just the thought of that encounter, as brief as it was, is etched in my memory forever. She cradled her son; a gut-wrenching shriek echoed around us, a sound that only the mother of a suddenly dead child could utter.

We shouldn't have been here. We worked on the other side of the bridge in the 18th District, but my partner Harry Gould wanted me to stop a traffic violator. So I activated the Mars light and pulled the driver over but not before he crossed the bridge and ended up in the adjoining 14th District.

After Harry wrote the ticket and I started to swing the car around to get back to where we belonged, we heard them. Three rapid gunshots rang out from the 1500 block of North Greenview Street.

"Did you hear that, Harry?"

"Yeah…it's not our beat but let's check it out."

I was happy to hear him say that because Harry had thirty-five years on the job and wasn't looking to be a hero at this stage of the game. I'm sure he remembered being the new kid and could sense my anticipation. I slammed the accelerator to the floor and rounded the corner in time to see the construction workers running toward Billy.

It didn't dawn on me until later that they were all wearing jeans and orange shirts, just like Billy. It turned out that he had been hanging around the site and wanted to dress like them too. According to the workers, Billy had worn the same clothes for the last three days.

Two of the workers had taken a liking to him because he was always watching and asking questions. One of them told me that Billy was very respectful and careful not to get in their way. The other worker said that it really seemed like the boy was grasping what they were telling him about their carpentry work.

Billy wasn't just a watcher; he was helpful. He volunteered to pick up scrap cutoffs and throw them into the dumpster in exchange for a "flat piece" of wood to make something for his mom. The guys let him pick out a nice scrap of common board and watched as he busied himself by carving into it with a large discarded nail. When the guys took a break, Billy showed them the finished product. The crew reviewed his handiwork and agreed on one thing. It needed a little touch-up to be perfect for Mom. One of the carpenters asked if he could add a little something to Billy's project. Billy agreed but told them not to ruin it. The carpenter cut the 12 x 12 piece of scrap into a heart shape and said Billy was overjoyed with the change.

He was standing against the fence, admiring this new version of the gift, when a car pulled up. The workers didn't think much of it when the four male Hispanic passengers motioned Billy to the car, figuring he must know them from the neighborhood. That was until the crew's foreman heard Billy yell out, "Hey, don't do that!"

It was a gang initiation, and like so many of them, entry into the gang requires a prospect to pull the trigger, not necessarily to kill someone but to at least shoot them. That way, they knew the guy could be trusted as part of the gang, and he was not an undercover cop or a police informant. It also let his fellow gangbangers know he could be trusted when things went bad with a rival gang.

Billy was wearing the wrong colors in this neighborhood. He lost his life at the age of twelve for some insane bullshit.

The beat car assigned to the job came from the 14th District. The siren wound down and stopped with a sudden grunt. Two older guys got out of the squad, wiping sweat from their brows as they came toward us.

"Did you guys get this on-view?"

"Yeah," said Harry, "I was writing a ticket on North Avenue when we heard some shooting."

Unbeknownst to me, Harry had already broadcast a description of the wanted vehicle and offenders that he got from some of the other witnesses on the street.

"All right, guys, we got it from here. Just write down your information and tell us what you know. Awww... too bad, it looks like the kid's gone."

It seemed so matter of fact to me as a young cop. The words were cold and spoken without any emotion. It gave me the impression that they had seen this story play out so many times, that it became commonplace and therefore had no effect on them. That brief encounter has played itself out over and over in my head for untold hours since that day. It's the kind of thing that haunts every police officer, whether they admit it or not.

The time came for Harry and me to get back to the other side of the bridge. Our end of the job was over, and my shirt was covered with blood. I didn't have a clean one, and it was too far to sneak home, but Harry would take care of that.

First, he had to ball-bust me. "You ready to get some lunch, kid?"

He didn't need to ask. I've always had the capability of eating anytime, day or night.

"Sure, Harry, but we should make it to go. I can't go to a restaurant like this."

"Ahh, I see what ya mean. Let's go to your locker and get a clean one."

"I don't have a locker, Harry."

Harry knew this as lockers were in short supply in the basement of the 18th District, and only a select few had them. Another requirement to getting one was to drop some cash to the secretary in the commander's office. This was a tactic employed by some to jump the waiting line.

"Well, we're about the same size. Let's see if one of mine will fit you; head into the station."

When we walked in, Harry led the way and was obviously doing so for a reason. He grabbed the loudspeaker from the desk sergeant and proceeded with his monologue.

"Attention all units currently in the 18th District station. I have an announcement to make. Please put down whatever you're doing and listen to this important message from beat number 1831. Let it be known by one and all that on this date, Probationary Patrolman Frank Goff was fully baptized. I don't know if he's of the Catholic persuasion, but he has been anointed. Come witness this event in person at the front desk."

Captain Harold Thomas was the first one to come around
the corner and look at my blood-stained shirt.

"That's an understatement. Do you have a prisoner to go with that, or…?"

"No, sir."

"Good." Then he shook my hand and went back into the watch commander's office.

A few guys patted me on the back. "Welcome to the club, Goff."

"The first of many," said one old-timer.

Now to most people, this scenario would seem to be strangely irreverent under the circumstances, but I would eventually become used to the "gallows humor," something frequently used by cops, combat vets, and emergency room personnel. It's a way of mentally separating yourself for your own sanity from the carnage you witness on the streets. Besides that, none of them had witnessed what I had today. But I'm sure at one time or another, we had a shared experience.

"Let's go downstairs and see what we can do to make you look presentable to the public."

"I appreciate that, Harry."

"Here ya go, try this one on. It's clean."

I was thrilled to put on Harry's shirt. Its center patch had the number 18 designator in the middle, framed by rockers that said Chicago Police Dept. My patch, on the other hand, had the letters A.S. in the center, which stood for Administrative Services. In other words, I was a probationary policeman, a rookie. Not a full-fledged "be on the street by yourself" cop.

The A.S. did have its benefits, however. Whenever I was on a call, and an attractive woman would ask what the A.S. stood for. I was quick to respond, "Available and Single." I can't remember if that ever worked out, but I always gave it a shot.

When we made it to the restaurant, I sat with the vet's patch facing out. On every call, I made it a point to turn so Harry Gould's patch was what they saw on my sleeve. Unless you're a rookie cop, you'd never understand the feeling. I'm just putting it out there for those who know.

The end of the shift came, and I drove home slower than usual. I had a lot on my mind. All the way, the only thing I could think about was Billy. I couldn't believe that I saw a kid go from life to death, looking at me with fear in his eyes and trust in his heart after I told him he wasn't going to die. He was probably thinking, *The policeman is here...he will save me.*

I was so disappointed in my performance that I couldn't adequately put it into words. I wondered if I had done something different... would the outcome have been the same?

Once in my apartment, I turned off the two lights I always left on when I wasn't home. I sat on the floor with my back to the sofa in the darkened room for hours. I relived the scene with Billy over and over and over in my head. *My lack of crucial first aid skills may have hastened if not caused his death*, I thought. I second-guessed everything I did on the street that evening. I also wondered why Harry didn't help me and show me what to do the right way. Or maybe he didn't because he could tell just by his experience that the situation was futile. I don't know the answer to that, but I truly believe it was the latter.

I sat there thinking about how long I had looked forward to becoming a policeman and now had second thoughts about that decision. Maybe at the age of twenty, I wasn't cut out for the job.

Being a cop put me in a position that many older guys wanted to be in. They still hadn't made it to the ranks of the CPD, and a lot of them were still trying to get on the job and expressing their frustration with the hiring process. After tonight, one of them could have my spot.

As much as I enjoyed the camaraderie and experiencing the thrill of the chase, I needed to do some soul searching. Would what I saw on the street today with the interaction of the salty veteran cops turn out to be me in a few years? Would I lose part of my soul and become so cold and jaded that the sight of a child bleeding out on the filthy street be just a normal part of my work night? If so, I had better make a decision while I was young enough to move on...and that thought remained with me until the following day at roll call on the second floor of the 18th District.

A guy I went through the Police Academy with was back from his days off. Eddie Griffin and I took turns driving to and from the Academy every day. Though we weren't partners yet, we knew that we would work together once we were off probation. I looked forward to working with him. Ed was a few years older and a Vietnam veteran — smart, single, and the guy who taught me to drink. We socialized a lot during our off-duty hours, which always included massive amounts of alcohol and good times.

Besides that, Ed lived only two blocks from me, so we could take turns driving to and from work most of the time, just like before. We drove to work separately on this particular day because I was coming straight from court.

When Eddie walked into the roll call room, he greeted me with his customary smile and usual comment, "How many felonies did you get while I was off, Dog Ass?" Now, depending on how the term Dog Ass was used, it could be a term of affection or denigration. I'm assuming this was not the latter.

The felony question was an inside joke. His good-natured attitude made me think that we'd have a blast working together in the future. So thanks to Eddie, I shelved the idea of leaving the job on the spot. I never told him what was on my mind, but I'm sure he would have talked me out of it at Mike's Bar on Webster or Sheehan's in Bridgeport.

Chapter 2: The Old Town Capers

We were working the midnight shift in Old Town. I was still on probation but lucky enough to get partnered with another younger cop. His name was Dave Chana. He had about five years on the job and was as aggressive as I was, if not more so. We hit it off right away. After taking our first report of the night, he liked that I didn't need to ask him for his Star number again for the reports I wrote the rest of the night. I memorized it and still remember it to this day — 14856. Dave was more than willing to stop anything anytime, anywhere, and teach me what I didn't know. That was a lot.

We were working in an area known as Old Town. It was unique in that it was known for an abundance of people from many different backgrounds. You name it, and Old Town had it. Old Town bordered the wealthiest part of the district known as the Gold Coast and, in particular, Astor Street, which was a few blocks east. With that being said, it was also a stone's throw from the poorest and most crime-ridden part of the district. The Cabrini Green housing project was a hotbed of activity around the clock. In addition to those demographics, we were only a minute's drive to all the bars and businesses on State Street, Rush Street, and Division Street. So it was a happening area.

Our night started like it normally did. We had already handled a tavern fight and two domestics, which is pretty typical for any shift on the midnights. Our next call was to go to the Henrotin Hospital at 939 No. LaSalle Street in regards to a rape victim.

The victim of the sexual assault was twenty-four years old and had been barhopping at several singles bars the area is well known for. She had a few cocktails, as one would expect, but wasn't drunk by any stretch.

The bad guy's modus operandi was to approach a young woman walking at night and say, "Oh Miss, you dropped something." When the woman stopped to look, he produced a handgun and forced her into a stairwell, where he proceeded to beat, rob, and rape her. Our victim was the second and, fortunately, as it turned out, his last victim....that I knew of anyway. She was new to Chicago and had just moved to the area from a small town in Indiana for a job in advertising.

We parked at the ER entrance, and the doors of Henrotin automatically opened.

"Excuse me, nurse, what room is our victim in?"

The ER nurse on duty was dating one of the older cops in the district and gave me a puzzled look.

"Victim? Which one are you here for, the gunshot, the rape, or the stabbing?"

"The rape."

"She's in there," the nurse answered, pointing to the second room as she'd done in this busy hospital hundreds of times.

I started to walk into the room where a curtain hid my victim from view, but Dave grabbed my arm.

"Hold on; ya just can't walk in there. She may not be decent yet, and she might not want to talk to a male officer. So ask her if she's okay with that or would like a female. But call out her name and identify yourself before you go in and see what she says."

I'm glad Dave stopped me, and he was right.

"Excuse me, Miss, it's the police. Can I talk to you about what happened?"

"Okay, just let me finish putting my clothes back on."

"Ummm....we might need those as evidence," I said, not at all prepared for her response.

"I'll talk to you about that when I'm done dressing...okay, you can come in now."

She was pretty and petite, maybe five feet tall and ninety-five pounds at the most. Her hair was shoulder-length, and at first, I thought it was auburn because of the red tint. But I learned later that blood had washed through her hair due to two separate wounds to her scalp, courtesy of her assailant's gun barrel. Her natural color was a sandy shade of blonde, which went well with her green eyes. Her name was #Sonja Bradshaw, and her pink blouse was torn open from the neckline to her waist area. Her skirt was filthy and wet with whatever she was forced to lie down in. I suspected it to be urine mixed with booze by the pungent smell.

"Miss Bradshaw, I'm sorry that we're meeting under these circumstances. I'm Officer Goff, and I'm here with my partner Officer Chana to find out exactly what happened to you and see what we can do to help find whoever did this to you."

"Thank you."

To my surprise, Sonja looked around me to see who Dave was, but he wasn't behind me anymore.

"Excuse me, Sonja."

I stepped out of the room and saw that Dave was talking to the admitting nurse.

"Hey Dave, don't you want to be in there with me, so I don't mess anything up?"

"Nah, you'll be okay. I'll look over what you write up, and if anything's missing, I'll let you know. You can add it later after you talk to her again. I'm not trying to jag you around, but sex crimes victims will tell you more in a one-on-one situation than when two of us are in the room, especially when it's two guys asking her shit. Ya know what I mean?"

Another lesson learned and one I'd pass on to newer officers.

"Miss Bradshaw, do you prefer I use that name or Sonja?"

"Sonja is better; it doesn't make me feel so old."

She forced a small but certainly not a genuine smile on her battered face.

"I get it. Now I've got one more question before we really get into this, and be prepared. I'm going to need each and every detail as best as you can remember it, no matter how embarrassing and ugly it is or how reluctant you may be to tell me. With that said, would you be more comfortable talking to a female officer, or do you want to talk to me about what happened?"

She looked at me for a few seconds without responding.

"If you would like a female officer, there's someone we can get in here, but I don't know how long that will take because she'll be coming from the Youth Division downtown. So it's up to you. I'll make sure we get her here as fast as possible, even if I have to pick her up. I think you may feel more comfortable under the circumstances or more inclined to say everything that happened to you."

"That's all right; I'm okay with talking to you."

"Okay, Sonja, I'm just going to sit here, and I may interrupt you to ask a question if I think it's important for clarification, but I'll keep that to a minimum. So just tell me what happened in your own words and how you would normally talk if you were telling it to your best friend. Use whatever terminology you're comfortable with, but we prefer the exact words your attacker used. Try to keep everything in chronological order from start to finish. I'm going to listen and take notes, and once you're done, I'll have some follow-up questions. Okay?"

"Sure, officer. What's your name again?"

I pointed to my name tag and said, "Goff."

"No. I can see that. What's your first name, or can't I call you that?"

She wasn't being smart. She was being respectful.

"My first name is Frank."

"Oh wow, that's my dad's name."

"Now you're making me feel old."

She put her hand out to shake mine. It felt like I was holding the hand of a child. My hand completely wrapped around hers, underscoring just how vulnerable she was. There was no need to bash this young lady in the head with a heavy steel gun; that was just evil being evil.

She smiled, and this time it was for real.

"All right, I left a bar called The Rush Up. It's on Rush Street, and I was walking toward my car parked in a lot near what looked like a school near there. It's a whitish-colored building. Do you know the one I'm talking about?"

"Yes, I know it, and you probably had to park on the north side of the building there. Is that where you were parked, on the north side?"

"Ummm...it would be the side where you would go towards Division Street, like where Mother's and those bars are."

"Okay, yes, that's the north side of the building ...go on."

"Well, it was darker on that side of the street there, but I could see my car. It was about four car lengths away from me. That's when a man came out of the parking area, and it looked like he was walking to one of the bars or something. He seemed nice enough because he nodded and smiled as I approached him. He had on a brown floppy hat with a blue feather in it. He pointed to what looked like a laminated driver's license on the ground just a few feet behind me. He said, 'Did you drop that?' I didn't think I dropped anything but seeing that it was lying face down, I thought it could be my new work I.D. So I bent down to pick it up, and that's when he grabbed me by my hair and yanked me up so hard it lifted me off the ground."

"Then what happened?"

"He put a gun in my face and told me to do exactly what he told me to do, and I would be able to go home tonight. He said, 'If you scream or start any silly shit, I'm gonna blow your fucking brains out right here on the sidewalk.' He dragged me down a smelly stairwell by my hair. I remember that it was all wet at the bottom. It smelled like a hundred different people must have pissed down there. I had an idea of what might happen, so I told him I had almost forty dollars in my purse and that he could have it if he would just let me go and that I wouldn't call the police."

"What did he say or do next?"

"He laughed and said, 'Bitch, what do you mean you're gonna let me have forty dollars? Shit, you ain't letting me have shit. I'm taking that money, I'm taking your jewelry, and then I'm taking your pussy, and it better be some good-ass pussy, or it's gonna be some dead-ass pussy. We understand each other now, bitch?"

Sonja stopped for what seemed like several minutes and held her head down. She began shaking, which led to vomiting on the gurney. A nurse rushed in and handed her a vomit tray, and quickly changed the sheet.

Sonja had tears rolling down her cheeks and apologized for what happened. I asked if she needed a break because she wasn't just reciting what had happened to her. Sonja was reliving the horrible experience in front of me.

"No, I just want to get this thing over with. So that's when he told me to take off all my jewelry, including my earrings and watch, and put them in my purse. He searched me for money and anything he could find and took my car keys that I had in my hand."

"Did he take your car?"

"Not that I know of because it was still parked there when those men brought me to the hospital."

"What men?"

"I'll get to that. They came later on, so let me tell you about this guy. He grabbed me by the front of my blouse and tore it open from top to bottom like some crazed animal. Then he pulled my bra down to my belly and started sucking on my breasts. His breath was horrid; then he started kissing me and putting his tongue in my mouth. He told me that I should have sex with him like I'm having it with my boyfriend."

"Is that how he said it?"

"No. Should I say the real words all the time?"

"Only if you are comfortable with them, Sonja. It's useful to us because sometimes bad guys use the same phrases or commands over and over, and it can help us link him to other crimes if he's done this before, and I'm pretty sure he has."

"I understand, but it's still embarrassing. His words are absolutely clear in my head. I'll never forget them. He said, 'Fuck me like you're fucking your boyfriend, cuz I wanna bust a nut in your sweet white ass.' When he said that, I thought he was going to try to rape me anally, but he didn't. Instead, he attempted to put it in through the front way. He was having a problem getting an erection, and he said it was my fault because I wasn't turning him on enough. So that's when he hit me in the head with his gun, and it started bleeding and running down my face. That made him mad, so he hit me on the top of my head, and I fell down in the muck. He told me, and I'm using his words…'Suck my big black dick, white bitch, or you is gonna die tonight.'"

"Did he hit you with his hand or the gun?"

"He used an open hand. Like a real hard slap with his palm."

Sonja was visibly agitated, and her body trembled as she recounted the event. I thought she was ready to throw up again or, worse, call it quits.

"You're doing fine, Sonja, just fine. Better than most women who have been through such an ordeal."

That seemed to reenergize her.

"I was afraid I was going to be killed and figured maybe if I did what he asked, he'd let me live. So I started to do what he told me to do, but I was so scared my mouth was dry, like I had cotton mouth. I started to gag, and that wasn't good. It really set him off. He went crazy and hit me in the head with the gun again and pulled me up by my hair. He stuck the gun in my mouth and told me to suck on it, and then ran it in and out of my mouth a few times, and I felt one of my teeth break, he did it so forcefully. Then he told me to spread my legs, and he shoved the barrel in there. It hurt really bad, so I screamed. I didn't mean to cry out so loud, but in a way, it's a good thing I did. Because the two guys I mentioned before were walking by and heard it. They looked over the railing where we were standing. One of them yelled something, but I'm not exactly sure what it was. My ears were ringing from the head pounding. I screamed for them to help me. That's when he hit me in the head again, right here. I think I have nineteen stitches altogether. These two young guys, like in their twenties, came running down the stairs, and one grabbed at the gun while the other one started punching him. That's when the gun went off. The guy that was beating me hit the taller guy in the face with the gun, then pointed it at them, and he got away. He was a lot bigger than they were too."

"Do you know if either of these two guys got shot?"

"No, the guy who was trying to get the gun from him had both hands around it. When he shot it, I saw the fire come out, and it went straight up."

"Then what happened?"

"The two guys helped me upstairs, and one took his shirt off to wrap my head up. I saw that my car was still there, but I didn't have my keys because the guy that attacked me took them. I was bleeding all over the inside of that man's car and felt so embarrassed. They were nice enough to drive me over here. One of them cut his hand pretty good when he punched the guy in the mouth. He was bleeding across his knuckles. I guess he cut them on his teeth. The other man was hit in the face with the gun and had a bloody nose. I'm pretty sure it's broken, so I thought they would get treated here, but they didn't want to stick around, I guess. If not for them, I'm not sure what that guy would have done. He was really mad at me for some reason."

"You keep saying the two men. I know you said they were in their twenties but did you get their names, or can you tell me any other way I can identify them?"

"No, I'm sorry. I never thought of asking because I thought I'd get to see them again while we were in the hospital. I remember them talking to each other, and one was named Tony for sure. I didn't hear the other one's name. They looked like maybe they could be Italian, if that helps. American Italians. They didn't have any accent."

Sonja gave me a surprisingly detailed physical and clothing description of the wanted offender. It matched the one the nurse had gotten from the two witnesses who had brought Sonja to the ER, only better. So Dave put it out over the air.

"Well, Sonja, the detectives will want to talk to you, and…."

"No, I'm done. I'm going to my job in the morning and quitting. I'm moving back home. I'm done with Chicago, and I hope you catch this guy before he kills someone. But I don't want anything to do with this. I don't want to see him or have to come back to this crazy city ever again. You have been very nice, and I'm sorry, but you'll have to catch him without involving me…please. I'm just really worried that he has my address in Indiana because all my IDs and my house keys for my dad's house are in my purse."

"Well, tell your dad he needs to change the locks, and hopefully, this guy is too scared or lazy to drive all that distance. He has plenty of potential victims to choose from right here, so I can't see that happening. By the way, does your dad own any guns?"

"Yes."

"Good. Now, what about your car? I can have it towed someplace safe for you."

"I'll let my dad and brother come back for it."

"Okay, Sonja, but what I'm gonna do is pull the coil wire on your car and bring it back here. Give it to your dad because he'll need it to start your car. This way, if the guy that attacked you comes back for it, he won't be able to start it."

Unfortunately, we didn't have any plainclothes tac guys to sit on the car and grab the guy if he came back for it at that hour. I told Sonja we would do our best to catch this guy, hoping she would change her mind when we did. Sonja had a friend waiting to drive her home, so Dave and I started on our mission. We were going to catch this evil prick.

Dave read over my report, and because he had made some notifications, I had to add that detail along with the offender's description. I was pleased when Dave read over it and nodded.

"Looks good to me. Now let's go find this asshole."

We checked the immediate area of the attack, including the basement stairwell, to see if the offender dropped his wallet or left any other clues behind. But there was nothing. Our beat was close enough to the attack that he might still be in the area looking for some easy female target, so we remained vigilant.

It was around 3:30 in the morning, near closing time for the 4 a.m. bars in the area. The other joints had already shut down at 2 a.m. Those still open would be giving last call, and the register drawers would be removed for counting. They would be loaded with cash, making it a great time for a stickup. So besides our rapist, we were on the lookout for stickup men.

Besides the obvious robbery incentive at that hour for those so ill-intentioned, it was a prime opportunity for the evil bastard we were on the hunt for to show his face. If not him, then some other pervert so inclined to grab a lone female leaving an establishment a bit liquored up. Like any predator hunting down his next victim, we were on the prowl but operating from the opposite end of the spectrum.

We hadn't been rolling that long when a beat-up green 1965 two-door Ford traveling northbound in the 1300 block of Wells Street in Old Town caught my eye. There were three occupants, two in the front seat and one in the rear. The driver was young, but the other two were mid-forties, as best as I could tell from the little residual lighting coming from the businesses that lit up the car to a degree.

"I'm gonna stop these guys, Dave." I made a quick U-turn.

"What are you going to tell them we're stopping them for?"

"I don't know yet, but they're up to something."

I sped up so we were directly behind them, no more than a car length. I hit the switch on the spotlight and filled the interior of the Ford with bright light. The rear seat passenger disappeared from sight. Why? As soon as the Mars light was activated, the driver slowed down to a crawl. He was moving at no more than ten miles per hour before shutting off the headlights.

The car kept going for another 100 yards or so to the 1400 block of North Wells Street. Instead of pulling over to the wide-open curb lane, he stopped in the middle of the street with the motor still running.

"Be careful, Frank. No good reason to shut those headlights off, and their plates are wired on. They ain't really pulled over either. These shitheads are gonna try something."

"I change my mind, Dave."

"On stopping them?"

"No. On giving them a reason for the stop. Let's get out, guns drawn, and get them outta the car. I'll tell them the reason for the stop once we neutralize them."

We approached the car from two sides. I was on the driver's side and Dave on the passenger's side but to the vehicle's rear. My gun was drawn, and Dave had the shotgun pointed at the rear window. As I got up to the driver's window, I could see the passenger in the backseat, lying face down. Thanks to the spotlight's beam, I could see a handful of shotgun shells in the ashtray. I ordered the driver to shut the car off and toss out his keys. He complied.

"Open your door and come out with your hands up. When you get out, lift your shirt and turn completely around once, slowly so I can see what's in your waistband."

He did as he was told, and I could see that he was literally shaking. He was not a problem at this point. Once the car door was open, I saw another set of license plates with wires on the front floor of the driver's side.

"You got a driver's license?"

"No, sir."

"What's with all them shells in the ashtray?"

"Oh, this don't be my car."

"I didn't ask you whose car it was. I asked you about them shells. They ain't invisible."

"Umm…I ain't never seen them before."

Though I was talking to the driver, my main focus was on the guy in the backseat. This was more than just your average traffic stop. I positioned the driver to use him as a human shield, just in case someone from inside the car took a shot at me. I sensed danger more than I ever had before.

But it wasn't just me. Dave must have felt it too because he moved closer to the rear passenger's window. He racked a round into the shotgun's chamber and slammed the slide forward with as much force as he could muster. Dave made it clear that we would not lose this one. There was no mistaking that sound for anything other than certain death at very close range.

"I've got these two covered from this side. Dave, you got the guy in the backseat?"

"Yeah, my shotgun is pointed right at his fuckin' head."

"Driver, what's with your buddy in the backseat?"

"Oh, he's just tired… he's sleepin' cuz we drove in from Michigan just now."

"He wasn't sleeping a minute ago. I want you to lay face down on the street, facing away from me. Hey front-seat passenger, slide over and get out of the car on my side. Lift your shirt and do a turnaround so I can see your waist area. Once you've done that, lay down facing away from me like your friend is doing. Lock your hands behind your head. I'm already nervous, and I don't want my gun to accidentally go off five or six times if I see either one of you make any snaky moves."

The passenger did exactly as he was ordered. Well, two of them complied and did so without confrontation. Maybe this would go down smoother than I thought, but I still had a bad feeling about Mr. Backseat.

"Okay, Dave, I'm gonna take this last guy out on my side. Keep that shotgun on him."

Dave stuck the shotgun barrel through the open window and poked the guy in the head with the business end.

"I can't miss this mother fucker from here."

"Hey, you in the backseat. Put your hands behind your head and sit up."

There was no movement or verbal response, and his hands were still under him.

I said it again and again. There was just silence without movement.

"Hey, Dave...the guy in the backseat has a shotgun. Light him up."

I didn't say it with the same urgency had I actually seen a shotgun, and Dave knew what I was doing. The guy threw his hands behind his head and sat up. His long gray overcoat gave cover to what he was trying to hide from us.

"No, no, no, don't shoot, don't shoot, man. I ain't touching no shotgun and ain't got no guns on me. I'll let you all check me."

It's funny how the mind works. I flashed back to what the rapist said to Sonja earlier in this shift: she'd "let" him have her money.

"What do you mean, you'll "let" me check you? You can't stop me. Now get your ass out of the car and keep them hands where I can see them."

I almost added the word bitch to that command but wanted to be more professional. He moved slowly, and his left arm went under and across his body, almost like he was reaching for a gun in a shoulder harness.

"He's reaching for something, Dave."

"Let him reach. This thing will blow a six-inch hole right through him."

"Hey, officer, I don't want to get out of the car without telling y'all something."

"Yeah...what's that?"

"Ahh....damn....officer, I have a rig on me, and as soon as I turn to get out, you're gonna see it. I'm telling you now, so there's no accidents or that you think I'm pulling it on you."

"You got a sawed-off shotgun under there?"

"Yes, boss."

"Is it loaded?" At that second, it dawned on me that I was talking just like the cop who questioned me eight years earlier while arresting me for wearing a sawed-off shotgun under a long overcoat on the corner of 63rd and Wood Street.

"Yes, boss."

"Did you hear that, Dave? He's getting out, and he's got a loaded shotgun under his coat. He's also been to the joint." Boss is a term often used by prison inmates when dealing with the guards.

"All right, step back a little, Frank, in case I gotta light this asshole up."

One of the guys on the ground yelled out.

"We ain't got no guns on us. Our hands are where you can see them, officers. He the only one with a gun."

I did take a precautionary couple of steps away from the car just in case Dave had to unload on this guy, but he'd be getting peppered from both sides if he tried anything crazy. I had a clear shot at him, as well as the two street inspectors at my feet, if they tried something.

Mr. Backseat came out with his hands locked behind his head and a sawed-off shotgun dangling from a sling under his armpit. Besides the uncalled-for wool overcoat, he had on leather gloves. The temperature at the time had to be in the mid-seventy-degree range. These guys were definitely on a mission of no good.

Once he was out, I could see that another sawed-off shotgun had been tucked partially between the backseat rest and the seat cushion. It was also loaded and lying in a manner that his body concealed it from view while he was on top of it. I don't know if he was planning to ambush us or was trying to duck the guns behind the back seat before we got up to them. Maybe we were too fast and too well prepared for what he had in mind. All I know is we won this one.

I took out the straight razor that I carried in the pen pocket of my uniform shirt and used it to cut the strap holding the sawed-off from under my guy's arm.

The wagon rolled by and transported our prisoners into 18, where the detectives were notified.

Detective Fornelli from Robbery came in to get pictures to add to the mug shot books they kept in the Robbery Unit and to talk with our arrestees. But they clammed up and demanded a phone call and a lawyer.

About an hour later, Fornelli informed us that our prisoners would be charged with the felony sawed-off shotguns, illegal possession of ammo, and traffic violations. The backseat offender would also be charged with firearms possession by a convicted felon, and his parole would be violated. It turned out that he had just been released from a penitentiary in Michigan the day before we arrested him. After serving thirteen of an eighteen-year sentence, he was on parole for shooting a Detroit policeman on a traffic stop. He had a rap sheet several pages long with a robbery conviction and several other gun arrests. We knew we had some bad guys; we just didn't know how bad they were until then.

My first thought was that they were going to stick up one of the upscale bars at closing time. But I found something in the pocket of the front seat passenger that led me to believe more sinister plans were in the works. A hand-drawn map showed an address on Astor Street. Then as now, some very wealthy and influential people resided on that block. This particular address belonged to the owner of O'Brien's Steakhouse in Old Town, and that was six blocks from our street stop. O'Brien's closed a few hours earlier.

On the passenger's side floor of the car, a gym bag contained electrical tape, rope, and strips of cloth that measured about six inches wide and three feet long. We inventoried those items along with the shotguns, the shells, and the map.

The following day I met with someone who, later in his career, would be known as one of the absolute best bosses in the Police Department. Tactical Sergeant Ed Wodnicki. I told him the circumstances of the stop as he read over my copy of the report.

"You guys nailed this thing up like a coffin. Nice job. I'm going to talk to the owner of O'Brien's. I know him pretty well, and he's a good guy. He's a friend of the police, and I'll see if he can tie this thing together. I'll get back to ya if I find out anything. By the way, when you get off probation, come and see me."

For a young cop, that last line was a huge pat on the back.

I was confident that we wrote up a nice tight case report. Extra tight, I should say. With the acknowledgment of Sergeant Wodnicki, I knew we had everything covered from a legal standpoint. The cases were severed, but all somehow ended up in front of the same Judge. I testified in each case, and I lost each one. Well, I shouldn't say I lost them. The Judge found the defendants not guilty. The stop was good, the circumstances called for what we did, and these were bad guys. They just happened to be bad guys that got hooked up with the right attorney. Not that the attorney was at the top of the food chain when it came to knowing the ins and outs of the law. I wasn't beaten on the merits of the case. I was beaten because...I'm not quite sure, but a federal undercover operation in Chicago was brought about by massive corruption in the judicial system. It was dubbed Operation Greylord. Ninety-three people were indicted, including seventeen judges, eight court officials, forty-eight lawyers, ten deputy sheriffs, eight cops, and a state legislator. The corruption was rampant and had been going on for years. Enough said.

Two days later, Sergeant Wodnicki met with me and told me he had talked with the owner of the steakhouse. He was unaware of any plot to home invade him or rob the business, but he did think he was followed home from the restaurant a week earlier. He went on to relate that some people in an older beat-up green Ford had been parked outside his restaurant and left at the same time he pulled out of the lot. They were behind him all the way to his home but passed him when he parked and talked to a neighbor walking his dogs. He said that the car came around the block two different times, but he thought they were looking for a place to park. He had taken the last available spot. He was going in his front door when he last saw them, and that was their third trip around. A woman was driving the car, so he didn't think much of it after that.

Dave and I received an Honorable Mention for this arrest.

Chapter 3: Gotcha

The following night, I worked with an officer who did things a little differently than most. It was the third, and I hoped the last time, I'd have to work with him. #Mike Patricks was a good guy with about fifteen years on the job. He always needed a little jumpstart to get aggressive, so he'd pick up a quart of orange juice and a half-dog of Smirnoff vodka right out of roll call. Mike sat in the passenger's seat while I drove around and every so often dumped a portion of the O.J. out the window until he had enough room to empty the full eight ounces of vodka into the vessel.

While I drove, I went into detail about the facts of the sexual assault the previous night, and Mike nodded in agreement.

"Yeah, this guy needs to be taken off the street."

About an hour and a half into our shift, Mike was red-faced and primed to do police work. Being on probation, I knew to keep my mouth shut about this. That's the way things were back then.

I turned down the side street where the attack had happened just to show Mike where it took place. I was stunned and could not believe the good fortune staring us in the face. The thug had on the exact same clothing Sonja described him as wearing, including the floppy hat with the blue feather.

"Hey Mike, look at this guy."

"I don't fuckin' believe it. He's wearing the same clothes you said he wore last night."

The wanted offender was looking south when we came down the street and didn't notice us. I think his eye was on the stewardess dragging a suitcase behind her.

"That's him, and if I'm right, he's got a gun on him."

"Okay, Frank, let me out here, and you come up on the other side."

Mike seemed to go from buzzed to being as straight as I was. He switched to full police mode. I'd have been drunk on my ass if I drank what he did in that timeframe.

Our target was moving toward the unsuspecting stewardess. The overhead street lighting was reduced because of the numerous tree canopies, so it allowed us some sneaking-up cover. That's probably the same thing our thug was thinking. Mike crouched, moving quickly along the sides of the parked cars. I jumped a fence and came around to be on the other side of him. I was glad that Mike had shut the radio off because our thug was within fifteen feet of his intended victim and ready to pounce.

"Hey miss, did you drop this?"

Bingo! That's our guy.

She ignored him and kept walking. Unfortunately for us, a loud-mouth partier saw Mike and thought it would be cute to point to his buddy and yell, "Hey officer, here he is, lock his ass up." For some reason, everyone who does this seems to think they're the first to say this stupid shit to a cop. It ruined our element of surprise, and now we were off to the races.

I knew there was no way Mike would catch him even though he was closer to the guy than I was.

"Call it in, Mike; I'll take him."

He had about a hundred-foot head start on me, but I was closing the gap quickly. #Leroy Fields made it to the first street south on Dearborn when Sergeant Wodnicki turned the corner, blocking his path. Leroy slammed into the side of the unmarked car, causing the gun to fall out of his waistband. I scooped it up before continuing the pursuit. I don't know if he meant to do it or was confused in all the chaos, but Leroy was running back in the direction we had just come from. He was running through Bughouse Square when Mike came out of the bushes and slammed into him hard. Leroy went airborne before crashing to the pavement and giving up.

While I was cuffing Leroy, Mike pulled his crushed cigar out of his mouth and looked at it while talking to me.

"Kid, you got a lot to learn. You gotta work smarter, not harder. Look at you; you're out of breath and all sweaty. While I look like I just stepped out of *GQ*."

Maybe Mike was right.

Once we had Leroy in custody, I called Sonja. She had returned to Indiana and did not want to come back to Chicago but took the time to express her gratitude to us for getting him off the streets. I let her know that her spot-on description is what got him off the streets, and we were just lucky. Fortunately for us, the gun case violated this guy's parole. He was a convicted rapist with two under his belt and three armed robberies. He had served twelve years on a plea deal for those crimes and had only been out on parole for nine days at the time of our arrest.

Fortunately for the women of Chicago, his case was heard by Judge James Bailey, a no-nonsense judge. He sent him back to prison on parole violation to serve out the remaining six years of his original sentence. The judge also gave him an additional four years on the felony gun charge we put on him to be served consecutively.

Later in our tour, Mike burst out laughing. He was laughing so hard, that tears streamed down his face.

"What's so funny, Mike?"

"You, that's what's so funny. You told me what a great job I did hiding in the bushes and not letting Leroy see me so he'd get close enough that I'd be able to pounce on him."

"Yeah…?"

"It wasn't good police work. I wouldn't have been there if I hadn't drank all that vodka. That shit gives me the squirts, and I had to piss real bad in the middle of everything, so I ducked behind the bushes. I'm not even halfway through it, and you guys are running right towards me. I still had my dick out and piss running down my pants leg when I shoved him to the ground instead of tackling him. If you hadn't jumped on him, he would've gotten away. Can you imagine the beef I would've got if I tackled him and pissed all over him? The newspapers would have a field day with that. I can see the headlines now: "Drunken Copper Knocks Man Down and Urinates On Him." He was right.

At least Mike was straight with me, and I've heard it said before — sometimes it's better to be lucky than good. We were lucky on this one and received an Honorable Mention.

Chapter 4: Wagon Man

#Billy Gray and I were working together for the first time. I was still on probation, and this would be my third time on the wagon. Based on my first two experiences, I knew I was in for a night of disappointment. All we'd be doing tonight is providing transportation services for either prisoners, dead bodies, or injured citizens to be taken to the hospital. In those days, wagons brought far more people to the hospitals than ambulances ever did.

Billy had been a wagon man for most of his career. The last twenty years, to be exact. It seems like once a guy gets a taste of being part of the wagon crew, he sticks with it for the rest of his time on the job. It's not uncommon for those who know him to adopt the moniker, both on and off duty, as "the wagon man" from such and such district.

It wasn't a job for me and not for most working cops. It's a dirty job at times, but the side benefit is that they're not usually assigned the types of jobs a beat car would get unless, of course, all the beat officers were down on assignments.

Billy was fifty-nine years old and, to me at that time, was an "old" man. He had worked the streets as a beat cop for twelve years and was no stranger to actually doing police work but would avoid it if at all possible. He planned to retire the following year and didn't want anything to jeopardize his pension.

He was telling me how he planned out his retirement and hadn't quite finished all the details when the call came out.

"1872...you got one for the Henrotin at 1799 N. Bissell. See #Patton regarding the daughter in labor."

When we arrived, Billy looked at the two-and-a-half-story white frame building and took a drag on his always-in-the-mouth cigar. "Kid, I'll bet you dollars to donuts she's gonna be on the top floor, and we're gonna have to haul her down, so grab the stretcher." He was right.

An excited woman came running out of the gangway.

"This way, hurry please, this way, she's upstairs."

"What did I say, kid? They can't come down when they feel it coming on? It's not like it's a surprise party, for Christ's sake. They know the baby's ready to make its debut."

Billy followed the woman in what could aptly be described as lumbering up the stairs. I was behind him and wondered how in the world we were going to make it down the stairs carrying a woman on a stretcher. Besides being an old man, he was overweight and carried about two hundred and forty pounds on a five-foot, nine-inch frame. He huffed and puffed on his cigar all the way up. I had a feeling I was gonna be on the bottom of the package on our way down.

Billy stopped at the second floor and started to walk in the open door at that level.

"Oh no, officer, she's up here."

Billy looked at me with that *I told you so* look, and we continued our trek up to the attic. This was July 16th, and it was hot and humid. I didn't record the temperature in my hospitalization report, but it had to be in the 90s.

At the time, our uniform pants were dark blue and made of heavy wool with white piping down the side of the leg. Our wagon, just like the squad cars, did not enjoy the benefit of being air-conditioned, so we were already quite uncomfortable, especially Billy.

"This way, hurry! The baby is coming out now!"

"Oh Christ," said Billy under his breath. "Well, kid, have you ever delivered a baby?"

I was stunned. I thought the senior officer was going to teach me while I stood by and learned from the pro. After all, he must have delivered at least a dozen babies in his travels.

"No."

"Well, you are today because it's on the way out."

The teenager was naked from the waist down, so I hadn't focused my attention down there until Billy said that. A tiny foot was poking out and not moving. I thought that it was dead and maybe just going to fall out.

"Maybe we should throw her on the stretcher and get her to the hospital right away, Bill."

"No time for that. Get down between her legs and get ready to catch it."

I knew babies were supposed to come out head first, but that's all I knew. This one was coming out backward. We were never taught anything about delivering babies in the academy.

"Can't we just lay her on a stretcher and get her to the hospital as fast as we can?"

"I don't think we should move her; that baby might die stuck in there like that but let's see what we can do."

We tried to move her onto the stretcher, but she screamed as loud as anyone I've ever heard.

"Get this motherfucker outta me!"

Whoa, I'd never heard a woman talk like that about her unborn baby, but then again, I'd never been in a delivery room. I'm sure the way the baby was coming out didn't help the situation. I still didn't want to try to deliver a breech baby. If it were coming out head-first, I'd have no problem. But this was dangerous. I tried calling the CFD, hoping to blow it off on them, but no ambulance was available.

The baby's leg was out all the way up to the knee.

"Listen, kid, I know you've never done this before, but there's no time like the present. Get down there and help the baby out. You're gonna have to rotate the body, so its shoulders are parallel to her stuff."

"Man, Billy, I thought I could watch you do it."

"Kid, I've done this so many times I could lay down there and have the baby for her. Now hurry up."

I did as Billy told me and pulled out my latex gloves. There must have been a dozen people up in that attic's tight quarters, and she was lying on a plastic baby mattress on the floor. I kneeled in a position where I thought I could look like I knew what I was doing but would just wait until the baby came out on its own. I started flashing back to images of little Billy lying in the street bleeding to death while I knelt over him. I was more determined than ever to see that this baby didn't suffer the same fate.

My knees were wet before I realized it. In my haste to get down there, I kneeled in her water.

"Hey Billy, I'm kind of pulling on this leg, and she's trying to push, but nothing's happening."

"Turn the baby's body like I told you."

"I can't. I got my fingers in here, and I can feel its other foot, but I can't grab it."

I was worried that the baby might die from drowning in bodily fluids or from lack of oxygen at that point or might be strangling like my brother, who almost died due to the umbilical cord around his neck.

"You're gonna have to cut her and do it quick."

Billy turned to the lady. "Hey lady, you got sharp scissors around here?"

"Yes… I will get it."

I carried a straight razor in the pen pocket of my uniform shirt for cutting through things in an emergency. This was actually the first emergency I would be using it on, though.

"I've got this." I held the opened blade to show him.

"Great, that'll work better than the scissors. Start cutting."

"I need to sterilize it first."

"Here, use this." Billy took some alcohol wipes out of his pocket, and I wiped the blade. He was still smoking his cigar, and the air was starting to choke me.

"What do I cut?"

"Just below her stuff; ya see that skin right there?"

I had to bend down to where my face was almost touching the floor and trying my best to keep my face out of the goo while waiting for direction from my mentor.

My patient was screaming like crazy, and I had to yell at her to stop. "Hey lady, I'm trying to help you, but I can't hear my partner."

Then I asked the crowd, "Can someone stick a rag in her mouth to bite down on? That might help."

Billy called out for someone to hand her a tennis ball lying on the floor. "Hey honey, squeeze that ball real hard when you feel pain." It seemed to work for a bit.

"Okay, Billy. I see what you're talking about, and it looks like it's starting to tear open there."

"Good. Just take the very tip of the razor and cut downwards towards her, ya know…but don't go deep. That skin is paper-thin."

I followed his direction and could see the toes of the other foot. I grabbed and pulled on them but lost my grip. That foot retreated into her a bit more. I had one leg out and didn't want to lose my grip on it. I still needed to rotate its body and also get a hold of that other foot again.

Once I did that, I thought things would go pretty smoothly. With one hand on the outside and one hand partially inside her body, I used only its legs to turn it sideways. I could feel its little butt and, using my forefinger, turned the baby completely on its side. It started coming out but took a little bit of tugging as the head was not coming as I expected.

"Don't pull so hard. You'll stretch its neck. Reach in there and help spread that area open, Frank."

I had everything spread as far as nature would allow, and blood was pooling around my knees. Then it happened. The baby's head just made a popping sound, and he was in my hands!

"I think I got it. He's a boy."

"Hold him up by his feet and slap his ass. That'll get the shit out of his lungs."

I didn't need to do that because he was already upside down, and he spit up and cried on his own. My patient had quit moaning and was now smiling. She looked weak but happy as I laid the baby on her chest. Everyone in the room clapped and patted me on the back. I was proud of myself. But that, too, would change.

We loaded our new mother and baby on the canvas stretcher, no different from the field gurney used by the military in combat and stained with just as many bodily fluids.

I was proud and couldn't wait to tell the other guys about delivering a baby once we got her to the Henrotin Hospital emergency room, where doctors and nurses tended to our patient. I made out the hospitalization case report and asked the nurse for the doctor's name for my report.

"Oh, you will get his name, all right. The doctor wants to talk to the two of you."

I didn't get why Billy suddenly walked out of the waiting area, but that was fine with me. I could answer the doctor's questions without my partner. Hell, I did all the work.

"Hello, officer."

"Hello, are you the doctor I will be putting down in my report?"

"Yes, I am, but I have a question for you. Who performed the episiotomy?"

"I don't know what that is. We brought the lady with the baby in."

"I know that. That's why I'm asking you."

His voice was stern, and I realized why my partner left the room so suddenly.

"Episiotomy… is that the cutting down there to make a bigger opening?"

"Yes."

I didn't want to give up my partner and say he told me to do it because he was close to retirement, and so I assumed full responsibility.

"That was me."

"What medical school did you graduate from?"

I knew I was in trouble and where he was going with this. He was right, and I was wrong, so I wasn't going to say anything in my defense.

"Do you know what you did? You performed a surgery, and not only that, you performed surgery without anesthesia, without sterilized instruments in a sterile environment, and I could go on. Shall I, Officer Goff?"

"No, doctor, you're right. I did everything you just said. I was wrong to do what I did; I just didn't know what else to do to help her."

"Why would you feel that you needed to do that?"

"I thought the baby might die if I didn't get it out fast enough because it was coming out feet first."

"The baby was breech?"

"Yes, sir."

He was quiet for a few seconds and told me not to leave. He went back into our patient's room and came back about two minutes later. They were a long two minutes too. I looked out at the wagon for my missing partner, but he wasn't in the wagon, and I didn't see him in the lot from where I was standing.

"Officer, what you did was wrong. I see by that AS patch on your shirt that you could lose your job over this. I don't think it needs to go any further than this room. Just don't ever, ever, ever do it again. Are we clear? Don't ever tell anyone, and I mean anyone, what you did."

"Absolutely. Thank you, doctor."

The doctor turned to walk away and, as if it was an afterthought, said, "Ohhh… by the way, you probably saved that baby's life. I just thought you should know that."

Whether that's true or not, I don't know. The doctor could have thrown me a bone because he could tell I was beating myself up over the incident. But now I was going to have some words with Billy Gray.

He was hiding on the other side of the wagon, smoking his cigar and not visible through the ER windows.

"We all done here, kid?"

"Yeah, we're done with the paperwork, but why did you take off? That doctor reamed me for cutting that girl."

"Well, how else were we gonna get the baby out of there? Did you tell him that?"

"We? I wasn't gonna tell him anything. He was pissed, and he was right. By the way, what happened to you when you did that?"

"Perform an episiotomy?"

"Yeah, that's what he called it."

"To tell you the truth, I never even delivered a baby the normal way. This was a first for both of us."

Billy had a good laugh at my expense and had me redo the hospitalization case report. This time, I omitted the surgery that I had so proudly performed from my report.

In today's world, I would have been fired, sued, and sent to jail.

Chapter 5: Doctor Whack Job

I wasn't off probation yet but would be in three more days, so when my partner for the day called in sick, Sergeant Bortko cleared it with the watch commander to let me work alone. It was the day shift, and I was assigned to a relatively quiet section of the district, at least during those hours. They both believed I was level-headed enough and could handle it alone. I felt like I had accomplished something. Just having their trust meant a lot to me. I was finally the Real Police and would do my best not to disappoint them. I wish I had Harry Gould's shirt now because mine still had the "AS" insert.

I don't recall exactly what drew my attention to the mid-fifty-ish-looking white guy with a pear shape and thick horn-rimmed glasses walking on the opposite side of the street. But something did. The temperature hovered around the mid-seventy-degree range, but it was pretty windy, and I could clearly see that he was sweating. Maybe that was it. I thought it odd but not that unusual.

The rearview mirror reflected that he had turned around as if watching me. People sometimes do that with cops. I drove another half block or so before my curiosity took over. It had become my thing that if something drew my attention and I looked at it twice, there must be a reason for it. So he needed to be checked out.

A quick U-turn caused the tires to squeal and pedestrians to stop in their tracks. That turn should have put me on the same side of the street as he was, but he had crossed to the other side by that time. Not in the mood for any cat and mouse games, I pulled my squad across the two lanes and was facing in the wrong direction of traffic at the curb.

This startled him, and it was clear that he was looking at me in the reflection broadcasted by the business window next to him.

He took off running, which made no sense. At five-foot-seven and two hundred twenty pounds of jelly-like softness, a majority of which was centered about his midsection, there was no way he was going to get away. The foot chase was over within a few seconds. Something he did just before that required some explanation. He frantically rolled his sleeves up when I first exited my squad.

"Excuse me, sir, I'd like to talk to you for a minute."

"Why are you harassing me?"

This caught me off guard. That was a common refrain more typically thrown at me by folks in the west end of the district. People at the east end tended to be more tolerant of the police.

"I'm the one asking questions here. Why are you running from me?"

"I wasn't running. If I were running, you wouldn't have caught me."

"You can't be serious. What's your name?"

"#Dr. Ronald Martin, you still didn't tell me why you're harassing me."

"Why are you sweating so much on a nice breezy day like today?"

"Is it against the law to sweat now?"

He was wearing a dark brown dress shirt and a yellow and brown hand tie-style bowtie that had been untied and hung loosely around his collar.

I figured this needed a bit more attention, so I went down on the air with a "hand waver" just so I wouldn't receive any other assignments until I finished with this guy. "Hand wavers" at one time were probably how we got most of our jobs, at least in the poorer parts of the district. Instead of calling the police on the phone, people waved their arms in the air to flag down a passing squad car, so there was nothing unusual about it.

"Why did you roll your sleeves up all of a sudden when you saw me coming?"

"What the fuck is your problem, Gestapo?"

I reached for his right arm, and he pulled away with a warning.

"I want your name and badge number. I have friends in your department, and they're going to hear about the way you treated me today. I'm a psychiatrist and counsel officers in the police department, in case you want to know."

"I ain't interested in that, but I am interested in your rolled-up sleeve."

I grabbed his wrist with one hand and the sleeve part of his shirt with the other. That's when he made the mistake I was hoping he'd make. He slapped my hand away.

"You just assaulted me, sir, by hitting my hand. That's battery to a police officer, and you're under arrest."

I placed him in handcuffs behind his back, looping one cuff through his belt as had become my routine. It keeps prisoners from slipping the cuffs around to the front of their bodies.

"Now it's time to see what you've been hiding from me."

I rolled his sleeves down. They were damp, and I thought that seemed out of place, given the weather conditions. Initially, I attributed it to him sweating, but that was ruled out almost immediately. My fingernails had turned red, and the smell of blood was in the air. I had no doubt in my mind that something bad... very bad... had happened.

"Well, this is interesting."

A closer examination of his black pants revealed some spatter that looked like it could be blood too.

"Who did you kill?"

"I didn't kill anybody, sir."

My antenna went way up with the "sir" comment. A few minutes ago, I was the Gestapo, and now he's calling me sir. I searched him and, after finding no weapons, put him in the rear seat of the squad car.

Looking through his wallet for some identification did reveal indicators that he may have done work for the C.P.D. or at least had some connections with the department's brass. That was no surprise. I always felt a percentage of them needed serious psychological evaluation anyway, so he might've been telling me the truth.

According to his driver's license, the doctor lived in a high rise near the Lakefront, but when questioned about that, he said he had moved to the suburbs and didn't have time to update his information with the Secretary of State. I wasn't buying it. We were less than a half-mile from the address on his license, and his psychiatry practice was located in the suburb of Oaklawn, Illinois, which was a long way from where we were.

I wasn't sure what to do at this point but I knew that I had to do something. It was too early to call detectives, and no violent crimes had been reported prior to or during my encounter with him in the area. I hadn't heard any complaints from his address during the shift, and I wasn't really going to arrest him for slapping my hand. So I thought the next best thing was to get him to tell on himself.

"I see by your wedding band that you're married. How long have you been married?"

"I'm not married anymore. I'm divorced."

"Ahh... sorry to hear that. Were any children involved?"

"No, sir."

"That's good. You know better than I, as a psychiatrist, how that can damage a kid for life, especially when one parent plays them against the other."

"Absolutely."

"Where does your wife live now?"

"Ummmm, she moved out of the country, sir."

There was that "sir" bullshit again.

I reached back over the seat and removed the keys from his front pants pocket. There were five in all.

"Two of these keys are car keys, for sure. What are the other three for?"

"Work. All three are for work."

"I see. Where are your house keys?"

"Oh, I lost those."

"Mmmm...hmmm."

Over the air, I gave out the address the doctor said he moved from and told the dispatcher I was relocating on a well-being check. Then we headed for the apartment he claimed he no longer lived in. All the while, he was fidgeting in the backseat, almost as if he was trying to break free of the handcuffs.

"What are you doing back there?"

"These cuffs hurt."

"Well, they ain't made for comfort."

"Where are you taking me?"

"Don't worry about it."

"Are you taking me to jail for real?"

"I'm curious, doctor. So what I'm gonna do is, go to the address that you said you don't live at anymore and try your office keys on the doors to the building and your previous apartment. You don't have a problem with that, do you?"

At first, he was agitated, and then his body went into that defeated head and body slump, and he shook his head from side to side.

"Do what you want. I can't stop you. Not now, anyway."

I pulled up to the building and created a parking spot right in front of it.

"You can't go in my apartment!"

"I'm not, doctor. I'm going to the apartment you don't live in anymore, according to you. But first, I have to get another car here to watch you while I go up."

"All right, all right. I wasn't totally honest with you, sir. Can I go up with you? It's just that my wife and I had it out, and, well, I thought I'd take a walk to cool off before going back. Maybe if I come back in with you, she won't act so crazy. You know I'm calm now, and I'm sorry about pushing you away from me. Could you please take the handcuffs off, sir? Everyone in the building knows me, and this is embarrassing."

"I'm confused. Now you're telling me you live here and your wife from out of state is suddenly back in the apartment?"

"I lied, but since we're here now, I am telling you the one hundred percent truth."

"The bracelets stay on; let's take a walk."

I proceeded to apt #505 with the doctor in tow, having to drag him as he slowed down to a snail's pace at times. After knocking on the door and not getting a response, I listened for any signs of life. There was absolutely nothing coming from inside the residence.

"Ahh, just as I thought, officer. She took off for her mother's house again. She always does this when we have a disagreement. She stays there a couple of nights, won't take my phone calls, and then comes back like nothing happened."

"Oh yeah?"

"Yeah, she does it all the time. So are you going to let me go? Or if you're taking me to jail for that little push, I'm ready to go now. I was wrong and I'm sorry, but if you're going to lock me up, can we please get it over with so I can be out for work by morning?"

"What's your hurry? You know ...I really appreciate you giving me permission to check on the well-being of your wife, so I'm going to unlock the door now. Which key?"

"I did not, and I'll say it again, I did not give you permission to enter my home!"

He repeated it several more times, his voice rising several octaves with each declaration. Doc didn't have to tell me which key would unlock the door; the first one turned the deadbolt, and he screamed out, "You have no right! You have no right!"

He was right, and I knew it, but sometimes I feel it's better to do what's morally right in certain situations than what is legally right. I'm not an attorney or a judge, but I'm aware that the "legally right thing" changes all the time. That's why there are local courts, appellate courts, state supreme courts, and finally, the Supreme Court. Each interprets its own definition of what is legal. The morally right thing to do never changes or needs interpretation.

It was too late; I was in, and I dragged him in before anyone came out of the apartments to see what the commotion in the corridor was about.

"Sit in that chair and don't move."

I placed a coffee cup and saucer on his lap.

"I'm gonna put these right here, and I better not hear them fall."

"You're gonna lose your job, and I can't wait to tell my friend #Deputy Chief Ballee."

That made me have second thoughts because he did have that Deputy Chief card in his wallet, and I was on probation. But I continued in my search for an answer to his blood-stained sleeves.

"Police…is anyone home?"

There was no response. The place was small, so it didn't take long to do a visible inspection of the premise. The living room, dining area, and kitchen were all connected without walls separating them. There was only one bedroom in the unit, so I slowly opened the door in case the woman was in there. But I could see from the reflection in the dresser's mirror that the bed was empty and neatly made. The whole place was spotless, and everything seemed to be in order.

I'm going to get a beef from this guy and get in some major trouble for doing what I'm doing if the place is empty. That thought kept running through my head the whole time. *Maybe she's at her mother's house.*

But the blood…that bothered me, and he offered no explanation. This place is too neat to have had any violent confrontation. I was worried now but not enough to stop.

Doc was quiet and sweating profusely. He stared at the only other room in the apartment, the bathroom door, which was closed.

"Police, is anyone in there?"

Again, there was no response. I attempted to turn the doorknob, but it was locked.

"Do you always lock your bathroom door when you're not home?"

He didn't answer. He turned his head, looked out the window, and started whistling. I had opened enough locked doors to know that if I slipped a butter knife between the stop and the jamb, I could hit the beveled side of the latch and force it open without damaging anything. It worked like a charm.

I was surprised, but not surprised if that makes any sense.

She looked to be at least fifteen years younger than her husband and was more attractive than I would suspect he could have gotten as far as outward appearances go. Her body was sprawled out in the bathtub, face up and naked. Her right leg and arm dangled out of the tub. The drain plug was up and void of any water. Judging by first impressions, it seemed highly unlikely that she had been taking a bath when she met her demise.

I looked back at her husband, who was staring at me. His facial features changed, and he looked like a different person, tense and angry. He ground his teeth and started growling like an animal.

"Relax, did you do this?"

"Look in the tub between her legs."

I had already looked but thought I missed something, so I bent over to get a better look.

That's when a crashing sound came from behind me, and without looking, I knew it was the chinaware that had been on his lap. He thrust his body forward, charging me with his head down like a bull, and let out a roar. Even with his hands cuffed behind him, he apparently thought he could win the battle he was about to take on. It wouldn't be much of a fight.

I sidestepped his attack without ever laying a hand on him. His head slammed into the corner of the marble vanity top, causing a pretty good-sized gash to open up dead center at the top of his forehead. Like with any head wound, blood spurted out all over the place, and he reveled in it. Throwing his head back and forth and from side to side, he fully intended on decorating the floor, the walls, the fixtures, and me with his blood.

I grabbed a towel and threw it over his head, and then sat him down on the floor. He was going to need some stitches, and I'm pretty sure he fractured his skull.

I knew the two supervisors working days — Sergeant Bortko, a great guy and very knowledgeable, and Sergeant Willems. I was working in Willems' sector but hoped Bortko would respond. Unfortunately for me, he was in the station on paperwork. Willems responded along with Officer Doody. Both were nice guys, but neither one of these guys would come to mind when you picture the stereotypical policemen. I'll leave it at that.

I thought back to something the doctor said on the drive over.

"Do what you want. I can't stop you. Not now, anyway." Was that a veiled threat? Was that why he wanted the cuffs off? Was this pudgy fifty-something gonna try to take me down? The thought was laughable but, under the circumstances, believable. At least with him sitting on the floor, another attack was unlikely. Besides, blood was pooling in his lap, and his wound looked like it took the fight out of him. I called for a squadrol to take him to the Henrotin Hospital while I waited on the sergeant.

I turned my attention back to the lady in the tub, examining the body for wounds. There were four — one under each breast, presumably puncturing the lungs, one in the heart, and one in the neck at the jugular.

I couldn't see any defensive wounds, and this puzzled me. The stab wounds were clean and precisely placed. I didn't learn until much later, after the autopsy and toxicology reports were completed, that she had high levels of a narcotic in her system.

It made me wonder why the good doctor hadn't just overdosed her on meds. That would have been quicker and cleaner than the mess I was looking at. Plus, he might get away with it if he made it look like a suicide.

Sergeant Willems arrived before the squadrol and asked me what happened. I gave him my version of the events, and he notified the dispatcher to send the crime lab and detectives to the scene. Then he turned to me and said what I came to learn was one of his favorite lines.

"You're gonna get in trouble. You have a bloody prisoner there. What did you hit him with?"

"I never hit him. He ran his head into the vanity and split it open by himself."

"Uhh...you're still gonna get in trouble."

Naturally, I was concerned because I initially went down on the air as a minor hand waver, and now I was in the middle of a homicide investigation. Detective Fornelli arrived on the scene. He relayed that he wasn't working but had just come from dropping a witness off after court. He would stand by until some homicide detectives were available. He took all my information and said he would take care of things until one of them could get there.

I related to him what happened. He was a very knowledgeable guy, and I trusted him when he said not to talk with anyone else about the case until I met with the homicide detective in charge. I thought I might receive my first Honorable Mention while working alone for this, but apparently, my sergeant felt that he didn't want to reward me for what he perceived as bad behavior and injuring a prisoner whom I did not injure.

His words kept ringing in my ears as I sat in my squad car, making out my case report. I was concerned that I may have stepped over the line in how I handled it. Still being on probation, I could easily be fired.

The dispatcher came over the air…"1814."

"1814 go." I could tell by his voice that something was up.

"1814 report to the watch commander's office immediately."

I don't care what anyone says; it's not a warm, comfortable feeling when you're told to report to the watch commander's office.

In fact, it's never a good thing. It's even worse when you're ordered to report there "immediately."

Captain Frank Nolan called me into his office after Sergeant Willems had scurried out of it. Apparently, the sergeant related his version as to what had transpired.

Captain Nolan was a big man with pure white hair and a great sense of humor, but he didn't look happy right then. I thought to myself, *I'm on probation, and I messed up the first time they let me out on the street unsupervised by a senior officer.* We didn't have FTOs in those days. I prepared myself for an ass chewing or maybe even getting fired. I wished this had happened three days from now. Then I'd be off probation, and it would be much more difficult to get the boot.

"Close the door, Goff. I understand that we let you out on the streets for a few hours, and this is the thanks we get for trusting you by yourself? We got a doctor in the hospital getting his head stitched up and his skull may be fractured. And a lady is dead in the bathtub. On top of all that, it's not even on your beat."

He was looking at me with eyes that never blinked, apparently anticipating some response from me. The only thing I could think of to do in that situation was to apologize.

"I know. I'm sorry."

"What the hell are ya sorry for? There's nothing to be sorry about until I hear the whole story from your lips to my ears. Proceed."

I told him the story as it unfolded and was honest about every detail.

Captain Nolan had a stern look on his face, almost as if he was trying to look angry and not doing a good job of it. In other words, he had a look in his eyes that put me at ease, as odd as that seemed. He leaned back in his chair and folded his arms. I no longer felt threatened by him.

"Ya did good, kid, don't worry about nothing. Anything comes up to the contrary, I'll take care of it. Your shift is over in two hours, right?"

"Yes, sir."

"All right, go home early, have a beer or whatever, and stay out of trouble till then. Don't say anything to anybody about this. Anyone asks you something, direct them to me. Got it?"

"Yes, sir."

"This will blow over."

I followed his advice and nothing ever came of the incident.

It wasn't until a year later that I learned of the drug found in the doctor's wife's system. It is called succinylcholine, and it paralyzes a person but keeps them conscious so they know what's going on. Apparently, the good doctor wanted her to know what he was doing to her as he murdered her. That's one sick bastard!

Dr. Martin was able to post bond through a very expensive and very connected attorney named Julius Echeles. Once the doctor made bond, he had himself admitted to a mental institution and died of natural causes before the case went to trial.

It turned out, the doctor had discovered his wife had filed for divorce. He was served the papers at his office the previous morning and ended his less than two-year marriage on his own terms.

Chapter 6: Working with Junior

I was working with John Creeley, aka "Junior." John was in his sixties, but to this twenty-year-old, he looked like he was in his mid-seventies at least. He earned his nickname by calling everybody "Junior." I don't know if it was because he couldn't remember the guys he worked with by name or because he was the most senior policeman in the district. He was as old school as they came and would retire in another year.

It seemed every time I worked with "Junior," he told me how I would be getting in trouble with the inspectors for one thing or another. I think it was more that he didn't like what I was doing and wanted to put the blame on someone else to get me to stop rather than call me out.

Just to bust his balls one day, I wore socks that had five different colors on the individual toes you slipped them into. After picking up our "power rings" on Fullerton, I parked under the viaduct and slung my three donuts over the gearshift. I saw him look at me out of the corner of his eye while he sipped his coffee. He was about to say something when I took off my shoe and put my foot up on the dashboard.

Junior couldn't contain himself.

"Haaaay brother, (Junior always exaggerated his 'hey' in that manner) you're gonna get fired if an inspector sees them socks on you. What's with them crazy colored toes? There must be something not right with you upstairs, wearing them goofy socks."

By then, he had other things to worry about because I was leaning forward and eating the donuts off of the gear shift on the column.

"What the hell is wrong with you?"

"What do you mean, John? I can't hold all three donuts while I'm drinking my pop. Me and Eddie do it all the time."

"You and that Griffin...there's another one that needs help. Ya know I won't let him drive because he's not right either. The two of you are both gonna end up getting fired if you're not careful. Now eat them donuts the right way and put your shoe back on before an inspector sees ya."

Our first call came over the air to see a complainant about a suspicious person. It was only three blocks from where we were sitting, so we got there pretty quick.

An elderly woman stood on the front porch of a two-and-a-half-story tall frame building. She smiled and waved at us as if we were her best friends.

"Hello, officers, hello. I'm so glad you got here so quickly."

Junior took the lead with his deep and blunt manner of talking. "What's your problem, lady?"

"Well, there are aliens in my house that shouldn't be in there."

"Who are these aliens to you?"

"I don't know them; that's why I called you."

"Well, then how are they getting in your house if you aren't letting them in?"

"I'll show you, officers, but be careful. They're very sneaky."

I started walking into the apartment when Junior stopped me from going any further.

"Let her go in first. Go in, lady, we'll follow you," he told her. But to me, he said, "She's cuckoo. Let's go."

I knew this woman deserved better than that and refused to leave. Junior was already walking down the front stairs to our squad while I was still engaging with the lady.

"How do these aliens come in, ma'am?"

She led me to a pipe in the wall that had previously been hooked up to a gas range.

"They come through there."

"I see."

By now, Junior had come back in and heard our conversation. He was willing to let me play this out, so that's exactly what I did.

When I was a cadet in the first district, a lady named Edith Brennan came in every day and sat on the bench in the lobby. She was always smiling and nodding at the officers. Edith was always well dressed with sparkling blue eyes that could look in two directions at the same. She would be tough to sneak up on.

The story was that she had been purse-snatched years earlier and had kept returning to the station daily in anticipation of her purse being recovered and the culprit arrested. When it came time for her to leave at the end of the shift, desk Sergeant Russ Madia had me call the "invisible squad" to watch her get home safely.

They did a hell of a job because she was never attacked again. They would come in handy on this caper.

"I see, ma'am. This sounds like a job for our Invisible Squad to handle. Would it be okay if I call them to take care of you?"

"Oh yes...please do that."

"Okay, I'll take care of it, but I'm also going to need your closest relative or friend's phone number so I can let them know what's happening."

She gave me her daughter's number, and I relayed to her what was happening. This woman needed help, and the daughter said she'd be able to come in about four or five hours and take her home to live with her family.

"Okay, ma'am, that was the invisible squad I was talking to on the phone, and they will be sitting in front of your house and in the back and by every window until your daughter gets here to take you home. Is that okay?"

"Oh yes, thank you so much, officers."

"Oh, one other thing. The invisible squad said I should stick a potato or apple in the end of the gas pipe so the aliens can't come through."

"Oh, let me get one. I have a potato in the bin."

I jammed it in the open end of the pipe, and we left a satisfied customer.

Once we got in the car, "Junior" looked at me and grunted. "Not bad, brother, but if an inspector knew you did that, you'd probably end up getting fired."

Chapter 7: I'm Glad I Didn't Ticket Him

Traffic ticket quotas. I'm sure everyone has heard that phrase, especially cops when they are accused of writing someone a ticket to meet their "quota."

Maybe some departments require it. Hell, I've known some district commanders who would come down on their supervisors if the beat guys weren't writing enough tickets, and then the supervisors would pressure their crews to write at least one a day "to make the boss happy."

I focused on making good arrests rather than writing folks tickets. That's not saying I didn't stop traffic violators; I did it several times a day while working in the district. I just didn't write them tickets. I figured I had already scared them when I pulled them over, so that accomplished what I wanted to do —change their driving behavior. If they were belligerent, I de-escalated the situation with great success in most cases. I'd always run their names for warrants, and if I felt the need, I'd ask for consent to search their vehicle. If they were clean, they were on their way.

Another reason I didn't issue them tickets was because, most of the time, they were folks who lived in my district. I used this as a prime opportunity to develop street informants or at least someone who might be willing to cooperate with me in the neighborhood when a crime went down or was about to go down. It was a tactic that worked with great success.

To accomplish this, I had business cards made up. After every traffic stop, I'd thank the driver for his cooperation and hand out a business card. I also gave my cards to the other occupants in the vehicle and let them know that I was out there working to help keep the community safe. I let them know that if I could ever do anything for them, they shouldn't hesitate to let me know, and I meant it.

A cop's reputation spreads fast on the streets. So I tried to leave everyone happy when I left. This led to developing a large-scale network of informants. They knew they could trust me as I showed them goodwill during my interactions on the street stops.

I didn't start my career with the intention of not writing people tickets. I figured I would do it because the job requires it in some cases. In many of our interactions with people, we, as cops, are given a lot of discretion. I used it quite often.

On a warm late August afternoon, I had just gotten off of probation and was working alone. I was cruising westbound on Armitage at Halsted. My light was green and I had just entered the intersection. A lady was crossing Halsted Street from west to east, pushing a baby buggy, when he came through the red light, almost t-boning me. I slammed on the brakes so hard and swerved to avoid the collision that I came within inches of hitting the woman. Thankfully, she made it to safety before my bumper clipped her.

I didn't even need to turn on my Mars light to pull him over, and he wasn't speeding, from what I could tell. He just acted like there was no traffic signal there. The driver immediately pulled over into the open parking lane to wait for me.

I jumped out of my car and was hot. Not only would he have wrecked me, but the woman and baby could have been killed. I was already doing a mental calculation of just how many tickets I'd be writing. The laundry list in my head went something like this: red light violation, unsafe vehicle due to his balding tires, cracked windshield, and improperly affixed license plates. That was just a start. *I'm sure I can find more,* I thought.

When I reached the driver's door, he had his wallet out and was going through it, looking for his driver's license.

"Good afternoon, sir. I'm Officer Goff. Do you know why I stopped you?" My tone was gruff and, I'm sure, sarcastic in delivery.

"Yes, sir."

His voice was quiet, almost a whisper. His hands were fumbling nervously as he located and handed me his driver's license. He didn't look at me; he just stared straight forward with his hands in the ten and two positions on the steering wheel. They were steady, and I could see that his knuckles were turning white.

His wife sat next to him, dressed in a dark-colored one-piece dress and wore a small corsage with an angel pin on her left shoulder. She was wiping a tear from her eye and telling the two children in the back seat to "hush up."

The boy appeared to be about seven and looked scared. However, his sister, about five years old, was smiling and waving at me.

"Sir, please look at me when I'm talking to you."

I wanted to see if this guy was drunk. Maybe his eyes were bloodshot. I didn't smell alcohol but sensed that something was not right.

He glanced up for a second and then looked down toward the steering wheel.

"#Mr. Quinn, step out of the car and walk to the rear, please."

Mr. Quinn did what I had asked but still wasn't making eye contact. He was dressed in what was probably his best church-going clothes, as were his wife and two children. He wore dark blue cotton work-type pants with a sharp crease and a white shirt with a blue tie. His shoes were of the black work-type rather than dress shoes and were well polished. Though his hands were scrubbed clean, they bore the black stain around the fingernails often seen on the hands of a mechanic.

I started to calm down and figured I'd just write him one ticket for the red light and give him a warning on the other violations. It didn't look like this family had money to spare.

"Okay, Mr. Quinn, what happened back there? Didn't you see the red light or…"

He kept his head down. I was stopped mid-sentence when I saw a teardrop hit his shoe. Then another. This was a traffic violation; no grown man is gonna cry over a ticket.

I'm not sure why I asked this question, but I'm glad I did, and it was something I carried with me throughout my career. I suggest all officers do the same on every traffic stop.

"Mr. Quinn, where are you coming from or on your way to right now?"

Mr. Quinn wiped his eyes with the back of his palm while still looking down. He reached into his shirt pocket and pulled out a card, and handed it to me without looking. Men are like that; they don't want anyone to see them cry. I didn't want to embarrass him, so I did away with the "look at me when I'm talking to you" thing and pretended not to notice.

It was a mass card. Her name was #Kelly Quinn, and she was three years old. I can tell you her full name and date of birth and death, even today. That's the impact this stop had on me, even though it's been almost fifty years.

The family had just come from funeral services for their Kelly. That's when I remembered that a hit-and-run driver had killed a girl in the district while she sat on her tricycle. The car had jumped the curb in the 1300 block of Cortland while making a turn too fast a week earlier. This was the girl.

A tide of remorse washed over me as I reflected on how I approached this man who was going through grief that I wouldn't experience until much later in life. The wording was what it should have been but was sarcastic in both delivery and tone. I was embarrassed by my unprofessional behavior in the way I acted. I vowed never to do that again, and I didn't.

I was twenty-one years old and had only been a cop for nine months. *I'm too young*, I thought, *to be in the business of lecturing folks like I have a handle on all of life's experiences.* Compared to this man and what he's gone through as a father, I was lacking. I wasn't married and had not lost a child up to that point, but I knew it had to be painful. Now I had to extricate myself from the first plan of action and make it a positive experience for all involved.

As it turns out, another beat car saw me and slowed down to check on me.

"Everything okay, Frank?"

"Yeah, Ernie, but can you do me a favor? I want to drive this guy home. It's only a few blocks, and then you can drive me back."

"Okay, I'll follow you."

I told Mr. Quinn I'd be driving him home and wanted to talk to his kids on the way if that was okay with him. He didn't know what I had planned but went along with it. The only reason he probably agreed was that I told him he wasn't getting any tickets, but I'm not sure.

"Hi kids, I saw your dad driving this car, and I remembered him from when we were growing up, so I just wanted to say hello. And I thought this was a cool-looking car, so he's letting me drive it to your house. Okay?"

"Yeah!" The kids were excited. Mr. Quinn slid over to the center of the bench seat, and his wife smiled at me as I put my arm around him. It was only a two-minute drive, but I think it left everyone with a good taste in their mouth. The kids were excited to see that their dad knew a policeman and said it several times. When we got to their home, Mr. Quinn got out on the driver's side with me.

"Officer, I know the only reason you're doing this, and believe me,

I appreciate it. You've made my children very happy. They've been through a lot, and so has my wife."

"I wish I could do more. You take care, sir."

Mrs. Quinn and the kids waved goodbye.

From that day forward, I made it a point to always ask everyone I stopped where they were going and where they were coming from. Some folks might find that kind of invasive. I think if they knew why I was asking, they would look at it differently. It's the right thing to do, and I think all cops should do it. You don't want to make the mistake I almost made on the worst days of a parent's life, burying a child.

Chapter 8: Area One Task Force

Several months later, we were off probation, and just as we planned, Ed and I became regular partners. We worked as partners in the 18th District and made a lot of good arrests. Because of that, we were given the opportunity to transfer to a specialized unit.

We had heard a lot of tales about the guys in that unit, and we looked forward to becoming a part of the "Big Red One."

As it turned out, everything I heard about these cops was true. To a man, they were absolutely the best group of guys I ever worked with. They were balls out in everything they did. You never had to worry about losing a battle as long as they were by your side, and there were plenty of those to go around.

When Eddie and I arrived for our first day in the Area One Special Operation Group, formerly known as Area One Task Force, I was impressed. All of the patrolmen were young, physically in good shape, carried at least two handguns, blackjacks, and two pairs of handcuffs, and many had knives on their belts and other assorted weaponry.

Everyone welcomed us with their particular brand of ball busting, and with that came their acceptance of us into a brotherhood on the spot.

It was our first roll call, so Ed and I took a spot in the back. Some guys have their preferences on where they stand at roll call in every unit, so we didn't want to step on any toes. We were called to attention where assignments and lunch periods would be designated.

Then it happened. He came into the roll call room, and I almost froze. There he stood with his Moe from the Three Stooges-style haircut and a crazed look in his eyes (it wasn't really like Moe's haircut, but it reminded me of it for some odd reason). I had seen that look before. It was back in the summer of 1968 when he attempted to kill me.

I had been riding in a '53 Ford and was sitting behind the driver, sixteen at the time. A guy I knew from school, "Marblehead," had just picked me up a few blocks away to go cruising. That's when he blew the stop sign at 69th and Wood. If that wasn't bad enough, he did it right in front of a squad car occupied by Patrolman Bobby Burns.

We thought Marblehead was using his uncle's car; at least, that's what he had led us to believe. Before he let us in to go cruising, we had to pitch in some money for expenses. After each of us had forked over some change for gas, we were happily on our way to see if we could pick up some girls from the Blue Island, Illinois area. We knew where a pretty large group of them would be gathered that day.

Bob Burns pulled us over, and Marblehead knew he had blown the stop sign, so he stopped pretty quickly. He casually got out of the car and started walking toward Officer Burns. We knew he'd be getting a ticket and hoped that wouldn't ruin our planned activities. Marblehead reached for his wallet to give Burns his driver's license but must have had a change of heart. He took off running and yelled, "It's hot!"

With that declaration, the other two guys jumped out and ran in different directions. I stayed put because I figured I'd tell the policeman the truth. The truth being that I did not know I was riding in a stolen car.

I could see him with his gun in hand and coming toward me.

"Don't fuckin' move, asshole, or I'll blow your brains out!"

I ain't stupid and figured this one out immediately. Since the other guys had a head start on him, I was the closest person. This made me most likely to be arrested, and I'm pretty sure somehow I would now miraculously become the driver of the stolen car for his arrest report.

I wasn't having any of that and jumped from the backseat, fearful of two things happening. The first one being that Burns was young, carried himself well, and was in physically good shape. I found out later that he was a former Marine. I knew if he caught me, he would beat the shit out of me for being in a stolen car but then give me an extra dose of ass-whooping for running on him. So I really needed to haul ass.

The second thing that concerned me was that he had a loaded gun in his hand, a crazed look on his face, and was saying unpleasant things to me. He might just do what he said and blow my brains out. He looked capable of doing either one or both. So I took off as fast as I could. He chased me and fired a shot. Now I don't know to this day if it was aimed at me or just to scare me, but I heard everything he was yelling as clear as day.

"Ya better stop, punk. The next one's in your fuckin' head." That upshifted me to high gear, and I made good my escape.

So this was our new sergeant. I didn't say anything to my partner Ed about my prior run-in with him. I didn't want us to get bounced from this prestigious unit because of me, so I held the secret for years. I had also been told that Bob Burns had a nickname which I won't report here, but it indicated that he was capable of going off at any time. I believed it because I witnessed it, and he had the ability to back it up.

Sergeant Burns stared at me longer than he should have. I thought for sure he was sizing me up. Did he recognize me? Was he waiting for me to say something? If so, he'd have to speak first, and I would just deny whatever he accused me of. Then he looked over at Ed, who was next to me.

"So you're Griffin. I heard about you from Jimmy Wadell. You're okay." Then he looked back at me.

"Goff, huh? Wadell didn't tell me shit about you. How fuckin' old are you?"

Oh boy, here it comes. He's trying to figure out my age and put it together with the time and location of the foot chase. He's on to me. He's testing me for sure, I thought.

"I'm twenty-two."

"Twenty-two. How the fuck did you get in this unit? Ya look like you're sixteen."

"Just lucky, I guess."

"Well, you two will be working for me, and by that, I mean work. There's no dog-assing on my team."

With that said, he told us what was expected of us and made it a point to meet for lunch after roll call. It was the beginning of a friendship I cherish to this day. Bob Burns and Ed Griffin are two of the greatest guys I've ever known and had the pleasure of working with.

I told Bob many years later and years after his retirement as a Captain about our little run-in in the late sixties. We were at Rivers Casino in Des Plaines, Illinois, having a beer at the Lotus Bar. Eddie Griffin was there too, and was about to hear the revelation for the first time. I had never told Ed because I came through the initial hump of meeting our sergeant and escaping unscathed, and it just slipped my mind. It didn't seem worth mentioning when I did think about it. I've always been good at keeping secrets and confidences when people have trusted me with them.

Bob was shocked and couldn't believe that it was me that he had chased fifty years earlier and even more so that I kept it from him for so long. Eddie took it calmly in stride as he did everything. At first, Bob was pissed that I hadn't trusted him enough to tell him when we were working together. There was a reason, and, as I mentioned earlier, he had a well-earned nickname. Again, I'll leave it right there.

Bobby Burns was no slouch and came back at me with a surprise that impressed me to the max and illustrated what a great copper Bob Burns was. That being the fact that he remembered the case even though he had made untold numbers of arrests between then and the end of his thirty-plus year police career and recalled every detail from 1968 until I told him 53 years later! He recounted the vehicle, the color, the location, how many of us were in the car, where I was seated, and even my direction of flight during the foot chase. That's a hell of a memory.

Over the years, Ed was promoted several times and eventually attained the rank of Captain. I was a Detective, the only rank I ever really wanted in the police department, and we moved to opposite ends of the city and, therefore, areas of assignment. I missed working with Ed, but we would often get together socially during our married lives and are friends fifty years later. I thank Ed for his greeting and his loyal friendship that day in the 18th District roll call room and over the years, or this book wouldn't have been possible.

Chapter 9: The 1000 Mile Call

While Ed and I were assigned to the Area One Special Operations Group, we, just like the other officers, had a dual purpose. That was responding to In Progress Felony calls and taking guns off the street on targeted street stops. It wasn't hard to get the guns. Our "humper" had eleven lines on which we would record our street stops until we grabbed a gun on one of them. We usually had a gun before the "humper" was completely filled out. Everyone in the unit was a top-of-the-line street guy, and I trusted any one of them in any situation.

With that said, one of the perks of the unit is that on a rotating basis, we got to work in plainclothes and an unmarked or, if available, an undercover car. When we were given one of those assignments, it usually meant that the Detective Division had a crime pattern that needed to be solved. Because they were short-staffed and didn't have the time to devote the manpower required, it would be given to us to handle.

One such evening Ed and I were given two crime patterns to look into. One was a rape/robbery and stabbing pattern that involved co-eds in the Hyde Park neighborhood near the University of Chicago.

The other was a much more serious matter that also involved the rape and robbery of young women near the school, but this one also involved the home invasion of the victims.

As usual, Ed and I ate lunch first because we planned to roll all night as the attacks in both patterns had occurred later in the evening.

We studied all the available case reports and noted that the offender in the rape/robbery/stabbing pattern had been described as a male black, approximately eighteen to twenty-five years old and five foot nine to six feet tall with a slim build and a purple earring in one ear. His weapon of choice in the stabbings was a Phillips head screwdriver. He claimed four victims in one month, and all were assaulted on a

Friday. This happened to be a Friday.

We learned later that this screwdriver was not only used to stab and threaten the victims but also used to gain entry to gated court-ways. The thug would unscrew the bracket that secured the lock on the entryway to the courtyard of the victims' apartment complexes. Once he gained access, he would screw the bracket back in securely and lock the gate. Then he waited in the dark for an unsuspecting victim.

He used the pointed end of the tool to press it against the young ladies' throats and threatened them with puncture wounds to the throat and chest if they didn't comply with his devious demands. In each case, they cooperated with him. But in his last assault, he upped the ante. Even though his victim did everything she was asked to do, he stabbed her in the breast before fleeing. He was getting progressively more violent and needed to be stopped.

One other thing caught our eye. The offender wore black and gray checked pants with a tight pattern. We knew that this was a very common uniform for dishwashers and cooks in the area's restaurants. Keeping that thought in mind, we hovered around "restaurant row" during the shift change. We stopped several guys and came up empty. They didn't have the earring or the screwdriver.

About three hours into the night, Eddie spotted something.

"Hey, how about this asshole?"

He was the right age, height, and slim build, and had a purple earring in his left ear. We jumped out, and Eddie grabbed him.

"Hey man, what's y'all grabbin' on me and shit for?"

"Don't worry about it."

I patted him down while Ed held the guy's hands behind his back.

"Frankie Lee (this was a term of endearment guys on our team used; we added Lee after every first name), he's got something wrapped up in a towel in his back pocket." Ed raised the guy's arms, and I retrieved it. It was a Phillips head screwdriver with an eight-inch long shaft.

"Nice call. I think we got our guy, Eddie Lee."

With that, Ed slapped the bracelets on him. Happy with ourselves for making the pinch so fast, we headed into our office to process him and turn him over to the detectives for a lineup. We'd be getting over to the bar early tonight!

Our unit did not have portable radios at the time. They were mounted in the squad car as well as in the unmarked cars. Once you were out of the vehicle, you were on your own. Fortunately, we were in our car when the emergency call came out as we drove our prisoner into our office.

Dispatcher: "Attention all units on the City Wide and units in the 21st District. We have a Home Invasion In Progress at 5032 S. Woodlawn, apartment number unknown at this time. The call is coming in from Bangor, Maine. The mother said she was talking to her daughter on the phone when two men burst into the apartment with her roommate at gunpoint. Use caution."

"Damn, Eddie, that's only three blocks away."

I hit the gas, and we arrived before any other cars. "You stay with the prisoner, Ed, and tell the backup units I'm gonna take the top floor, and they can fill in on the other floors. Hopefully, we can get lucky again."

I passed several apartments on my way up, each with its own genre of music or television coming from them.

On my way to the apartment I intended on going to, I stopped short. Something drew my attention to a different one. It was a male and a female voice. The words weren't clear, but I sensed it was the right apartment. I listened, and it felt like they knew someone was outside the door because they stopped talking. There was no television noise or any other signs of life coming from the other side of the door now.

My heart started pounding, and I tried to control my breathing to hear them. Somehow, I knew this was the right door. The wooden floor creaked underneath me as I edged closer. That may have been the giveaway. I listened for a few more seconds…they were by the door, and I'm guessing trying to hear what I was doing. I know it's impossible, but it felt like I was so close to them that I could feel their body heat in the chilly hallway.

I gave it my best shot and knocked but didn't get a response.

I figured that the occupants were probably university students, so I didn't knock like the police. I tapped on the door like a wimpy college student might. I did it again, and there was no response. So I tried something else, hoping that if I had the right apartment and the victim was a student, my next line might work.

"Hey, it's Frank from school. I got those books you loaned me."

My ear was pressed against the door now. Even though it was whispered to her, I could hear a male voice say, "Tell whoever it is you're taking a bath."

"I'm taking a bath right now."

"Well, you ain't taking one now if you're at the door. Just take these books quick. I don't want to have to pay for them if someone steals them. My car's double-parked out there, and I don't want to get a ticket if the cops come by."

Now I knew I was at the right apartment. I had my gun in my hand but behind my back. I was in plain clothes and young-looking, so if they saw me, the college student thing should work.

The chain lock slid open; it was game on now.

Next, the door lock clicked open, and a young woman ran out to the hall totally naked and grabbed me around the arms and body in a bear hug. "Please help me." She had a death grip on me.

My arms were momentarily pinned to my sides as she held on so tightly. He grabbed her hair to pull her back in and pointed the gun at me. I yelled "Police" and fired once from the hip with her still holding on. He fell back into the apartment. The gunshot startled her so much that she took off running down the stairs. I'm sure she didn't know which one of us fired and wasn't going to wait around to find out. Fortunately, our victim ran into the arms of arriving 21st District tactical officer Al Fashingbauer.

That's when #Ann Johnson, the woman I had encountered who is an occupational therapist, relayed to the responding officers that her roommate had been taken by the second offender, who was armed with a butcher knife, to a liquor store around the corner to cash in her traveler's checks.

We knew we had to get to them quickly because if the other home invader saw all the squad cars at the apartment building when they returned from cashing out the checks, he'd never come back into the building, and he might kill our second victim just to keep her quiet.

Two uniformed 21st District officers named Charlie Brown and Harold Pointer, both great cops, volunteered to go to the liquor store. They knew which one she was talking about because it was on their beat.

The second victim #Mary Jones was standing in line with the armed offender very close behind her. She had her traveler's checks in hand, so she was easy to identify. Pointer and Brown grabbed the thug at gunpoint and immediately handcuffed him. He had the knife at the ready, but it was no use. They were too quick for him and did a great job.

I could hear one of the cops from the 21st District directing my partner up to the apartment I was in.

"I'm in here, Ed."

"Hey, Frankie Lee...are you done shooting people up here?

One of the coppers from 21 is watching our prisoner. What the fuck happened? There's a naked girl wearing some coppers jacket crying downstairs."

"I think we just solved the second crime pattern, Ed."

We needed additional information for our report and needed to know exactly what had transpired. Ed and I interviewed the victim after she was released from the hospital. She was bruised up a bit and, of course, traumatized by what had happened, but thankful that things turned out the way they did instead of what the thugs had planned on doing to them over the next day or so.

So far, only Ann had been sexually assaulted. Mary was to be raped once they returned from the liquor store with the money and some alcohol. The home invaders had planned to spend the night and possibly the next day with them. But first, the girls would have to cook dinner for them. After dinner, they would be sexually assaulted and probably again the following day.

To make sure the girls didn't attempt to escape when they went to bed for the night, they were going to tie them up. The victims would be forced to sleep next to the thugs so they couldn't leave their sides. If they woke up to find that either of the girls had tried to escape, they would both be killed.

Ann Johnson relayed to us that she had been grocery shopping for her and her roommate at the A&P Grocery store. When she returned home and walked into her vestibule, she was followed by the two men. One was armed with a handgun and the other with a large knife. They asked her if she lived alone, and she told them that she lived with a roommate. They asked her if the roommate was a man or a woman, and she told them it was a woman. They asked her if she had any dogs up in the apartment, and she told them she did not.

In my opinion, she gave them just what they wanted to hear, and that was all the wrong answers.

The thugs forced her up the stairs at gunpoint and told her to use her key to open the door. She complied, and upon entry, her roommate was talking on the telephone with her mother in Bangor, Maine.

Unknown to the bad guys, the roommate had already alerted her mother to the problem. "Mom, some men just burst in with guns. I'm scared." Fortunately, the home invaders were far enough away from her that they didn't hear what she had said.

One of them pointed the gun at her and said, "Tell whoever you're talking to you have to go."

She told her mom that she would have to hang up and told her she loved her.

At that point, the home invaders took all the money the two victims could come up with and ransacked the apartment, looking for and taking other valuables that they loaded into a pillowcase.

It wasn't enough, and they demanded more.

"This little bit of money and jewelry ain't gonna save your asses. You have to come up with more money, or you're both gonna get the shit fucked outta y'all, and then we're gonna kill your asses."

The two thugs pulled a sheet off the bed and started cutting it into strips. Fearing for both her and Ann's life, Mary Jones told them she could cash in her traveler's checks and give them the money. That seemed to calm the thugs down a bit because it was a fairly large sum. The guy with the knife thought it would be a good idea to take her to the liquor store, buy booze, and cash in as many of the traveler's checks as they could at that location. So he took Mary with him so she could do that.

These men were desperate and agitated. They had home invaded, raped, robbed, and injured women in the past, and there was no doubt that they would do it again. One of them was on the run after escaping from a penal institution.

Their M.O. was to follow their victims home on foot from grocery shopping, as each victim had been prior to being home invaded. This way, they knew their victims had some money on them with probably more at home. They would be provided with food, sex, and a clean, warm, safe place to spend the night while the law was looking for them.

Thanks to the quick actions of the frantic mother who called the police in Bangor, Maine, this crime pattern was solved. The Bangor Police informed the mother that Chicago was way outside their jurisdiction. She would have to call the Chicago Police to respond to the location. They provided her with our emergency phone number, which was PO-5-1313 at the time. The mom relayed what little information she had to our dispatcher, who put it out on the air. Fortunately, we were close by. As I said before, it's better to be lucky than good.

The offender I shot survived his wound and went on to claim that he cooperated with us and that he was actually a victim too. He claimed that he told us where his partner had taken the second victim. He also claimed that to get this information from him, we had tortured him by stepping on his wound and shoving a gun down his throat, and threatened to finish him off in the apartment, among other dastardly deeds that never happened.

This is a common refrain from thugs. It's something you not only get used to but come to expect. The problem is, they often get attorneys who, whether they believe them or not, will file a bullshit civil suit on their behalf, knowing the City has deep pockets when it comes to paying out bad guys and will, with rare exception, always settle out of court.

The attorneys, on the other hand, are handsomely rewarded for little or no real work being performed on the case. I can see why they do it for monetary reasons, but the moral reasons are lacking. I've had many conversations with attorneys who have filed these types of suits, and they can read through their client's B.S. story as well as anyone. But as many will tell you, "Cash is King."

The thugs went to trial on our case and received sixty-five-year sentences from Judge Francis Mahon. They took pleas on the other cases, some of which included concurrent time rather than chancing consecutive time on each case. They deserved life without parole, but cops are not in the position of determining sentences.

The first offender we had arrested with the screwdriver was identified in two of the four cases, though we knew he committed all of them (DNA was not a thing back then). Two of the coeds, including the one stabbed in the breast, had relocated out of state and were not interested in coming back for a lineup. The offender copped a plea and received twelve years from Judge Cousins.

Chapter 10: My First Night on Midnights in the 15th District

I was going to be moving from the South Side of Chicago, where I had spent my entire life, to the North Side. Marriage was also in my plans. I requested a transfer to the 15th District in preparation for that move. To my dismay, I got my wish a month sooner than I had requested. I wanted time to let my partner Ed know but was waiting until all the paperwork went through first. I knew he'd successfully persuade me out of making the transfer request. I was pissed, but at least I got the district I wanted. The bad thing is, I went straight to midnights.

Unfortunately, after working for several years in Area One SOG, where the hours were 6 p.m. until 2 a.m., this was an adjustment and not what I bargained for.

I reported to the desk sergeant for my assignment and was greeted by a handful of guys I didn't know personally but had seen in court on plenty of occasions over the years. They were hard-working street cops and knew their stuff. They made me feel at home right away.

My first night on the midnight shift would be with Charlie Gardner. Charlie was laid back in a way, but aggressive as any young cop I've ever worked with. I liked him immediately. Charlie always seemed to be laughing, and if he wasn't laughing, it was only because his attention was drawn to something that caught his eye on the street.

The night started like most with the usual calls. Charlie was driving because he worked the area for a while and certainly knew it better than I did.

As we drove northbound on Cicero Avenue, the traffic started backing up due to the bars starting to shut down. It was close to 3 a.m., and the streets were full of people.

Moving stop and go through a maze of double-parked cars and jay-walkers, Charlie spotted something.

"Aw shit… look what we got here, Frank."

A black female in her twenties came running up to our squad, screaming. She had a gash over her left eye that caused blood to stream down her face. She was shoeless, and her blouse was torn open from the right shoulder down to her exposed breast.

"Help me, officer, please help me."

"What happened to your head?" Charlie asked.

She started pointing while breathlessly telling her story.

"Them men, them men, see 'em? That one walking around the corner, he busted me in the head with a gun and tried to drag me into their car. Then he took two shots at me. See it? It's that blue one that's making the turn. Right there, get 'em before they get away. He still got my purse in there too."

We were stuck in traffic, but so was the blue car she described.

"I'll get out here, Charlie, and take the guy with the gun."

"All right, be careful. I got the car; he's making a left turn on Adams."

I ran around the corner just in time to see the guy with the gun walking west on Adams. He didn't notice me as he had his eye on another female walking just ahead of him, drinking from a beer bottle. I guess he thought she might be an easier target than the one who fought him off.

These guys were aggressively hunting females tonight.

I got within twenty feet of him before announcing my office. "Police, put your hands up."

He turned halfway around and raised the arm facing me in the air. I could only see one side of his body as I moved closer. His body and the lack of residual lighting available in that landscape obscured his other arm. I had the feeling that he was weighing his options. I was alone and had the drop on him. But that didn't seem to matter to him. He was going to make a move; at least that's what his eyes and body language were telling me.

"What you want? I didn't do nuffin'. Why is you pointin' a gun at me?"

"We need to talk to you about bustin' a girl in the head tonight with a pistol. You carryin' a gun?"

"Naw man, I ain't packin'. Whoever told you that is bullshittin' y'all."

"Keep your hands up and turn all the way towards me so I can see both of them."

"Okay, be cool. I'm doin' like you say."

All the while, he was dropping the hand I couldn't see because he already had the gun in his hand. He leveled his pistol at me, and I heard a click.

I returned the gesture and fired. He dropped instantly. A scream and loud commotion came from my rear. It was Charlie Gardner wrestling with the driver, who was now out of the vehicle and resisting Charlie's efforts to handcuff him. Charlie was screaming loud enough so everyone could hear that he was just trying to cuff the guy who was fighting him off.

"Put your hands behind your back. Stop resisting."

Charlie had been wrestling with this guy since he pulled him from the car. Things escalated dramatically when the shots were fired, and Charlie was in a fight for his life. He was winning at the moment, but neither of us knew if this guy was armed or if he was as homicidal as the first guy.

At that point, a decision needed to be made, and any hesitation could end in tragedy.

If I went to assist Charlie, the locals would most likely trample the crime scene and steal the gun. That's not unheard of. If that were to happen, it would look like I shot an unarmed man. On the other hand, if I didn't make a move, Charlie could be seriously injured or worse. I chose to do the latter, and we were able to end the physical part in seconds.

But the crowd was growing more brazen, fueled by the prisoner screaming that the police had just killed his brother. In a way, I can understand why he went into full crazy mode. He had just witnessed what had happened between his brother and me, and even if you're a bad guy, that's a pretty traumatic thing to see.

The street was overrun with drunken tavern goers, police haters, and curious passersby. We knew it wouldn't be long before the two of us became targets of the angry mob.

Charlie had full control of his prisoner, and I went back to check on the offender I had shot to see if I could offer any lifesaving aid. There was nothing I could do.

I called in shots fired by the police, and units started screaming in. It didn't take long before the "real police" had cleared the area to a point where we had full control once again. Within minutes, yellow tape markers were put up, and officers stood in a formation around the perimeter, protecting the crime scene as well as ourselves.

The first cop to arrive was Sergeant Petrousonis, whom I hadn't met yet but was our sergeant that night.

"What the fuck happened? This guy's dead over here. Did you shoot him?"

"Yeah. Charlie has the other guy that was with him; they're brothers."

Sergeant Petrousonis looked at the guy Charlie was holding down on the front end of the car.

"What the fuck? That guy's head is bleeding. Did you shoot him too?"

"No."

"What the fuck? Did Gardner shoot him?"

"No."

"Why's he bleeding?"

"He was resisting."

"Who's the broad standing by Gardner? Her head's fuckin' bleeding too. Did you guys hit her in the head?"

"No. She was that way when we met her."

"Okay, well, why did you shoot this guy?"

"He pointed his gun at me, and it misfired. I returned fire, and this is how it ended. His gun is underneath his body and still locked in his hand."

"How do you know it misfired if it's underneath him?"

"Because I heard a clicking sound when he spun around."

"Aren't you the new guy from the Task Force?"

"Area One."

As it turned out, the gun did not misfire. The clicking sound I heard was the hammer being pulled back into position to fire the weapon. It was a single-action pistol that needed to be cocked before firing. It was in the full cocked position when it was recovered.

"All right. I'll call the Dicks (Detectives in Chicago) and the crime lab. Lieutenant Martin is the watch commander. He's gonna want to see you in the station. Are you okay?"

"I'm fine, but you better check with Charlie. He was wrestling with that guy for a bit."

Charlie Gardner was okay, and I'm glad he was with me that day. He is an outstanding policeman and protected me from an assault that would have come from behind had he not been so quick to take this guy down.

We drove into the station, and when I walked in, apparently everyone at the desk and in the building knew what had happened. The desk sergeant pointed to the watch commander's office and said, "Lieutenant Martin wishes to speak with you, sir."

Lieutenant John Martin was the boss that night, and I hadn't seen him at roll call because another lieutenant had handled that.

"Lieutenant, I was told that you wanted to see me."

"Yes, I do. I don't know you. Who are you, and where did you come from?"

I introduced myself and told him I transferred in from Area One.

"I see that you have a five-year bar on your sleeve, but you look like you should still be in high school. Well, welcome aboard. Relax, Goff. Can I get you a cup of coffee or something?"

"No, sir."

"Okay, tell me everything that happened from start to finish. Don't leave anything out, and don't make anything up. The Dicks will be here to talk to you, and I want all our ducks in a row before they get here, or the state's attorney or anyone else, for that matter. You're going to have to talk to all of them."

I proceeded to recount the events of the night exactly as they happened. My mind was clear, and there was nothing that I was unsure of or didn't recollect. When I finished, Lieutenant Martin looked at me and said, "Are you nervous?"

"No, sir."

I wasn't nervous or worried about the outcome of the investigation. I was just glad Charlie and I weren't hurt. It was over, so there was no need to fret.

"So, have you told me everything you can remember about this shooting?"

"I've told you everything in the exact chronological order that it transpired out there."

"Perfect, don't change a thing. That is absolutely perfect. Now, I'll tell you what's going to happen from here just to prepare you for what's going to seem like a lot of bullshit and scrutiny, but don't let it worry you. I don't want you to get rattled or second-guess yourself. You did the right thing out there."

"I know what to expect, Lieutenant, and I'm fine with it."

"Have you been through a shooting investigation before?"

"Yes, sir."

John Martin reached across the desk and gave me a fake forehand and backhanded slap across the face and nodded. I knew he was solid from that second on.

The shooting was ruled a justifiable homicide. The state's attorney, the detectives, and the Office of Professional Standards all concurred.

The victim was treated for her injuries and moved on with her life. The surviving brother's case was adjudicated accordingly.

The backstory to this case was that the two brothers had recently moved to Chicago from the South. They didn't have jobs but decided that they didn't need them. They were going to establish themselves as gangster pimps in the big city and make their money the easy way. By taking the money from women who earned it.

Their plan was to kidnap females off the streets and hold them in a location where they would force them into working as prostitutes. They wanted to amass a stable of at least a dozen girls and believed that if they worked them long enough and often enough, they could live quite well off of the untaxed cash that the girls would generate.

Charlie and I received an Honorable Mention for this case.

The only reason I put this particular chapter in the book was so that I could tell the story of what happened in the following chapter. It will illustrate the dilemma police officers across the country face on a daily basis. That is the ever-present uncertainty of reacting properly in a given situation.

When should an officer use deadly force, and when should he hold his fire? Remember, in virtually every case where there are reservations, the officer is forced into making a decision in a second or less. Only the person standing in the officer's shoes at that particular moment in time, experiencing danger, whether real or perceived, can make that judgment call. Graham v Connor, a U.S. Supreme Court decision, is one example.

A cop's decision to use deadly force takes all things known and unknown into account. The initial call or cause for the encounter. The sights, sounds, surroundings, and nature of the environment are all computed at lightning-fast speed in the officer's mind. Thoughts of his/her family or loved ones make cameo appearances in that thought process. Are there innocent people, especially children, anywhere in the line of fire who may be hurt if the officer fires and misses the target?

At the same time, officers calculate the situation's outcome if they're wrong.

What if they violate department policy?

What if their actions violate the law?

How will the community terrorists react to his/her actions?

How will the anti-police, corrupt media, along with money-hungry lawyers chomping at the bit for an easy settlement from a city payout, portray the cop's actions?

In every case where officers are forced to use deadly force, it isn't they who choose the date, time, location, or day of the week for such a response. It is the bad guy's actions that lay the groundwork. Officers only act upon the threat or perceived threat they were faced with at the time. Keep in mind that the time span can be as short as a fraction of a second. That's a heavy burden for an officer to carry, given the authority vested in them to do their job under some extremely dangerous circumstances.

If people only knew how many times cops hesitate and put their own lives in danger to avoid using deadly force, they'd appreciate the fact that when an officer does have to resort to that extreme measure, it's because the bad guy left him no viable alternative.

With that said, I want the reader to keep in mind the mental gymnastics that were going on in my head the following night in the next chapter.

Chapter 11: WTF

I reported for the midnight shift the following night. In those days, they didn't give you a thirty-day rest period after a shooting like officers get today. Depending on the boss, you would get the following night off, and in some cases, I heard of guys getting a few free days.

The desk sergeant, Bob Warner, looked surprised to see me when I walked in. "Goff, what are you doing here? We're carrying you working the desk, but you don't really have to be here. You got a free day; go home."

Apparently, in the confusion of things, no one told me that this was something they had arranged. The last thing in the world I wanted while working was to be assigned to the desk and would be happy to go home, but that isn't what happened.

Hugh Nightingale was an extra man on the desk because his partner had called in sick at the last moment. As I learned later, Hugh hated to work inside; he was a street cop.

"Hey, Sarge, if he's here and wants to work, I'll go out with him. We can put my car back in service since it's so busy tonight."

Hugh looked at me and said, "I mean, that's if he wants to work," posed almost as a question. I had already made mental plans on where I was going based on this "freebie" night. But with Hugh looking at me like he needed to be rescued, I agreed that I would work.

Sergeant Warner went into the watch commander's office and cleared it with Lieutenant Zaprzalka, who came out and introduced himself. He was a well-seasoned older guy with pure white hair and deep blue eyes. "Goff, didn't anyone tell you you'd be carried tonight?"

"No, sir."

"Well, ya made the trip in all the way from the South Side, so if you wanna work, we can use another car, but it's up to you."

"I'll work. I've got nothing else to do tonight."

"Okay. Nightingale, take good care of this guy, will ya?"

"Absolutely, boss."

Hugh was overjoyed at getting out from behind the desk.

"I hate pushing paper and talking to these assholes that call the station all night for bullshit. I'm glad you felt like working. My name is Hugh Nightingale."

"Nice to meet you, Hugh."

"Just for agreeing to partner up tonight, I'm buying lunch." He made sure to jab a finger in my chest, which I came to find out was a habit of his, anytime he wanted to make a point.

Hugh and I hit it off well and eventually became partners for a few periods after that. Hugh was a great guy, and we laughed all night working together. Hugh had the neatest handwriting of anyone I had ever met. His case reports looked like they were printed on a press. Each letter was perfectly formed. Some of the things that impress me may seem strange, maybe because neat handwriting is a skill I lack.

"Are you hungry right now, Frank? Cuz I know a joint that's just like a little trailer, and it's still open. They got great cheeseburgers, and we can get there if we haul ass. I'll drive."

"Sounds good to me."

That was probably the fastest I had ever ridden in a squad car when we weren't on an emergency call. We got there three minutes before closing, and the guy had already put the closed sign on the door. But when he saw Hugh, he laughed and shook his head. He spoke in broken English.

"You late, you late today, Hugh."

We ate lunch, and true to his word, Hugh picked up the tab. The cheeseburgers were the best I ever had.

We took in a couple of calls and handled them accordingly. Surprisingly, we didn't have to arrest anyone yet. Then around

3:30 a.m. Hugh, who had been quiet for about fifteen minutes, spoke up. "Hey, if you don't mind, can you tell me how that thing went down the other night?"

"What do you want to know?"

"Ah, it seems weird, but I know we're close to where it happened. I just want to see if you can walk me through it. I've never had to shoot anyone, and I hope I never will, but I'd like to get some insight or your perspective and see what it was like."

I didn't respond right away because I was trying to process the scenario in my mind without having to repeat any specifics over and over to get to the crux of his inquiry.

What was it like? he wanted to know. I didn't think I could answer that question because my response might seem a bit odd.

On the previous night, an Office Of Professional Standards (The Civilian Review Unit) agent came into the district to partake in the shooting investigation. Her name was Ruby Rogers. I hadn't met her until that night, but I have to say she was very professional, thorough, and knowledgeable. I had heard a lot of negative things about OPS, but this was not at all what I experienced with Miss Rogers.

One of the questions Ruby asked was how I felt after being involved in an OIS (Officer Involved Shooting). My response was as follows:

"I don't think I can articulate what you think I should be feeling about this, Miss Rogers, or what might be considered the appropriate response to your question. But here is what I will tell you. I once heard it said that 'He that pulls the trigger, feels no pain.' I can tell you right now with absolute certainty, that has not been my experience, and I hope it never is."

I answered her question honestly, and she seemed satisfied with the response.

As a side note, Ruby Rogers handled a number of false allegations made against me over the years, none of which were ever sustained, and rightly so. We came to respect one another in our respective positions, and I think she is a wonderful and classy lady. Ruby became a supervisor in that unit and surprised me when she attended my retirement party many years later. She even gave a little speech on my behalf.

"All right, Hugh. It happened up there a few blocks."

It just so happened we were driving on Cicero Avenue, like the previous night, and were also northbound.

"Hugh, we were right about here when a woman …just like this woman who's bleeding from the forehead now and coming towards our car, stopped us."

It was déjà vu. It was literally happening again.

"Police, that man in the brown striped shirt just bust me in my head with a pistol."

Hugh, who was driving, looked at me incredulously. "Am I in your dream?"

"You gotta arrest him before he gets away. He gonna run up in that building for sure."

I notified the dispatcher and jumped out of the car. We were on the exact same street as the night before and only seventy-five yards west of the original incident. Hugh was coming up from the rear but was still fifty yards behind me when the offender turned into a three-flat building. The radio was off, so he didn't hear me coming up behind him. Once he got into the building, he made it up the first flight and then started up the second landing when I came through the door. Thoughts of the previous night flashed like quick still shots from an old movie in and out of my head while I hoped this guy wasn't as crazy as the guy from last night.

He looked down at me without saying a word and kept walking up the stairs. That wasn't a good sign.

"Police! Stop right there and put your hands in the air."

He didn't say anything as he turned to face me.

The victim was right; he had a gun. It was a large framed revolver in the front of his waistband. *This will be easy. He's cooperative, and the gun is in plain view. His hands are above his head, so all is well.*

I kept moving up the staircase in a slow and cautious manner but was about four or five stairs below him. My gun was pointing directly at his chest when Hugh ran into the vestibule.

The bad guy suddenly reached for his gun and pulled it out.

I was shocked and couldn't believe the man in front of me was in my gun sights and making the same move that another fool had made just about twenty-four hours earlier. I hesitated for a moment, and a dozen scenarios raced through my mind.

No one's gonna believe me. I can't shoot first. I'm going to need some clear and convincing evidence that I had to shoot, and the only way to be sure of that is to let this guy get one off at me. If I don't, the powers that be will think I'm trigger happy or just plain crazy. They will never believe what is actually the truth. Same cop, same street, same time, same scenario, two days in a row, and I wasn't even supposed to be working the street tonight.

I don't know how fast the mind works relative to speed in identifying and analyzing a critical situation and then formulating a plan of action. I only knew I had about a half-second, and every one of those thoughts I mentioned raced through my mind but left as quick as they came.

As dumb as a move like this seems, I wasn't going to shoot him just because he pulled a gun from his waistband.

I would be totally justified, as I was in fear for my life and facing an armed offender who was drawing down on me. I also decided that I wouldn't let him get one off either if I could help it and time it right. I would wait until he raised the gun toward me and then shoot. That way, the high-velocity blood spatter on his forearm and weapon would corroborate its position at the time I fired my Python.

But all of that was wasted energy. I wasn't forced to make that decision. Thankfully he never pointed his gun at me. Instead, though it was a boneheaded move on his part, he pulled the gun out and threw it to the floor.

By then, Hugh had rounded the landing and recovered the gun.

"I got his gun, Frank. Did that asshole pull it on you?"

"No, Hugh. Not at all. He was very cooperative."

I was so relieved but still angered that the guy on the stairs would place us both in such a precarious position for nothing.

I was ready to go off on him because he didn't have any idea of the level of high-intensity stress that he had put me through; or how close he came to winning a toe tag.

"What were you thinking, buddy?"

Even though I was enraged on the inside by his action, I could see that he wasn't a bad guy. He didn't present himself that way, and I'm glad I read him right.

"Officer, I'm sorry. I just wanted to get rid of the gun so you wouldn't shoot me." He was as sincere and apologetic as anyone could be.

This is exactly why I put both of these chapters in the book. It illustrates the split-second decisions, dilemma, scrutiny, and backlash officers face when everyone and their grandmother Monday morning quarterbacks an officer's actions.

Shooting the bad guy the night before was a blessing, as hard as that is to believe. If I had not been involved in that, the man standing before me would have surely been killed, and as you will see, he wouldn't have deserved what he came within a millisecond of getting.

During my interview with my prisoner #Leroy Mills, he relayed the following to us regarding the woman that claimed he busted her in the head with a pistol.

First of all, it was his legally married wife and not a stranger, as she led us to believe. They had been married for ten years. Mr. Mills had two jobs and had never been arrested. As far as what happened tonight, Hugh and I agreed he wouldn't be going to jail.

Mr. Mills worked a day shift job for the railroad as a switchman, and because he wanted to move his family out of this neighborhood and into a house, he had taken a part-time job as an armed security guard that checked I.D.s in and out of a warehouse three nights a week. This happened to be one of those nights. Mr. Mills wasn't due home until 5 a.m.; however, there was a power outage at the warehouse, and they had sent the employees home except the full-time security guard who worked inside.

Mr. Mills said that when he arrived home early at 3:10 a.m., the front door to his apartment was closed but unlocked. This surprised him because he and his wife both grew up in this neighborhood, and his wife was very security conscious. In addition to that, her purse was sitting next to the nightstand in their bedroom.

He went into his twin daughters' bedroom, thinking maybe his wife had fallen asleep as she had done on several occasions. But she wasn't in there either. He kissed his sleeping daughters like he always did when he came home from work and then checked the bathroom. He waited a few minutes, thinking his wife would return shortly and had probably just gone to the downstairs neighbor's apartment for something.

Mr. Mills said that's when it dawned on him that an acquaintance with whom his wife was once very friendly in high school was released from the penitentiary earlier that day. He went by the name of #Jumbo Brooks. Jumbo had served sixteen years for his part in a murder. Mr. Mills also knew that there was a welcome home party for Jumbo at the corner tavern that had been planned for him and that he knew his wife had received a flyer for that party. But she said she was not interested in going because Jumbo was a "bad dude," according to her.

It was clear to me that he did not like Jumbo and didn't want to associate with any criminals. He wanted to bring his daughters up right and set an example for them as to what kind of man they should let in their lives in the future. He expected the same from his wife.

Mr. Mills said he decided to go down to the tavern that would be closing at 4 a.m. and get his wife out of there if that's where she was. He knew if he didn't get there quickly, she might decide to accompany some of the players to an after-hours joint.

Because Mr. Mills didn't drink, and for that reason had never been inside that tavern, he was leery about going in unarmed. He knew a lot of the hood rats hung out there, and most had reputations in line with Jumbo's. So, he took his service revolver in with him for his own protection.

Mr. Mills said that when he walked in, he saw Jumbo and his wife dancing. She was being overly friendly and, according to him, "disgracefully" over-friendly. He did not elaborate anymore, so we didn't ask.

"Officer Goff, I'm being straight with you. I grabbed my wife by her arm pretty hard and jerked her away from Jumbo. I told her to get her ass back home with her babies and don't gimme no shit. That's when Jumbo got in my face and told me I better let her go cuz he ain't through dancing. Then he pushed me backward away from her. And then told me if I didn't get my ass out of there, he was gonna whoop my ass. So I pulled my gun and told him to back off. That's when I got hit from behind with a bottle."

He bent down to show me a large bump on his head.

"That's when I turned around and saw it was my own old lady. My wife was taking the side of a killer! The bottle had busted when she hit me, so I thought she might try it again, and I reached for it. She pulled it back so I couldn't grab it outta her hand, and she hit her own self in the forehead. It started to bleed a little bit. I told her to get her ass home, and she left out and went home, and I thought that was the end of it."

But that wasn't the end of it, as Hugh and I soon learned.

"Well, that's not what she did, Mr. Mills. She ran out the door like you said, but she hid on the side of the building until you left. Then she waited for either Jumbo to come out or a police car to come by."

This meant that Hugh and I happened to come by at just the right time for her to make her claim. She acted as though she didn't know her "assailant" and claimed he hit her in the head with the gun.

"Officer, go ask anyone in there and look at my gun. There's no blood on it or me. I wouldn't hit her with the gun and take a chance on losing my job or my kids. Please go ask someone; just don't ask Jumbo."

"I assume Jumbo will be a big guy?"

"Officer, Jumbo is every bit of six foot seven and three hundred pounds of mostly muscle. No brains, just muscle."

Hugh called for a backup car to hold onto Mr. Mills while we went in to talk to the patrons. As usual, nobody saw anything or knew what we were talking about, including the bartender and Jumbo. As far as we were concerned, it was case closed.

I didn't arrest Mr. Mills for a number of reasons, but let's just say it was because he was within his one-hour time frame that security guards are granted so they can carry their weapons to and from their homes to a place of business without fear of arrest. Of course, an armed guard would be in violation if they entered a liquor establishment in that time period. But I used my discretion because no one saw anything and we couldn't establish with absolute certainty that he was in the liquor establishment since no one other than Mr. Mills had said he was there.

Hugh Nightingale concurred that there was no call for an arrest. It was a "he said, she said," and my observations of the wound to the complainant's forehead were more consistent with a cutting instrument than with blunt force trauma.

***

"I'm sorry."

"Sorry for what, Hugh?"

"If I didn't ask you to drive over here, we could have avoided this bullshit."

"I don't look at it that way, Hugh. We made a friend in Mr. Mills… I think. And anytime we can make friends out here, they are always potential sources of information in the future when something bad happens in the neighborhood or as witnesses in our defense if they happen to see what went down."

Hugh looked at me while lighting up a smoke. He took a long drag on it before he spoke.

"You know what? You're right. Mr. Mills thanked me when I took the handcuffs off of him and shook my hand, and I could tell he meant it. It was firm, and he clasped one hand over the outside of my hand. I think that shows real sincerity."

"Me too."

I only saw Mr. Mills twice during the following year. The last time was when I stopped while he washed his car in front of his building. He was waiting on a moving truck and was exuberant over the fact that his divorce was finalized. As rare as this was back then, he was given full custody of his daughters. His ex-wife chose to move in with Jumbo and basically abandoned her kids.

I've thought about Mr. Mills time and again over the years and am happy that I held my fire that day, or I would have never known Mr. Mills or the true story behind the initial "hand waver" complaint. If things had gone the other way, two little girls would have lost their father, who wanted nothing more than to make sure they were safe and cared for in a rough neighborhood. He would have been portrayed as a criminal who attempted to kill a policeman. That would have been a travesty. I'm sure under their dad's guidance, his girls turned out to be happy, productive young ladies. At least I hope they did, but you never know…all you can do is hope.

Chapter 12: Who Am I?

Dispatcher: "Beat 1525."

"1525 go...."

"1525, see the complainant regarding a suspicious woman, supposedly emptying the garbage at 1577 No. Latrobe."

"10-99."

"Let us know if you're gonna need a backup, 1525."

"10-99."

I pulled up to the brick bungalow and observed the front door slightly open. A nervous-looking sixty-something woman frantically motioned for me to come inside.

"Good afternoon, ma'am. Are you the one who called?"

"I am. Come in, officer but hurry. I don't want her to see me talking to you."

Once inside the neatly kept living room, it was clear that this lady watched all of the goings-on in the neighborhood. There were two sets of binoculars. One was hanging on a hook by the front window, and one hung on a hook by the rear kitchen window.

"I'm Officer Goff. How can I help you today?"

"Just let me check real quick to make sure she's not watching us."

The complainant dashed to the back, side, and front windows to look out.

"Okay, I don't see her. Hi, I'm #Mary Grabowski. The reason I called is because the young man that lives next door to me, and has from the time he was about ten years old, recently inherited the house from his mother who died a few months ago. His name is #Kenny Kentsen, and he's about thirty. Now he's always been a little strange, and maybe that's because he was an only child, if that can account for anything. He went to private school, and he never played with the other kids in the neighborhood."

"Okay, but who is the lady, and what's the problem with emptying the garbage. Does she throw it in your yard or trash can…or what?"

"Oh no, nothing like that. For the last three weeks, a woman, a nurse to be more precise, comes out and empties it."

"Okay, and …?"

"Well, every evening, just before the sun goes down, she comes out in the full nurse's uniform, including her nurse's cap. Then she stands next to his garbage can and lets out a blood-curdling scream. She throws the trash into the can and slams it down really hard. Then she runs down the alley all the way to the corner with her hands waving around over her head, screaming like some kind of nut. Then she runs back into the house and slams the door real hard. She does it so hard my windows actually rattle."

"Have you talked to Kenny about her?"

"I have not seen Kenny since his mother died, and I don't know if something's wrong or not over there. If something's wrong and she's the nurse caring for him, I think something needs to be looked into because she's more like a crazy person than a nurse."

"Okay, I'll go next door and check on Kenny, and I'll have him give you a call."

"No, no, I don't want them to know I talked to you."

"Okay. I'll take care of it."

"1525…"

"1525, go ahead."

"1525 is relocating to 1579 N. Latrobe on a well-being check."

"1525, you are relocated."

The brown brick bungalow was exactly the same as Mrs. Grabowski's and obviously built by the same builder. So I was already familiar with the interior layout.

A male voice answered my knock.

"Yes, who is it?"

"It's the police."

"What do you want?"

"I want to talk to Kenny, but I don't want to talk through the door and have all your neighbors hear our business. Are you Kenny?"

"Yes. Give me a few minutes, and I'll let you in."

I waited by the door and could hear him talking to someone, but the voices were muffled. It was probably the crazy nurse.

The door swung open, and a very slender-looking young man stood there. He was Caucasian but seemed to have albino features. His hair was a white-blonde color, and it was combed back but short in length. He reminded me of David Bowie, except unlike Bowie, he had two blue eyes, and they were ice blue. His skin was as white as I've ever seen. I suspected that he rarely came out in the sunlight. He was dressed in a black and blue plaid shirt with a tight pattern and buttoned at the top. His pants were black, as were his highly polished shoes.

"Hello, Kenny. I'm Officer Goff. How are you doing today?"

I couldn't help but notice a large drafting table in the center of the living room. There were several very detailed blow-ups of mechanical images drawn in pencil that detailed a larger scale image of the smaller mechanism.

"I'm okay."

"Wow, that's quite a setup you have there, Kenny. Drafting was one of my favorite subjects in school."

"It's how I make my living. I work out of my house. This is for the Sears catalog coming out at Christmas. It shows how the mechanics of this toy work the operating features of the Atlas Missile set they will be selling."

"Very nice freehand work, I gotta say. I couldn't do it that precisely."

"No one can. That's why they hired me."

"I see. Well, Kenny, I'm here because some of your friends wanted to know if you were okay. You know, in good health and everything because they hadn't seen or heard from you since your mother passed away. So I'm just here to see…."

"What friends are you talking about?"

"I didn't get their names; it just came over the air from my dispatcher. He must have talked to them."

"The reason I ask is that I don't have friends, and I don't want friends."

"Well, maybe you have people who care about you, and you don't realize that they are concerned with your well-being. I understand that you have a nurse that comes and goes from here. Maybe that's why they were worried. Are you being cared for by a nurse?"

I could see Kenny was getting a little uneasy and fidgeting with his shirt's top button.

"Is the nurse here now, Kenny?"

"No, she left for the day."

"Did she also leave her medical bag and sweater I see on the chair in the next room?"

Kenny turned and looked at where I had pointed and honestly seemed shocked.

"Oh… she must have come back while I was working. She only uses the backdoor, and when I'm concentrating, I don't hear what's going on around me very often."

"I understand. What's her name?"

"Well, she's my sister."

Something was off because the longtime neighbor said he was an only child. I wondered why he would say that.

"Great, does your sister have a name?"

"Yes, it's Kendra."

"Well, I'd like to talk to Kendra. Will you call her for me?"

"I'll have to get her. She must be in her bedroom, or she would have answered the door."

Kenny disappeared around the corner and grabbed Kendra's sweater, which had medical pins and badges on it.

I could hear the two of them conversing but couldn't see where they were, but it sounded like they were behind a closed door.

About a minute later, nurse Kendra came into the adjoining room. Like the neighbor had said, she was dressed in the full nurse's uniform, including the sweater and nurse's cap. She had on her white nurse's shoes and picked up her medical bag, sliding it over her left forearm the way women often do before speaking.

"Hello, officer… are you alone?"

That question seemed out of line and a bit concerning. She looked like Kenny, so much so that they could be twins. Everything was identical to Kenny's except for her hair being longer. It only took about a second to realize that she looked so much like Kenny because Kendra was Kenny.

"My brother told me that you wished to speak with me, officer… what can I do for you?"

She moved closer and swayed to and fro, thrusting her padded bra within a few inches of my chest. She was flirting with me!

Her voice didn't sound like Kenny's. It was soft and very feminine, as were her gestures.

Was there a nurse here who was harmed or maybe even dead, and Kenny covered it up by assuming her identity? Or was Kenny just a nut job? I had to find out before I left.

"Yes, I do need to talk to you. Are you Kenny's sister Kendra?"

"I am, and yes, I'm single if that's your next question."

"Okay. It's nice to meet you. Are you taking care of Kenny for some medical issue?"

"That's a doctor-client privilege thing, so I'd rather not say. You understand, don't you, officer?"

"Yes, I know about the privacy issue, but I really wish you would help me out here. Do you work at a hospital as an R.N., or are you an L.P.N.?"

"I'm an L.P.N."

"Okay. Where did Kenny go?"

"He's in the bedroom."

"Will you get Kenny back out here for me so I can talk to him?"

"Sure, wait here. I'll see if he's decent."

"Great."

I didn't know how Kenny planned to pull this off, but I wasn't in any hurry.

Kenny came back into the living room and was dressed as he was during our first encounter.

"Did my sister answer all of your questions, officer?"

"Well, no, Kenny. I wanted to talk to both of you about another issue, and maybe we can resolve it to everyone's satisfaction. In other words, I need to talk to both of you together."

"Okay...Kendra...Kendra, will you come here? She's got that damn television on. I'll go get her."

It wasn't long before Kendra presented herself to me once again and, as expected, without Kenny.

"Kenny says you wanted to talk to me about a problem of sorts."

"Yes, but get Kenny back in here."

"I'll get him."

Kenny came back into the room and was back in his Kenny clothes, but he had forgotten to remove the wig.

"Officer, she is driving me crazy with this back and forth stuff, and when I get stressed out, I have migraines that interfere with my work. Just tell me what the problem is, and I'll tell her."

"Either you both come out here together, or I'm going in that bedroom to make sure everything that's going on in this house is on the up and up."

"If you want us together, you will have us together. Kendra, get your ass out here right now!"

Kenny went out of sight for about two minutes. When he came back this time, he had lipstick on the top and bottom right side of his lips and had hurriedly and sloppily put on blue eye shadow and powder on the right side of his face. He was wearing his black pants and a blonde wig that was now moved, so it only covered the right side of his head. He had one white nurse's shoe on his right foot and a black men's shoe on the left. He was wearing the nurse's sweater over his arm and one shoulder but had his man's shirt on the way you would normally wear a shirt. I knew where this was headed. I would be talking to a male side and then, when called for, a female side.

Since Kenny thought this was normal, I'd play along. So I questioned them individually.

"First, I have to explain the problem. Besides people worrying about Kenny's well-being, there seems to be a disturbance problem that is quite upsetting to some of the neighbors involving you, Kendra."

Kendra spoke first and turned her female side toward me. "Like what?"

"Kendra, folks are saying that when you throw out the trash, you always slam the lid down with a loud bang and then take off running down the alley, screaming and waving your hands over your head. This concerns them because they think someone is attacking you or that you might have some other problem that causes you to do this."

Kenny's side: "I've never heard her do that."

"Well, it happens. Multiple people have reported it, and that's why I'm here."

"Kendra's side: "He's right, Kenny. I have done it. I find it's the only thing that helps."

Kenny's side: "Helps what?"

Kendra's side: "Helps with your headaches."

Kenny's side: "Is that how you make them go away so fast?"

Kendra's side: "Yes, it's the only thing that works for you."

Kenny's side: "That's why you're the nurse, and I'm the patient. Thank you, thank you, thank you."

"Kendra, does Kenny take any medication?"

Kenny's side: "She won't tell you, but I will. I take lithium."

"When was the last time you took it?"

"I take it every day."

"Did you take it today?"

"Kendra, did you give me my lithium today?"

"Kendra's side: "I have it in my medical bag." She produced the prescribed lithium and handed it to Kenny, who took it without water.

"Before I go, Kenny, I have to take a quick look around the house and basement. Is that okay?"

"Sure."

A fifteen-minute search of the home didn't yield any other persons present. But I did find a telephone book and noted a relative, as well as the name of the doctor who prescribed the meds to Kenny. I notified them as to what was happening at Kenny's home. The relative promised to take care of it, and the doctor said the sister nurse thing had been going on for years and was not a result of the recent passing of his mother. I reported the findings to the neighbor and told her that there was a mental issue going on and that no one was in danger in the home at the present time.

Out of curiosity, I stayed in the area and particularly Kenny's block, as often as I could. Like clockwork, just as the neighbor told me, the nurse came out. I was able to witness the bizarre trash emptying ritual in person ten minutes before my shift was over.

I don't know if that was the last time it happened or if the neighbors just got used to it and accepted the behavior, and stopped reporting it. I never heard any more reports after this incident.

I hope Kenny, who seemed like a nice but odd guy with some problems, got the help he needed.

Chapter 13: Tyrone Deel

I was riding alone that night when she flagged me down. I would have normally had a partner, but he took a tour of duty as he had spent the last nine hours in the courtroom on a jury trial.

That's when the "Hand Waver" flagged me down.

"Hey, officer, a boy's just been run over by a car that took off."

"1531…"

"1531, come in."

"1531, I just got a hand waver who told me a child has been struck by a hit and run vehicle in the 4800 block of Quincy. Get fire rolling."

"1531, 10-4, an ambulance is on the way."

When I pulled up to the scene, I was heartbroken. #Tyrone Deel was lying in the street. He was seven years old and one of the local kids I had talked to on numerous occasions. His body was twisted in a way that I knew was not good. He had been run over by a speeding motorist who had taken off moments earlier. The only description witnesses could supply was that it was an older four-door maroon Chevy with a male black driver.

Tyrone was the son of a local drug dealer but was different from the rest of the boys in the hood, at least in my eyes. He had a spark about him; he was good-looking and bright. In another environment, he would flourish, but not here.

I had a penchant for Hershey bars and always kept a few in my squad car to share with a few of the neighborhood kids. These were the ones who would wave me down and ask if I had any "Hot Sheets." Those were the daily bulletins we were handed out at roll call with pictures of wanted offenders on one side and a list of license plates from stolen vehicles on the other side. Most cops had several and would gladly pass them out, me included. But, I'd also give candy to the kids and tell them if they saw any license plates to let me know. I knew nothing would come of it, but it made the kids feel important and just a little boost to their self-esteem.

Tyrone was the son of a dope dealer known as "#Pitbull Deel." He was called that because of the two Pits he owned that guarded his dope spot on Quincy Street. They were also quite vicious, just like their master.

Deel and I started off on the wrong foot a few months earlier when I first met him. It was in response to a man selling drugs in the 4800 block of West Quincy Street. His street name, Pitbull, and physical and clothing description were given out, along with the fact that two pit bulls were protecting the abandoned auto in the empty lot where the drugs were hidden.

With such detailed information, I knew that the caller was legit and acted on the information. I was working with Hugh Nightingale at the time, and because the other cars in the district were down on assignment, we didn't have a backup.

Deel was standing at the front of the lot and about fifty feet from the abandoned car.

"Good evening, sir. We got a call that drugs were being sold here. Do you know anything about that?"

"Ain't no drugs being sold here. Somebody bullshittin' y'all."

"Nice looking dogs. Are they yours?"

"Yeah, they be mines."

"Well, do me a favor because they don't look so friendly. Call them away from the car cuz I need to check it out."

"I ain't callin' them away from shit."

I pumped a round into the shotgun.

"I won't ask again. Call them away from the car, or I may be forced to kill them, and I don't want to do that. They're just doing what dogs do. So it's up to you."

"Punk, you ain't gonna do shit, and you knows it, so stop acting all bad and shit and go about yo' business."

"You done?"

"Man, get the fuck outta here."

I looked at Nightingale and shook my head.

He took a long drag from his cigarette, which he always did before making some profound statement.

"If I were you, I'd believe him. He don't bullshit. Just move your dogs so they don't get hurt."

"You crazy as him, y'all know you ain't gonna…."

I proceeded to the abandoned car hoping the dogs would move or he'd call them off. This was a lot owned by the city and not anyone's private property.

Bang. Bang.

"What the fuck! Y'all kilt my dogs! Y'all kilt my motherfuckin' dogs!"

"Just one; the other one ran away."

Nightingale took another drag on his cigarette.

"I told you."

"You got any weapons or drugs on you, sir?"

"You the one that kilt my dogs…"

"I asked you a question, and I'm not gonna ask a second time."

"No, the drugs is in the car, but they not mines."

"Go get them, so I don't have to hurt your other dog if he comes back, and I might let you drop them down the sewer."

Deel brought a small handful of tin foil packets up and said. "That's all."

"Hand them to my partner. When I check the car and find more dope or a gun, you go to jail, and your other dog will be put in the cage unless I have to kill him too."

"Okay…I be getting the rest; they ain't no gun, that's why I got my pits, but don't fuck with my dog."

Deel produced a plastic baggie that had about forty more tins.

"Dump everything down the sewer, and don't be dealing no more shit out here. Your neighbors are tired of it. They'd like to live in peace and tranquility. Do you understand me?"

"Yeah… but you kilt my dog…"

"Don't worry about it."

"Don't worry about it? Is that all you gotta say, man?"

"You ain't going to jail, so just do what I said and don't be dealing so open and notorious out here. The good people in the hood don't appreciate it."

I notified my supervisor that I had to destroy a dog, and he pulled up within minutes. It was Sergeant Spicer, a top-of-the-line guy who handed me a Misc X card to fill out, and that was the end of it.

Deel moved his street operation indoors after that.

Unlike the other cops in the 15th District, I never had a problem with Deel from that day forward. I'm sure in today's environment, I'd be fired, sued, and probably jailed for what I did back then. But at the time, it was very efficient based on time and energy expended and the standards in getting the job done. I really felt bad about his dog, but without him calling it off, that thing could have torn me apart, and I'm sure the other one would have helped him.

Back to little Ty. The times I stopped and talked to this kid, he was always grinning about something, and seemed like it was a big thing for a cop to stop and talk to him like a buddy. Ty told me of his dreams of becoming a fireman someday. He said he'd be a cop, but his daddy wouldn't like that. Ty was really sharp and picked up on every little thing I did when talking to him.

"Hey, officer Goff, I see when you pull over and talk to me, you take yo' other pistol and move it to the front. I know why. That's so if some dude run up on you, you can pull it faster than the other one on your side there."

He was right.

***

Ty was in tears and a lot of pain. His little body was twisted and the lower half was rotated almost a full 180 degrees behind him.

"Hey Ty, how you doin', buddy? You're gonna be okay. You hear that ambulance coming? You're gonna go for a ride. Now, you don't have to wait till you're a fireman to go riding with all those lights and sirens. I'll tell them to blast it a few extra times for you." Ty let out a weak laugh and looked up at me with the scared but innocent eyes of a child.

"Is you going with me?"

"You bet I am, but I'll be following you in my squad car, okay?"

I did, and he was admitted to Loretto Hospital with one broken leg, a fractured pelvis, a broken ankle, and some internal injuries. His father and mother were nowhere to be found.

The following day I was working a different beat, about a mile from where Ty lived. But I happened to pass a store displaying Easter baskets. One of them was set up with a fire truck in it. I thought of Ty and immediately went in and bought it for him.

On the way home from work that night, I stopped at the hospital. Even though it was after visiting hours, no one stopped me. Ty was asleep, so I put the gift on the nightstand and left. The following day was Easter Sunday, so I'm not sure if they celebrated it or not, but either way, I was sure he'd get a kick out of it. It was loaded with candy, and the fire truck was metal, not some cheap plastic crap, so he could play a little rough with it as kids tend to do.

About a month went by before I saw Ty again. He was playing with some other kids when I rolled up on him. He was casted from his waist all the way down one leg but was surprisingly able to stand on his own, though he should have been in the wheelchair he was next to.

"Hey, Ty! When did you get out of the hospital?"

"Do you got a hot sheet for me? I got out this morning."

"No, but I got a candy bar, and I only have one, so don't let the other kids see it. I see your buddies have all written things on your cast, and it looks so full up I don't see a spot for me."

I gave Ty the candy bar. As he started to unwrap it, I saw his dad walking up to us. He slapped it out of Ty's hand and told him to "get yo' ass back up in the crib and don't be talkin' to no fuckin' police."

Ty hobbled back toward his apartment building but stopped about halfway and turned back toward me. His face showed the disappointment I was feeling at that moment. His dad started walking away from the squad but stopped when I called out to him.

"What you got to say? You kilt my dog."

"Mr. Deel, you have an intelligent young son there who can be more than you or any of your family members are or will ever be. He wants to be a fireman someday. If you don't do something different, he's gonna end up just like you, your brother, or your cousin who was killed by the police. You slapped a candy bar to the ground for what? To show what a big badass man you think you are? Well, you didn't let him enjoy the chocolate bar, but I hope you didn't throw away the Easter basket I left him at the hospital."

I was pissed and drove off before things escalated.

About an hour later, I drove down Quincy Street again as it was on my beat. Mr. Deel came running out and waving his arms above his head. My first thoughts were that something terrible had happened to Ty, but that was not the case. Deel spoke to me in a hushed tone.

"Hey, officer, in about a half-hour, can you meet me behind the building at Fifth and Cicero?"

"Why would I do that?"

"Please, officer, I can't talk to you in front of my peoples."

"Okay."

As he walked back to the lot he formerly dealt drugs from, he played the game. "Yeah, and don't be talkin' to my son anymore, mo-fo."

I read between the lines and did meet up with him. The gesture of kindness I showed his son made a big impression on this hardcore thug. He became my best informant for the time period I spent in the 15th District. Except for Hugh Nightingale, no other coppers knew.

As for Tyrone…tragically, he was the victim of a homicide when a bullet meant for his father struck him three years later while visiting family on the south side. R.I.P., Ty. You deserved a better life.

Chapter 14: Always Take a Peek

Ever since this happened to me, I tell coppers why they should always "take a peek."

It was hot and humid, and the a/c in our squad was out, as usual. We had just finished a two-block long foot chase assisting another beat car and had to do a little battle with the parolee who didn't want to go back to the joint. We were on our way in, but I was dying of thirst. The #Brother's liquor store a block away was the closest place to grab something cold to drink.

"I'm getting a pop before we go back to the station. Hugh, do you want anything to drink?"

"Nothing now. I'll get a cup of coffee when we get in."

Maybe it's just me, but drinking something hot after what we just went through seemed counterproductive.

Reaching into my right pocket as I came through the door

was a big mistake. My service revolver was on my right side in a low-slung position and had shifted to cover my balled-up fist full of change inside my pocket. I needed it out as fast as I could, and after one tug, it was still locked under the pressure of the holster and gun.

The guy sticking up the liquor store had one clerk at gunpoint behind the register with his arms over his head and the other on the floor face down.

I ripped my backup gun from the cross-draw position with my left hand faster than I ever thought I could while my right hand remained stuck in my pocket. If this was a quick draw contest, I was a loser. But I got lucky. The bad guy chose not to shoot. Instead, he dropped his gun on the counter and threw his hands in the air.

"You got me, officer, you got me."

I was thankful for his immediate cooperation, but his surrender was short-lived.

"Oh no, you don't, mutha fucka."

The clerk at the register grabbed the heavier end of a sawed-in-half pool cue with one hand and the guy's afro with the other and slammed his face into the counter, where he proceeded to beat him about the head and shoulders as viciously and as fast he could.

"Yo, hold up! Drop that club now!"

"This mutha fucka said he was gonna blow my head off, officer."

"Yeah, but he didn't, so stop whoopin' him. I'll take it from here."

I recovered the loaded small-caliber pistol from the counter and cuffed the stick-up man.

"Did anyone get hurt in your store?"

"No, officer. He just came in a minute before you did."

"Okay. This guy's gonna need to go to the hospital. I'll send my partner in to get your information."

"Hey, hey, officer," piped up the stick-up man. "Isn't you gonna arrest him for bustin' up my head and shit?"

"Your hands were still on the counter, so he probably thought you might go for the gun."

"Oh, c'mon, officer. You know I ain't that dumb with you pointin' that big ass gun at me."

Hugh was lighting up a smoke as I came out with the handcuffed prisoner, who was now bleeding profusely from the top of his head and down both sides of his face.

"I thought you went in for a pop."

" I did, but this guy was robbing the place when I walked in."

"I see you had to fuck him up a little."

"Not at all. He didn't resist me, and as a matter of fact, he's the most cooperative stick-up man I've ever arrested. The victim got a little carried away, so this guy is gonna need stitches. Call for a wagon to the Loretto, then get the info from the victim. I'll wait here for the transport."

I had the offender sit down against the storefront and out of the sun. he looked worse than he was.

As usual, when the police are on the scene of a crime, the crowds start to form up, especially when you have a prisoner covered in blood.

Within a minute of Hugh calling for a prisoner transport to the emergency room, our supervisor came tearing around the corner with the squealing tires and racing engine of Beat 1530. It was Sergeant Petrousonis.

"What the fuck happened here, Goff?"

"He was sticking up the liquor store when I walked in on him."

"Did he have a gun?"

"Yeah, it's in my pocket."

"Did you shoot him in the head?"

"No, that's the victim's handiwork."

"Oh, good. I'll meet you in the station."

"Hey officer," piped up the stick-up man once again, "when we get to court on this shit, is you gonna tell them how when I saw you, I laid the gun down?"

"Absolutely, cuz you and me are cool. You did the right thing, and I'll let the judge know."

I kept my word, and he was sentenced to four years by Judge Mahon.

Chapter 15: The Bulldick

I got lucky a few months after arriving in the 15th District. I was asked by Sergeant Eddie King to move upstairs to the tactical team. This is something a lot of young cops looked forward to because it got them out of uniform and the everyday paper jobs and domestics. It freed them up to concentrate on the heavier duty criminal activity in their areas.

I wouldn't be on Eddie's team because it was full. I'd be on another team until he had an opening. That was fine with me. I just wanted to be in plain clothes. The team I went to had a great reputation as hard-working cops and was loaded with great guys — Joe Cannon, Norm Lysiak, Mike Scornavacco, Don Rouzan, Skip Adams, and Curtis Baker, to name a few.

This was the day I would meet my new partner. I had heard a lot of stories about this copper but had never formally met him. To his inner circle, he was affectionately known as "The Bulldick."

For those who don't know what a Bulldick is, it has nothing to do with one's anatomy. It is a term used long ago to describe the old-time station house detectives who worked out of each district. They wore suits, fedora hats, and, weather permitting, long overcoats. These were the guys who went after the worst of the worst. Besides their duty weapons, they were heavily armed, often carried short-barrel shotguns, blackjacks, iron claws, and were the last guys you wanted to see if you were on their shit list. In fact, they could be the last guys you ever saw.

His name is Vic Grimm. At six foot one and one hundred and ninety pounds, this former Marine was the type of copper you wanted to have your back in any tough situation.

Vic had served honorably in Vietnam after enlisting in 1969. He was a member of the Elite Force–Recon Group while serving and did so for three years. I knew I was in good hands as not only was I working with a great copper, I'd be surrounded by these types on the team.

Vic walked in and looked me up and down, then spoke in his trademark baritone voice.

"So you're the guy I'm gonna be working with, huh? Well, I know who's buying lunch tonight."

He held out his hand and, making direct eye contact, said, "Vic Grimm...Bulldick."

After a few minutes of ball busting by the rest of the crew and listening to some district crime information relayed to us from the guys on the watch, it was time to hit the mean streets of Austin — a.k.a., the 15th District.

After grabbing a shotgun and radio, we settled into the unmarked squad. Vic wanted to know if I preferred to eat lunch before we rolled for the night or wanted to do it mid-shift to break up the night. We both preferred the former, and Vic, who was driving, headed over to a hideout-type of restaurant on North Avenue. I had been there twice and was aware of its reputation. The food was excellent, but many of the patrons tended to be of the mob variety, and by that, I mean the Chicago Outfit.

We recognized a few of the gangsters sitting at a table for six. They knew we were cops, and we knew who they were. One of the guys sitting with a side profile looked very familiar, as he should have because I had watched him while I was a kid living in Englewood. He was the star of a television show called The Wild Wild West. His name is Robert Conrad, and he was apparently very friendly with the group as they ate, drank, and laughed together. He turned and nodded at us, so we acknowledged the gesture.

After dinner, I asked for the check as that was what the Bulldick expected of me. The waitress told me that Mr. Conrad picked up the tab and left a healthy tip. She further went on to say that he told her that he understood our position and accepted our appreciation without troubling us to come to the table. We left with a nod, and he returned it with a wink. I thought that was a class move on his part.

It wasn't long after when we monitored a police chase that had been going on for a good twenty minutes or so. It started on the city's near north side before heading into the downtown area. From there, it bounced all over the Kennedy and then the Eisenhower Expressways with the driver going up and down the on and off-ramps, trying to lose the police.

The Black 1978 Oldsmobile had just blasted through a roadblock that two squad cars set up on one of the entrance ramps going west.

At the speed it was traveling, it would reach us in less than two minutes. So Vic positioned our unmarked car on one of the westbound ramps of the Eisenhower, and we waited.

A half dozen mars lights lit up the highway as the chase moved toward us.

"Let's put a box around it," said the Bulldick, and with that, we were joined by several marked units and another unmarked car with the same tactic in mind. We surrounded the car on all four sides. The car slowed down from an estimated ninety miles per hour to about sixty miles per hour.

The driver caught on to the tactic and decided to break out of the box by slamming into the lead car, almost like a pit maneuver. This caused both the squad car and the Oldsmobile to spin out.

The offender's vehicle went over a divider at about 6200 West on the x-way and came to a halt momentarily. The driver threw the vehicle in reverse and slammed the accelerator to the floor, squealing the tires. The rear bumper struck a traffic control device so hard that it flew off its base and sailed through the air and into a civilian's vehicle that had come to a stop during the commotion.

For a moment, we thought the chase was over, but that was not to be. The Oldsmobile's tires were smoking as it burned rubber and came racing forward. A tactical officer from the 12th District was the first to be struck. He was a plainclothes officer and slightly to my right in front of me.

Vic was able to jump out of the way. The explosion from his .44 Magnum revolver was deafening. He fired two rounds at the tires on the passenger side of the car. If he hadn't taken this precautionary move in the heat of battle and shot anywhere else, officers would have been in his direct line of fire. In the heat of the moment, that was good thinking on Vic's part.

Officer Rick DeFelice was on the driver's side and, because of the position of other officers, including me, opted to do the same thing that Vic did. He fired six rounds at the tires in an attempt to stop the madness.

The plainclothes officer who was struck went airborne and flew past my position. He let a few rounds go but was firing from the ground and was still in the direct path of the moving vehicle.

I had no place to go at this point. If the car was allowed to continue on its trajectory, the injured officer lying on the highway would be struck a second time. That was an unacceptable proposition.

I was hit head-on by the vehicle and, while being thrown across the hood, fired two shots into the driver before hitting the pavement. I can't explain the sensation of sliding across the hood while hearing multiple gunshots from unknown directions and waiting for one to impact my body, and wondering what would happen when I hit the ground from a speeding vehicle. I didn't know where I was gonna land as my momentum continued sending me on a trajectory I couldn't control. The vehicle suddenly slowed and rolled up the embankment before coming to a halt. The driver was no longer a threat.

The madness was finally over. The driver wasn't the only casualty; we also had injured officers. One of them was an Oak Park police officer who had come to assist us since that suburb bordered Chicago. An unknown officer who had fired at the vehicle shot him through the hand. Apparently, the officer who fired that round wasn't as tactically smart as Grimm, DeFelice, and the other injured officer. DeFelice was struck in the chest by his own ricochet from the spinning wheel of the auto he was firing at. I had injuries to my thigh, stomach, and right hand, but we were all lucky compared to the first officer struck by the vehicle. He required immediate surgery to reattach the muscles in his leg and had to undergo physical therapy for his injury.

As a cop, you wonder what goes through a person's mind when they do crazy things like this. In retrospect, it would seem like the driver was on a suicide mission. I can't think of any other logical explanation.

At worst, pulling over and being cooperative with the officer will get you a speeding ticket and a warning at best. So why not pull over and take the ticket? Why endanger so many lives and cause property damage to so many vehicles? I don't recall how many vehicles were struck during this rampage; I just know there were many.

All of the chaos that ensued was so unnecessary and all brought on by the demons in someone's fragile mind. This is what we learned later through the ensuing investigation. The driver had recently been forcibly evicted for nonpayment of rent, had been fired that day, had a car repossessed, and learned of an abrupt end to an engagement to be married. Admittedly, that's a lot for anyone to handle, but it's not the end of the world.

Some people just aren't equipped to handle that volume of problems all at once, and that's a shame. I think of the lives put in danger because of the selfish actions of another and wish people would seek help when they face problems and don't think they have the ability to handle them on their own. It would make for a better outcome all around. I hope the driver has found peace.

I disagree with so many of the bosses, politicians, and laypeople who believe police should not shoot at a moving vehicle. When that vehicle is being used as a weapon, the only difference between the car killing someone or a bullet doing the job is about three thousand pounds.

Chapter 16: Slick Willie

The Bulldick and I were driving westbound on Lake Street in slow-moving traffic due to the accident at Laramie. I was still relatively new to the 15th District at the time and still hadn't met all the players.

Suddenly there was a loud thud on the roof of our squad car. I thought for sure one of the railroad ties had come loose from the elevated train system above us and wondered why Vic hadn't stopped the car to investigate. He didn't flinch; it was almost as though he didn't hear it, but I knew he had.

"Have you met slick Willie yet?"

"No."

"You're about to."

Vic slammed on the brakes. That caused the object of my suspicions to roll off the roof and down the windshield, leaving an oil slick as he continued his forward momentum onto the hood. He eventually landed on the street in front of us.

"That's Slick Willie."

The man was naked and covered in cooking oil. His only clothing items were a pair of beat-up mismatched gym shoes and black leather gloves. He took off running southbound as Vic, without any fanfare, continued driving as if nothing out of the ordinary had just happened.

Slick Willie was just one of the local characters. We were soon to meet another nut job operating in the district. This one must have gotten his idea of concealment from the old Flash Gordon series that featured "The Clay People." Their bodies bore a clay-like epidermis instead of normal skin, allowing them to blend into the surrounding sidewalls of caves, hills, or even the ground. It was the ultimate in camouflaging in an outdoor environment.

A call of a Burglary in Progress came in. Other units were now in a foot chase of a male black that had climbed through a woman's bathroom window.

We saw him in the distance for a brief second before he made a turn into a group of schoolgirls waiting for the bus at Washington and Central. In his attempt to slow his pursuers down, he grabbed one of the girls and threw her in front of a moving bus. Then he disappeared behind the school.

Officers went to the injured girl's aid while Vic and I abandoned the squad car to search for him on foot. Walking through the alley behind the Siena Girls High School, I encountered an older man emptying his garbage. He didn't say anything to me. He just pointed to the top floor of the building next to the school.

"Hey, Vic. I think he's up there."

We proceeded to the top floor and looked behind the abandoned refrigerator. Nothing

"Let's check the roof, Vic."

A built-in ladder was attached to the sidewall, so up we went. Men's clothing was scattered about the roof, and it appeared to be what our bad guy had been wearing, but he was nowhere to be seen on this flat roof.

I kept walking and went over a two-foot-tall firewall that helped surround the airshaft in the building and separated the front half from the back half of the apartment building.

"Hey Bulldick, come over here. I don't know where the hell this guy went. I can't find him anywhere."

I stood within five feet of our offender, pointing down at him so Vic wouldn't accidentally step on him when he came over the wall.

Our guy was completely naked but covered at the same time. In an effort to conceal himself from us and blend into the newly resurfaced rooftop, he opened a five-gallon can of liquid tar left by the workers. He dumped it all over himself, and I mean from head to toe. He lay motionless even as we stood over him talking.

"It looks like he got away, Frank."

"You're right. I see his clothes over there. He even took off his pants, so he's gotta be running around naked."

"Watch yourself; there's a shitload of liquid tar spilled all over the place."

"Since he's naked, I hope he didn't get any of that tar on his Jones."

"I know. You remember that roofer we had that accidentally spilled it on his leg?"

"How can I forget? The poor guy had to have his leg amputated."

"I gives up, officer, I gives up. Please take me to the hospital right now. I got this shit all over my Jones, man. I needs help quick."

"I think it's too late, my man. The doctors will have to remove it."

"Oh lawd, please get me to the hospital, please."

"We'll see what we can do for you, but I can't make any promises."

The wagon was called, and we were fortunate that someone tossed a sheet from a window because the wagon guys were not gonna get stuck trying to clean tar out of the wagon and were looking for alternatives. The only material they had was a body bag, but they didn't want to waste it on him.

After very painful and painstaking clean-up work provided by the good nurses at Loretto Hospital, it turned out that was the worst punishment he'd receive. The pitch in the tar burns the hell out of the skin, so he was marked up pretty good. He spent less than two days in jail because a psych evaluation put him in a mental ward for a brief period. Since he was on parole after serving seven years of a ten-year sentence for sexually assaulting two women, I don't think he was as crazy as he acted.

He was able to con the psychiatrist who evaluated him and was released to a halfway house, where he struck again one week later. This time, they violated his parole, and the crazy act didn't work. He got an additional six years.

Chapter 17: Red Dog

Cruising through the hood and catching eyeballs is the norm when you're riding five deep in two unmarked cars. The locals pick up on us right away. They know someone or something is going down. As a practical matter, it's easier to sneak up on a target location in that fashion than the usual five unmarked squads we'd be rolling in.

It was a typically warm summer evening on Chicago's west side. Our tactical team was on the path to do what we did at least once a week, and that was to take down a gangbanger's dope flat. This one was on Jackson just east of Central.

Everyone on the team carried two guns, and at least two of us toted 12 gauge shotguns loaded with 00 buckshot. We didn't wear vests back then, which was hazardous to our health, but we did have tools in our war chest that worked to our advantage. One was the element of surprise, and the other was the skill to make a quick and decisive entry by way of the sledgehammer and the Chicago bar.

As soon as we rolled up on the apartment building, the lookouts on the street started chiming in from every direction.

"Five-O be rollin' up, Five-O be rollin' up."

The alert had been sounded to our intended targets, so we needed to get up to the apartment ASAP. Half the team moved up the three flights to the front door as fast as our feet would carry us, while the other half took the back door.

"Police, we have a search warrant. Open the door now!"

We could hear excited voices coming from inside the apartment.

"Police is out there; dump all that shit."

The unmistakable sounds of people running and a toilet flushing gave us cause to make an immediate forced entry.

Stieben blasted the door with the sledge, nearly taking it off at the hinges. We ran into the apartment and were met by a flurry of activity.

One guy was flushing dope down the toilet that hadn't refilled enough to make a clean second flush. Another had to be brought down, gun in hand, with a shotgun butt to the forehead. There were at least a dozen people in all, and half of them were children under the age of six. It took a few minutes to get everyone into the living room, where they could be controlled, searched, and disarmed.

Once we got the adults in handcuffs and the frightened children settled down, we began a systematic search of the premises.

A plastic bag had not flushed all the way down the toilet drain as the air in the bag kept it afloat with its one hundred and twenty-six tins of brown heroin. We recovered a sawed-off shotgun and four handguns in addition to the one butt head had when we entered.

An hour into the search, it was nearly over when I found a brass-colored metal box pushed into a corner and under a pile of shoeboxes. It contained a purple-colored velvet bag that looked similar to a Crown Royal bag. Inside was a brown and white substance with a gritty texture. I had never seen dope like this before, and it was a substantial amount, I'm guessing approximately one pound.

Since this was Stieben's search warrant, I brought it to him for clarification.

"Hey, Stieben, I found this in the closet, but it doesn't smell or look like any dope I've ever come across."

"Let me see that shit."

Stieben took a small handful and rubbed it between his thumb and forefinger before taking a whiff.

"I never saw shit that looks like this either; there's an odd smell but not like coke or heroin."

Stieben took a small amount and rubbed it on his gums to see if it would have a numbing effect. I know that's crazy. I've never done it. It could be poison, and even if it wasn't, you never know what your reaction will be to it. Plus, there are no quality control and safe-testing standards when it comes to dope. But it was something I have witnessed more than a few coppers do in the past.

"Well, it sure ain't any kind of cocaine cuz I ain't numbing up, but it might be heroin. I'm gonna take a little taste and see."

Stieben lifted his open palm with the substance in it to his lips as he walked into the living room where the adults were seated. With the bag in one hand and the suspect dope in the other, he spilled about a teaspoon's worth into his long red beard while giving it a taste test. This was not a good idea, and it was made clear when one of the ladies screamed out in horror.

"Ohhh, Lordy. Ohhh, my God! I can't believe what I'm seeing up in here! The police be eating my child, the police is eating up my child! Lord, don't tell me the police can eat my child!"

I'll never forget the look on Stieben's face.

"Hey, Red Dog… if I was to take a wild guess, I'd say that what you got stuck to your lips and beard are the cremated remains of this lady's child."

I'll end the story here.

Chapter 18: Crashing the Commander's Car

Lieutenant Timmy Daly had been newly appointed as commander of the 15th District, and I couldn't be happier. He was a guy I not only knew but actually respected as both a man and a boss.

He had been in charge of the wildest group of coppers I ever worked with, and they were the guys of Area One SOG.

Timmy took all of the idiosyncrasies of each cop in stride. That was a tough assignment for anyone, but he knew to a man they were hands-down great cops who could be trusted to handle anything thrown at them. Believe me when I say we had a lot of crap thrown at us.

When the guys in 15 learned that we were getting a new commander, some were anxious, and others were happy to see the current commander leaving. I was among the latter group.

Commander Daly proved himself to be a boss who took a great interest in his cops. By the end of his first week in the district, he knew every single officer by first name and face. In addition to that, he knew all the hotspots in the district.

I looked forward to introducing him to my partner so he would know how tight Vic Grimm and I were, just for future reference, if you get my drift. Vic was a great cop but operated on the edge, so to speak. I thought it would be a good thing to have a friendly commander who understood him, but Vic, unfortunately, wasn't around.

He had been injured and was on medical leave after being kicked in the hand by a thug we arrested after a car chase that ended up in Oak Park. His hand was broken in two places.

The guy was wanted for abducting a young woman into his car at Cicero and Division when she got off work at Leaf Candy Company. He had attempted to sexually assault her, but a passerby called it in to the police and scared the guy off. Fortunately, the woman was able to jump from the moving vehicle, albeit naked from the waist down, before he took off at a high rate of speed.

A beat car responding to the call was on him in seconds and chased him west on Division when we picked them up at Laramie and took over the lead.

Within two minutes, the offender crashed into a tree and bailed out on foot. Vic caught up to him in a rear yard and tackled him. This thug fought like a wild man. It was obvious he didn't want to go to jail. Once we got him cuffed up and transported him in for processing, Vic told me that his hand was broken, but he waited until we were finished processing the arrest before he sought treatment.

A week later, we were working the day shift. Vic was off, and I was paired with Curtis Baker.

Curtis was a great guy for whom I had much respect. Although we hunted for a pinch all day, we came up empty. That's not good when you're on the tac team, but sometimes it happens.

Curtis had been telling me about some mechanical problems he was having with his car and that it was still in the shop. He said he needed to call his house and see who could come and pick him up.

"Nonsense, Curt, I'll drive you home."

"Nah, I don't want to put you out none, Frank. I know where you live, and I'm in the opposite direction. I'll call home."

"Don't make me bitch slap you, Curt."

"All right, man, I do appreciate it. I'm gonna throw this stuff in my locker, and I'll be back with ya."

"I'll be in the lot, Curt."

That's when Commander Daly saw me walking out the door as he came in.

"Hey Frank, I need a big favor from you. You getting off now, or are you going back out on the street?"

"No, sir, I'm off now."

"Good, I know you're a south sider too. I need you to drive me home if it wouldn't be too much trouble for you."

"Sure, but I'm driving Curtis home too, and I'm in my pickup truck, so it might be tight."

"Oh no, I mean in my command car. I go on furlough, and I want to leave the car in the district for the acting commander. You can drive it back to work tomorrow for him."

"Okay."

We drove Timmy Daly home, and afterward, Curtis moved up to the front seat.

"Hey, Frank, I was listening to you and the commander talking like you were old school buddies. How come you didn't let old Curtis know that?"

"Because you, like everyone else, would be telling me to ask for shit."

"Does the Bulldick know?"

"I'll tell him when he comes back off IOD but let's keep this between us."

"I can do that." Curtis had a sly grin. He knew something the other guys didn't, and I hoped he would keep it that way.

"Hey, Frank. Are you hungry?"

"I'm always hungry. What do you have in mind?"

"Since we're down here in the commander's hometown, how about a Ricobene's steak samich? I'll buy."

"Sounds good."

I got a little worried when some guys from the 2nd District came in just as we finished eating. Curtis knew both of them but hadn't seen them for several years, so they played catch up. A half-hour later, I had to break my silence.

"Hey Curtis, I hate to break up this little tea party, but we got the commander's car."

"Oh yeah, let's get going. I'm sorry, I didn't realize I was talking so long. I came on the job with those guys. They've been partners since they got out of the academy a lifetime ago."

We jumped on the Dan Ryan Expressway and were headed south when I saw the two young boys in the green convertible Jaguar about three car lengths ahead of us.

The top was down, and they looked too young to be driving. I also saw a sticker in the window from a very wealthy suburb of Chicago.

"I'm gonna get next to these guys, Curt, and get a good look at them. See if you can tell if the column has been peeled."

"Oh, I see. You see young black guys in a nice car, and you think they done stole it, huh, Frank?"

"Exactly!"

Curtis was busting my balls. He's black, and we constantly messed with each other in those days. Not just him and I but everyone on the team and, in fact, the entire district and every place I worked as a cop.

No one was ever butt hurt back then because we were men, not the boys of soy. It was good-natured bonding that true friends are capable of.

I got right next to them. "How's the column look?"

"It ain't peeled, Frankie boy."

"I'm gonna get on the other side and see if they have keys."

Once I lined up on the opposite side of the car, they knew we were eyeballing them and changed lanes.

"They have keys, Curt, but it's got a big pink flower on the key ring. This ain't their car. I'm gonna stop them."

"In the commander's car?"

"Yeah…look at them. What do you think?"

"They look too young and dumb, and they ain't dressed for that car. Besides that, they sweatin' bullets."

"I'm gonna stay on this side so they can't get off and head to the projects. Then I'll stop them when we get past, just so they don't have a good place to run."

"I'm with ya on that cuz there's no way I'm gonna catch them young boys if they take off."

They suddenly changed lanes and tried to get off at Pershing Road, but I had blocked them. Now I turned the lights and siren on. They took off south on the expressway and then down the shoulder, exiting at Garfield. I stayed to the left side so they wouldn't turn east towards the projects, and it worked. They headed westbound on Garfield.

We called the chase in but were alone until we got to Ashland Avenue. That's when two beat cars came flying from the north and caused the teens to swerve left to avoid a collision. They turned south and drove another block before taking a right turn too fast and crashing into a parked car. We were on them. As a matter of fact, we were so close that I drove the commander's car into the left rear bumper of the Jaguar, causing minor damage to the Jag but breaking a headlight and smashing the bezel area on the commander's car.

Curtis was out in a flash and caught the passenger mid-air as he leaped up and over the door that had been jammed shut by the impact.

The driver was pinned in by the steering wheel.

"Hey Frank, the motherfucker's got a gun on the floor. Be careful."

"I see it, Curt."

Curt's prisoner tried to break free but was quickly slammed into the street.

"Damn, this one's got a gun too, Curt."

By then, a wagon crew pulled up, and with a half dozen squad cars on the scene, we had more than enough help.

"Hey Frank, the car ain't reported hot, and this boy is saying it's his uncle's car."

"It's hot, I'm sure of it. The owner just doesn't know it yet."

"I'm with you on that. I just got the registration back, and it ain't the name this boy gave me."

"That's all good, Curt, but we're out here with a smashed-up commander's car a good hour after we dropped him off."

"Oh, yeah. How we gonna explain this one?"

"I know a copper from SOG, Jack Bloore, who does great bodywork as a side job. I wonder if I can get him to straighten this out so nothing comes of it. I know he's got the paint and can do the work. We might be able to take a bezel and headlight off a pool car without anyone seeing us."

"Hey, I ain't too worried. The commander is your buddy."

"Let me think on it, but I'm gonna finish looking through the car."

Curt took information from our prisoners while I searched the car. When I opened the trunk, I had to jump back. I never expected to see what I saw. She was naked, blindfolded, and gagged with a woman's tee shirt.

The girl was seventeen years old and had just graduated from high school. She currently lived in Oak Brook, Illinois, and had gone downtown to apply for a job as an intern at a prestigious company. After her interview, she returned to her car in the underground parking garage at about eleven in the morning. That's when the two fifteen-year-old thugs approached her from behind and forced her into the trunk at gunpoint.

They drove over to one of their girlfriend's homes to show her their prize.

According to our victim, she thought she was going to be okay when the teen girlfriend opened up the trunk. But instead of helping her, she told her boyfriend they better do what they were gonna do before the police caught them.

But before they took her to the next location, she demanded that they give her the victim's shoes, watch, rings, bracelets, necklace, and the ankle bracelet for herself. The boys did that and then stripped her down and gagged her while tying her hands behind her back with a shoelace. They only wanted the money from her purse and the car.

After taking these items, the girlfriend told the boys that they'd better kill the victim after they were done playing with her because she had seen all of their faces.

The boys told our victim that they would not kill her if she did what they told her to do for one week. They just needed to make money off her. Once they made a thousand dollars, she would be driven to a location, and they would let her out of the car and give back her keys.

She thought they were going to ransom her for a thousand dollars to her parents, but that was not the case.

They planned on taking her to the uncle's house, and they told her that she'd be put in a room there for as long as it took her to make a thousand dollars. They said she would be rented out for sex to men whom the uncle knew, and once he collected enough money, they would blindfold her and drop her off in a safe place with money for a phone call home.

They then left the girlfriend's house and were on their way to the uncle's when we spotted them.

It was a pretty good pinch, but I had something else on my mind. How was I gonna tell the commander we were out way past the time we should have been with his car, and on top of that, I smashed it up.

I wasn't gonna need to call him. I heard his voice behind me as I was draping our victim with whatever we could come up with. He pulled up as the passenger in a station wagon.

"Hi, Frank. I heard you guys call numbers on the air. Are you and Curt okay?" Now, this is a boss!

"Yeah, we're fine, but your car's got a little…"

He cut me off. "Don't worry about the car. I'll take care of it. So you guys got this hot car. Any guns or anything?"

"Well, yeah, we got two guns and a naked kidnapping victim in the trunk."

"Oh my God, is she alive?"

"Yes, sir, but we need to get her covered up and over to the hospital as soon as possible."

Timmy Daly got out of the car, and everyone on the scene knew him and were apparently fond of him by their interactions as he came through the gathering.

He talked to the girl and told someone to grab some blankets in the back of the station wagon. Then he helped wrap her up.

Our victim was transported to the hospital, and her parents were notified. Unfortunately, her parents felt she had gone through enough and did not wish to pursue the matter on her behalf. It was too traumatizing, and they didn't want her name to get out in public.

When I spoke to the father, a pretty wimpy guy, he told me the thugs would be punished enough on the gun charges. Little did he know about the court system in Cook County.

A sad note to this story is that my friend and co-worker Curtis Baker Star #12212 was shot and killed while off duty. He was stopping an armed robbery while being outnumbered three to one on June 2, 1984. All three subjects were arrested and charged with his murder.

Chapter 19: Taking the Neighborhood Back

The night started like so many others when you're on the tac team. We hung around the office for a bit and made game plans for the night. First and foremost, where were we going to eat dinner before we rolled for the rest of the evening shift? Second, where were we going for drinks after work? Once that was settled, it was on to police work.

Our team met at Victor's Pizza on North Avenue, where we discussed how we were going to handle one of our "tips and clues," as we called them.

At roll call, we were given a number of assignments to look into regarding criminal activity, but one, in particular, stood out. Residents in the 5200 block of West Kinzie Street were complaining again about all of the drug dealers and gangbangers shooting up the block in a turf war over the sale of drugs at that location. Most of the decent people who lived on that street wouldn't let their children out of the house to play because of the threat of violence and drug dealing.

I say it stood out because just the night before, we had conducted a raid on a home identified as being an integral part of the criminal activity by members of the local street gang.

We thought we had put an end to the dealing for a while because that's what usually happens after you make a number of arrests at a particular location. Apparently, business was too good to shut down, so they started back up.

The honest, hard-working families in this area deserved better, and we were going to see that they were protected from this crap. Good surveillance perches by police in this area were few. I'm sure that was a major contributing factor in why they chose this spot to set up shop.

We decided that the maximum number of cops we could sneak into the area was four, and we'd have to do it under cover of darkness. We needed to position ourselves in such a manner as to first clearly identify who the shooters were. And second, who was dealing the dope, and where had they hidden it on the street.

Tom Flood and Ronnie Stieben joined my partner Rick DeFelice and me. We were able to secure our cars in a safe location where the gangbangers wouldn't suspect that the police were close by. It would be easy to blend into the shadows, and we could approach from the alley on foot.

I chose the concrete basement stairwell of a two-story brick building next door to the gangbanger's safe house. A driveway situated between the two structures would allow me a clear view of the criminal activity being conducted at that location. Rick was behind me, and Ronnie and Tom were to the rear of the lot and out of sight. Prime surveillance real estate was limited and the spot I chose only had room for two people. The other guys would wait for my signal and move in to make the arrests.

All things don't go as planned, and we have no control over that. We were forced to play our hand out earlier than expected when one of the drug dealers and a customer came walking down the driveway toward the rear of the lot. They would have to walk right past me, exposing our positions.

As they came closer, Rick backed out of the stairwell and went to tell Ronnie and Tom. I ducked down as low as I could. Tom came up and was right behind me, while Rick was about twenty feet to my rear and standing in the unlit backyard. They didn't see him until it was too late. Rick was on them and jammed his gun in their face. "Police, don't say a fuckin' word."

They didn't. Both raised their hands, and one stated: "We ain't the ones with guns."

Rick holstered his gun and grabbed them by the collars

With his two prisoners in tow, he headed over to Ronnie to conduct a pat-down for weapons. Rick started patting down one and Ronnie the other.

About thirty seconds later, the drug dealers out front became suspicious and called out to the gangbanger Rick and Ronnie were occupied with.

"Don't say a fuckin' word and keep your hands where I can see them until I'm done searching you."

"Hey officer, you know I'm cool with y'all; you just doin' yo' job." The pat-down was in progress when I could see five of their gang members coming down the driveway in our direction. The first three had guns in their hands. Tom was behind me but couldn't see them at this point.

"Hey Tom...we got five guys moving towards us, and the first three have guns. Let the other guys know."

I didn't want to engage in a shootout if it came to that while in a cramped concrete surrounded stairwell, so the only way out was to step in front of them.

Tom yelled one word out to Rick and Ronnie — "Guns!"

At the same time, I jumped out and announced my office.

"Police..." that's as far as I got. They raised their guns, and two of them started shooting. I returned fire, and the shooter closest to me went down while the others ran towards the street. Rick saw I was in trouble, fired two rounds from behind me at the fleeing shooters, and then jumped a fence to come up on them from another angle.

Tom continued up the short driveway and was joined by Ronnie in what they thought would be a foot chase. I started to handcuff my guy and remove the gun from his body for safety concerns. But things changed when I heard a barrage of gunfire erupt at the front of the driveway. It was directed at Tom and Ronnie. Instead of trying to get away, two of these thugs decided to shoot it out with the police and had waited for them to come to the front of the driveway, where they would be in plain sight and without any cover.

My partners were met by a hail of bullets, and Tom went down, landing on his back and still firing.

"Tom's been hit," Ronnie screamed as he fired at the assailants.

Ronnie was sure Tom had been shot and stood his ground next to his partner, drawing fire towards himself in an effort to keep the shooters from shooting at Tom anymore as he lay there. I ran up to join them, but one shooter had been dropped, and the other was running away.

Tom, as it turned out, wasn't helpless and hadn't been shot. He had dropped to the ground as a tactical move to present a smaller target. That took some serious balls on these coppers' part; that's why I loved working with them. Most guys in that situation would have sought refuge, but Tom and Ronnie were in a firefight they would take to the end.

The guy they shot, started to reload, and not wanting to be outgunned, Tom, who was blasting away with his .45 caliber long colt revolver, grabbed a speed loader and jammed six more rounds in the cylinder. In the confusion, he dumped his five spent rounds and one live round. He quickly reloaded and continued firing (count your rounds as you fire because it can make the difference between living and dying on the streets). Tom's single live round could have made a huge difference.

The third guy saw that Rick was coming up the gangway to get them from behind and fired at Rick. Both he and Ronnie returned fire. Rick fired two rounds, and Ronnie fired one. The shooter was hit or tripped, but either way fell to the parkway about fifty yards to our west and rolled in between parked cars. Rick ran down there to engage him, but the shooter had made good his escape in the darkness. There was no sign of blood, so we couldn't follow a trail.

Once the shooting was over, there wasn't a single person on the street anywhere to be seen. An eerie quiet had settled over the 5200 block of Kinzie. Everything I just explained above took place in a matter of maybe thirty seconds.

When you're involved in a shooting with that many assailants and rounds being fired, it's possible to get caught up in sensory overload.

After all the noise and adrenaline-pumping action had settled, the night air was still. The normal sounds of the neighborhood started creeping back in. One of the first things I remember was hearing a cat meowing in the darkness and hoping he wasn't lying somewhere wounded by a stray bullet.

When Tom stood up, we could see a half dozen strafe marks on the sidewalk from the rounds fired at him. They were definitely trying to kill him.

It wasn't long before some of the neighbors opened their windows and started yelling. To our collective shock, they weren't bad-mouthing us as we expected. Instead, there were words of praise and encouragement. "Thank you, police!" "Amen, amen!" "About time you got them motherfuckers!" "Thank God!" and the best one of all was, "I hope no police is shot!" They didn't want to be seen, only heard. Their choruses broke the still night air and seemed to come from nowhere but everywhere all at once.

The offender that miraculously survived this shootout was the one Tom and Ronnie had engaged. He was hit five times in all. Two of the rounds from a .45 caliber semi-automatic had struck him in the head and leg. In addition to that, he was shot twice in the abdomen and once in the chest. Those rounds came from a .45 Long Colt Revolver.

When the surviving offender was finally physically able to appear in court, we were called to testify. I was shocked to see which attorney would be representing our defendant. It was the same female attorney I had seen at the 95th, a high-end restaurant located in the Hancock building.

The fact that she was having a nice dinner there was not my concern. The fact that she was having what appeared to be a "romantic dinner" with a judge a number of years her senior *was* my concern. He was the same judge who would be hearing our case! They had dinner a few nights before he heard the case in a bench trial. Coincidence? I think not.

I voiced my concerns to the assistant state's attorney who was handling the prosecution and wanted to get a substitution of judges. He agreed with me on principle but said we would not be able to get one based on my observations.

When I questioned him on this, his response was as follows: "It is not uncommon for members of the bar to socialize and especially minority members of the bar. There's not a whole lot of them, so they tend to socialize with one another quite often." I can buy that, but this looked pretty shady on its face, and my skepticism was on point.

Cook County isn't referred to as Crook County for nothing.

The case was called, we testified, and in a very short bench trial, the defendant was found Not Guilty! If this had gone to a jury trial, this shooter would have been found guilty without a doubt, and I'm sure that's why the decision was left up to a friendly, and I suspect compromised, judge.

With that outcome, we knew the next step in the ghetto lottery would be a civil suit. We were sued, and the same criminal attorney who handled the case was now handling the civil side. The city settled the cases for $30,000. When I asked why they settled when I knew we could win at a civil hearing, the city attorneys told me that fighting it would be more costly than making the $30,000 payouts.

That's the Chicago way. I believe that the immediate first aid we rendered to the thug and the quick response by EMTs was the only reason one of them survived this shootout.

As they say, "No good deed goes unpunished."

Flanked by Lt. Nick Nickeas on my right and "Downtown" Bobby Browne

Captain Ed Griffin and Captain Bob Burns

1984 – Cook County State's Attorney Award for a record 309 consecutive felony trial convictions

Carter Harrison Honorable Mention Award

Public Housing Tactical (left to right): Ken McNeil, Scotty Alberts, Bob Bradford, me, Sgt. Joe Kosala

The SPUTAC Posse (left to right): Freeman, Erbacci, me, Orr, Washington, Bradley, Marquez, Mingo

With Det. Walter Smith – The "Godfather" of Traps

Blue Star Award ceremony

Jimmy Arceo 014th District

Sgt. Jimmy Hanson – the "unflappable one"

My partner, Akki Mares – also known as "Hon"

Detective Bob Fischer

Vic "Bulldick" Grimm

Rick De Felice

Mike Mondane – Fastest Cop" in Chicago

Chicago

2 officers shot in drug operation

Two undercover police officers were wounded in a shooting Wednesday night on the South Side, police said.

My partner Scott Freeman and me

S. Side Gun Battle

$92 Million Dollar Drug Bust in Chicago Lawn

One of many multi-million dollar seizures our undercover team made in the Organized Crime Division

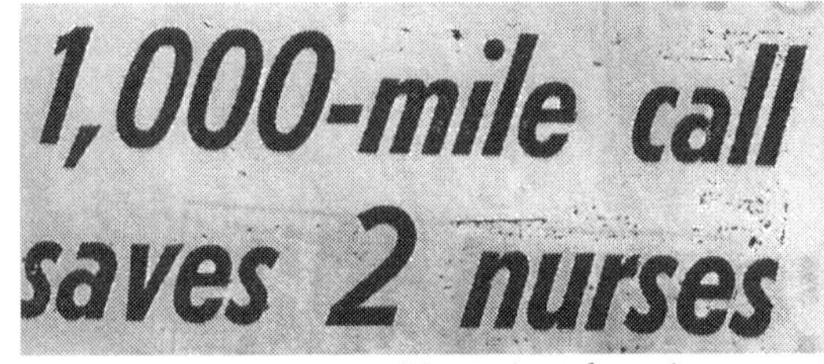

1,000-mile call saves 2 nurses

Commented Sgt. Fanning: "That's got to be the longest emergency call this department ever received. Look wh those guys had already done. If the policemen hadn't arrived, it possibly would have been worse."

Home invader crime pattern solved

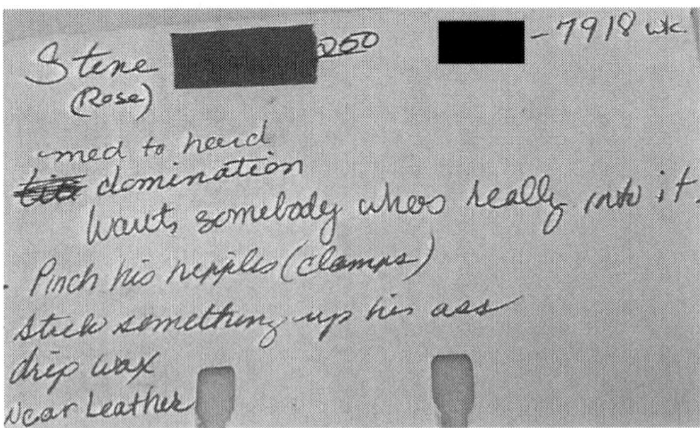

My insurance policy Rolodex cards from call girl operation

Chapter 20: If Something Draws Your Attention Twice, Check It Out

It's something I tell cops across the country, Mexico, and Canada, whenever I'm conducting Pat McCarthy's Street Crimes Seminars.

Good cops develop a street sense when they're working. They are constantly eyeballing people, locations, and situations that seem out of place. The following is a prime example.

This particular case took place in the 14th District, which had some great street cops. Guys like Jimmy Arceo and John Lyons come to mind. Arceo was the kind of cop that all cops should aspire to be like. I've heard him praised by good citizens, as well as street thugs he's locked up. That's the mark of a great copper.

I was fortunate enough on this day to be working with the other one, Johnny Lyons. It had been raining all day, not a heavy rain but steady. The wind was whipping pretty strong, and that may be what caused it. It was our second time coming down the block on Oakley. The first time was about an hour earlier, and then, just like now, I noticed that the French doors on the front of the house were still open.

"Hey John, pull over. I wanna check something out."

"The open doors?"

"Yeah… you saw them the first time too, huh?"

"Yeah, I thought maybe the owners might have just gone in the first time, but now…I don't think so."

"1422."

"1422 go."

"1422, put us down on an open door… possible burglary at 2099 North Oakley.

"You're down 1422."

There was no damage to the door, and everything in the house was neat. Nothing seemed out of place, so we continued to the second floor, which was nothing more than a glorified attic in various finishing stages.

"Hey Frankie, it looks like the wind just blew them doors open. I know those French doors, if they don't catch just right, that can happen."

"Yeah. I don't see anything wrong; maybe we can get a neighbor to call the owner."

I thought I heard movement coming from behind a small locked door on the knee wall side of the sloped roof in an area about three feet high.

"Did you hear that, John?"

"I thought I heard some type of scraping. You think they lock their dog in there?"

"It's padlocked."

I started banging on the door to see if I could get any kind of response, animal or human.

"Police, who's in there?"

No response, but we knew something was back there.

I grabbed a piece of copy paper from the desk and stuck it under the door. A dog or cat might step on it, and I would feel it as I pulled. But to my surprise, the full sheet wasn't stepped on. Instead, it slowly pulled out of my grasp until it disappeared. That was creepy.

"Whatever's back there is human, John. See what's in that toolbox."

John handed me the biggest screwdriver he could find, and I started prying the hasp off the framing.

"How you gonna justify breaking in there?"

"Maybe the burglar did it." He knew what I meant.

With the hasp off, I crawled into the tiny space. There was a double bowl, the kind animals have for solid food on one side and water on the other. There was also a blanket, a baby mattress, and a child's training potty. I went in as far as I could before seeing a small opening to my right and shined my flashlight down to the far end of this dark stretch of wall. It was about fifteen feet long, and she was huddled at the farthest end against the wall, giving me a side profile. She was a child and held a stuffed monkey against her face.

"C'mon, honey, I'm the police. I'm here to help you."

No amount of coaxing could get her to respond or come out. John gave it a try, but she was not budging.

"I'm gonna crawl down and get her, John. Go see if there's any fruit or candy downstairs and toss it to me."

It took a while, but the banana and the cookies did the trick. She ate them with gusto but resisted my efforts to pull her to freedom, as much as her frail body allowed.

A follow-up investigation was conducted, and it turned out that she was not a child. She was a twenty-four-year-old, four-foot-seven-inch tall, sixty-six-pound woman with a physical and mental disorder. Her sister and her live-in boyfriend were her caretakers, received SSI and other benefits, and locked the victim in that space. They were charged accordingly, and the woman became a ward of the state.

Tragically, on October 5th, 1992, Officer John Lyons Star #3124 was killed in the line of duty. Another one of Chicago's finest, gone too soon. Rest In peace, my friend.

Chapter 21: The Annual Reading of the Thanksgiving Day Caper

We can't all be off on this holiday, so none of us were thrilled about working on Thanksgiving Day, but someone had to do it, and it was our turn in the box.

Most of the restaurants that we'd normally be dining at were closed for the holiday, so a lot of the guys brought bag lunches that were nothing more than mini versions of their holiday meal.

I chose not to. I look at trying to find a good place to eat as another version of hunting. It's the same way I approach working the streets.

Newly promoted Lieutenant #Arturo Diaz held roll call today. It was the first one he would be conducting as a watch commander, and he looked anxious.

Someone had slipped a case report into the C.O. book, penned by an officer in the 25th District regarding a violent Thanksgiving Day domestic, along with the normal court notifications and other bits of interest regarding crime problems in the area. A notation in the book helped make this case report look as though it came directly from the district commander's office. So he was sure to read it out loud once we settled in.

"Can I have everyone's attention? Since all other notifications have been made, my last order of business is to read a case report that may be of interest to you as the holiday of Thanksgiving is upon us. It concerns domestic disturbances and what you may encounter during your tour of duty. It's a battery case report with a secondary classification as Aggravated/Other Weapon used. The date, time, and location are of no importance, but the fact that it occurred on Thanksgiving and involved a turkey leg as the weapon of choice should be noted."

He shared the responding officer's narrative in the body of the report, word for word.

"Victim was having some turkey leftovers for dinner with her boyfriend/fiancé. They got into an argument over who would eat the last turkey leg. Offender/boyfriend struck the victim across the face numerous times with the meaty end of the turkey leg, causing bruising to her face. Offender then pulled down the victim's pants and panties and inserted the small knuckle end of the turkey leg into the victim's anus for approximately four inches. Offender then told the victim to enjoy the leg and fled the scene. "The victim was transported by Chicago Fire Department Ambulance #35 to Saint Mary's Hospital emergency room where Dr. #Sewell removed the turkey leg from the victim's rectum. The leg was then photographed and documented by Evidence Technician #Fagan of Bt#2509 and Bt# 2520, and Bt#2590 on the scene. R/O advised Domestic Violence Information and also advised her to obtain a warrant."

When the watch commander finished, he had a big smile on his face and was expecting a few snorts, retorts, and laughs. We all sat there stone-faced. He expected it to be an icebreaker. It wasn't. We all stood up at the same time and left the room without a word. We had just broken in our new lieutenant. Domestic violence isn't funny, and our silence let him know it.

Chapter 22: The 25th Wedding Anniversary

They were brother and sister, two nice, clean-cut hardworking suburban teenagers from Palatine, Illinois. They were the kind of kids parents dream of calling their own. I'll call them Mark and Caren. Mark was seventeen, and Caren was just shy of her sixteenth birthday.

The two of them had worked part-time jobs all during the school year, and when school let out for the summer, they worked full time. They had some special plans. They loved their parents and appreciated all the sacrifices made for them, so they wanted to do something extra nice for their twenty-fifth wedding anniversary. Their mom had just beat breast cancer, and that had been taking a toll on the family for the past two years. It seemed to hit dad especially hard. But now, things were looking up for the first time in a long time, and the kids wanted to give their parents a special treat.

Mark and Caren had been putting their money together every payday for the past four and a half months. As soon as they cashed their checks, they put most of their money in a cigar box. After eighteen weeks of saving, they had enough to buy tickets for a play their mom had been talking about going to see for months. She could never get them because the show was always sold out. Unknown to their mom, the kids paid a scalper more than face value to get them just in time for her mom's anniversary celebration.

The kids wanted to do even more. They tried to book a room at the Waldorf Astoria Hotel in Chicago but were told they couldn't without a credit card.

Not to be deterred, Caren called her aunt (her mom's sister), and she agreed to let them use her credit card. In return, they gave her the cash payment in full. The room was booked.

The kids made arrangements for dinner at Chez Paul restaurant via a gift certificate before the play and would return the following morning to pick up their parents.

On this muggy summer night, Rick DeFelice and I had been working non-stop at the Cabrini Green Housing Project. But there was nothing unusual about that. The projects go 24/7 — they never shut down. They may quiet down during certain hours, but they are never peaceful.

We were assigned to the tactical unit here and had also been partners for a while on the 15th District tactical team. We not only worked together; we were friends outside of work. Years later, our sons would work together as partners on the same 15th District tactical team Rick and I had been partners on. We worked in plain clothes in both spots, but everyone knew who we were when we drove an unmarked squad car. Fortunately so, because that's how we were alerted to what was happening that night.

Rick and I stopped at the firehouse at Division and Larrabee just to say hello to the firemen. We made it a point to do that at least once every shift. And it's a good thing we did. It put us at the right place at the right time.

A delivery truck came flying up the street eastbound toward us, blasting his horn to get our attention. An older guy jumped out, yelling, "There's a kid laying on the street back there, and a bunch of guys pulled a girl out of the car and dragged her into the building right there." He was pointing to the 714 building.

I knew the building well — 714 W. Division Street. It was a fifteen-story tall public housing unit that had between a thousand and twelve hundred residents at any given time. A good number were criminals of varying degrees.

I was driving and Rick had the radio, so he put it out over the air. When we pulled up, the "roaches" scattered. They were stealing everything possible from the kid's car.

Mark was face down on the street. A chunk of concrete that crushed the left side of his skull was next to his body. A fire ambulance returning from a call immediately scooped him up and took off for the hospital. He didn't look good but was able to point to the building and say, "My sister."

If we were lucky, these thugs might have dragged the girl into one of the vacant apartments because most of the locks were broken, and it would allow us easy access to gain entry. But just in case, I grabbed the sledgehammer.

We had no idea where Caren was. People in the building were aware of the goings-on but wouldn't call the police. It's not that they didn't want to help; many did. They were just terrified of the gangs that controlled each building. There would be hell to pay if word somehow got out that they called the police.

On the other hand, if we were already on the scene, sometimes righteous folks gave us hints as to where we needed to go. They'd do this by a head tilt, eyes looking in a certain direction, or a whisper. As an experienced officer, you know to never acknowledge their gestures in any way as you don't want the wrong person seeing you give them a nod or a thank you. You just move on and hope they steer you in the right direction. They usually did.

I knew of two empty apartments in this building. One was on the thirteenth floor, and one was on the fifteenth.

We headed up the stairway in search of Caren. In the projects, experienced coppers never use the elevator. It is a trap. If a gangbanger wanted to attack you in the elevator, all he had to do was open the doors on one of the other floors and shoot down on you or up at you, depending on where you were situated. On top of that, if you were riding the elevator and were in a position below where they pried the doors open, it would be easy to drop a Molotov cocktail down on you, and there would be no escape because that stops the movement of the elevator.

On our way up, we encountered the decent people every so often, and they'd motion us where to go using the gestures I previously mentioned. We got lucky on the 13th floor and started down to the vacant apartment number 1310. But before we got more than a few steps in that direction, a young girl, maybe fourteen years of age, shook her head "no" while holding her hand in front of her chest so no one could see. She pointed up. We trusted her and continued up two more flights.

On the 15th floor, a young gangbanger was coming out of the vacant apartment in question. He was only about twenty-five feet away when he saw us. I don't know about Rick, who was physically in better shape than me, but I was running out of steam. We had run up fifteen flights as fast as our legs would carry us. Like Rick, I wore two guns, had extra bullets, two sets of handcuffs, and carried a sledgehammer. I'd hit the apartment door before getting in a foot chase with this punk.

The gangbanger yelled "Police" back into the open apartment door and took off running. Neither of us chased him. It turned out Rick was winded too. We wanted the guys who were still busy with our victim.

As soon as he yelled to his homies, we knew we were on the right path. There was only one way in and out of this apartment, and that was through us. That is unless they decided to jump out of the window from the top floor to avoid being arrested, which would have been interesting. We had them, or at least most of them, and they could not get away. Hopefully, Caren was still alive.

We burst through the door with guns drawn, and they scattered like the low life vermin they were. One guy was still sporting wood as he pulled out of her from the rear. Another kneeling in front of her had been forcing her to orally copulate him. They jumped up; we assumed to attack us, so we dropped them right where they were. I had the backdoor guy, and Rick had the other one. It was over in seconds. As they lay motionless on the filthy floor, I cuffed them up.

Caren was naked and on all fours. Her face was beaten bloody, and blood trickled from her right ear. She had been stripped of all of her clothing except for her shoes.

Rick stood in front of the only door in the apartment while I secured our first two prisoners. Rick would not let anyone get past him while I was occupied; I was quite confident of that.

During our brief scuffle with our prisoners and the fact that we had to use some serious force to subdue them, our victim did not move or respond in any way. She stayed on her hands and knees. I was sad and angered like never before. She was obviously in a state of shock.

I can honestly say that in all the years I spent on the job, this was the only time I wished someone would come after me with a weapon in his hands. But no one did.

Seeing only the two of us, the other three tried to overwhelm us by numbers, apparently thinking they'd make good their escape before assisting units arrived. They were wrong.

I realized pretty quickly that we weren't fighting grown men. These were younger thugs. They may have been young, but they were strong and determined. They were the same size as Rick and I, but you could tell by their faces that they were teenagers. At that moment, age didn't matter. All five, it turned out, were juveniles — even the two who were six foot and six foot one.

Sergeant Joe Kosala was first to arrive, followed by Officers Stieben and Bradford.

"What's with her, Franko?" asked Kosala.

"She's the girl they dragged out of the car, but I don't see her clothes anywhere, and she hasn't moved from that position since we got here."

"Okay. I came up from the back, and I saw some clothes lying on the ground, like they were thrown out this window."

Kosala went over to our victim and bent down to look at her face while he spoke, but she didn't respond. He put his arms around her to help her up. Initially, she resisted and then screamed. Kosala assured her that we were there to help, not hurt her; for the loss of a better word, she became malleable.

She was completely beaten down on the inside. It struck me how quickly such violence had been heaped upon her in such a short period of time. I would estimate that it was no more than twenty minutes from the time she was dragged out of the car until we found her.

"We gotta get something to cover her up. I don't know if it will do any good, but it's worth a try. I'm gonna knock on some doors. But just in case no one helps, Stieben, go down and grab her clothes before they disappear."

Bradford only spoke up once. He was a quiet guy but a serious copper. He looked over our badly injured prisoners and said, "Y'all look way too good for what you did to her. I'm sure I'll see ya again sometime." I'm sure he meant it.

I put my arm around our victim. She was so fragile, so tiny in stature. Her body shook, so I held her tighter, but it didn't help. She felt like a baby in my arms. There was no need to bust up this innocent child like they did. Only pure evil could do that. I wondered how people so young could muster up so much hate for people they didn't know and then do such a thing to her and her brother. In a sane world, violence like that should never happen.

I did my best to console Caren by reassuring her that she was safe now. We wouldn't let anything else happen to her. I know she heard what I was saying, but she wasn't responding verbally. Every once in a while, she shook her head, indicating yes or no responses, but not every time. I knew she was really bad off mentally when she never asked about her brother. She had seen him fighting, and I would have thought she'd be concerned about his fate, but she never spoke to us in a full sentence. The detective who eventually followed up on the case got a little more than we did, but not much more.

Within a minute, Kosala came back to the apartment with a blue bedsheet someone was kind enough to donate, and we wrapped her in it. Bradford and DeFelice walked her down the stairs while Kosala and I stayed with the five prisoners and waited for them to be transported to the hospital before they could be processed. They had sustained some serious injuries while resisting arrest.

We learned the details of exactly what happened that night. Mark and Caren had driven their mom and dad to the front door of the Waldorf Astoria Hotel. Once there, they kissed them goodbye and handed their mom the theater tickets wrapped up in a box with a corsage for mom and a boutonniere for dad. They also gave them a gift certificate for the Chez Paul restaurant.

Mark and Caren's parents told us later that they were speechless. They couldn't believe all the planning and the execution that went into making their 25th anniversary so special.

This is what happened, according to Mark.

As the two kids drove home, they reveled in how they were able to pull off such a big surprise for their parents. They were joking around about how their dad had practically begged them to stay and have dinner, but they told their parents that it was their night to enjoy without teenagers being in the picture. As it turned out, they should have heeded Dad's offer.

Mark was at the wheel, and since it was his dad's car, he was driving extra carefully. They drove westbound, and at 714 W. Division Street, Mark had to stop for a stop sign. He could tell the area was pretty rough but felt safe in his dad's big 1978 Mercury.

Three teens were hanging out near the sign and weren't hiding the fact that they were looking into the car. This made Mark uneasy, but he couldn't drive away because, by that time, three other guys ran from across the street and were now standing in front of his car and motioning for him to roll down the windows. He started inching the car forward, hoping to get them to move out of the way. Instead of moving, they slammed their fists down on the hood and started yelling at him.

It was at about that time when one of the teens threw something through the passengers side window with such force that it shattered the glass and cut his sister's cheek wide open.

He remembered someone reaching in through the window to take his sister's purse, but he still couldn't move the car because the other part of the gang was still standing in front of it, yelling and banging on the hood.

Caren held onto her purse and, for a brief few seconds, fought off her attacker. Suddenly, the car door swung open, and two guys yanked the purse from her grasp. She screamed as her fingers twisted in the strap, breaking several of them.

The thieves weren't satisfied with their bounty. Now they wanted Caren and pulled her out of the car. Caren was pretty easy to handle at five feet tall and in the ninety-pound range, but she fought like a little tiger. It was long enough to give her brother time to come to her defense, and that he did.

It was Mark against six thugs, and he was going to protect his sister at all costs. He waded into them swinging, according to the truck driver witness. Three beat on Mark while the other three carried his sister into the project building. One of the three was still fighting with Mark, who was able to stay on his feet during the battle. Discouraged by Mark's unwillingness to go down, one of the other attackers grabbed a chunk of broken concrete and slammed it against the side of Mark's head. He dropped immediately. Then they rummaged through his pockets before taking off into the same building that the others had disappeared into, according to our witness.

Mark's injuries were severe. He suffered a fractured skull that required forty-two stitches. Mark, unfortunately, lost vision in one eye. He had a broken eye socket and a fractured jaw.

His sister was admitted to Henrotin Hospital with severe internal trauma both vaginally and anally. In addition, she suffered three broken fingers, two broken ribs, and a broken nose. She needed seven stitches across her upper right cheek.

Psychiatric care was recommended for a period of time after that. Caren was unable to testify, but I testified as a witness to a portion of the sexual assault that I witnessed.

The truck driver witness was excellent and came to every single court date he was asked to attend, even though he lost a day's pay every time. He was always there, and on behalf of the victim's family and me, we say, "Thank you, sir. James Arceri, you are a hero!" (Real Name)

I don't know, but I hope Mark and Caren went on to enjoy the rest of their lives and that good things happened to them along the way. Those kids deserve every break in life they can get.

Since all of the offenders were juveniles, they were tried and sentenced under juvenile guidelines. Not one of them did more than three years! This is why Chicago, and particularly Cook County, has a raging crime problem.

Chapter 23: Let Them Eat Cake

The mother was angry. So angry that even though she didn't have a telephone in her tenth-floor apartment at the projects, she wanted an arrest made. So she walked two blocks to the nearest working telephone, or so she thought. Virtually every telephone within walking distance of the projects had been broken into and vandalized beyond repair. This one was no different.

As I turned left on Larrabee, she jumped in front of the unmarked car, waving her arms frantically. I hit the squealers so hard it laid rubber for ten feet.

My partner Rick DeFelice and I had just returned from our second gun arrest on this muggy night and were hoping to have a few cold beers without any more interruptions in a couple of hours.

"Officers, stop. Stop, please. I needs help, and I needs it now. My boy have to go to jail and maybe his sister too, but mostly he got to be locked up tonight for what he done did."

She looked too young to have a son who needed police intervention, but that wasn't unusual in the projects. Seasoned cops will always refer to the projects as the "Jets." There were countless numbers of children having children in the "Jets," and that's often the source of the crime problem here.

"How old is your son, and does he have any weapons that you know of?"

"He just turned ten yesterday, and he must have a knife."

Why do you think he has a knife, and what did he do that you want us to lock a ten-year-old up for?"

"He ate cake!"

"Are you telling us that you would like the police to take your son to jail for eating some cake?"

"That's right. He stole it without my permission and done ate it and also done took some more and fed it to his damn sister!"

My partner and I shared a look. We knew this was going to be good.

Rick took a long drag on his stogie.

"Let me think about this for a minute."

He took another long drag and acted as if he was in deep thought. Then feigning an expression of deep concern, he nodded to her.

"I know, I know exactly what you're going through. I got kids at home. You want us to kick his ass too?"

"Damn straight, I do. Y'all could whoop on that little motherfucka till he snots on hisself."

Over the years, we've seen a lot. But it doesn't matter how many years you have on the job; no cop has seen it all. This was another first. Without saying a word, we had mentally formulated a plan of action. In times like these, our minds tend to work in sync.

"All right, I have to do a quick pat-down of you before we let you jump in the backseat."

"Oh, that's okay. Y'all cool, and I trust y'all ain't gonna be grabbin' all up on my shit."

"Yeah, you don't have to worry about that."

She was braless and preceded to pull up her tee-shirt so high it covered her face. She had shorts on and dropped them to the hairline.

"Yo, I didn't mean all that. I was talking about your pockets and waistband area."

"You can check my pockets. Go on and put your hand in there and feel all around. Just don't be touchin' on my virginia."

"Just pull out what you got in your pockets. Your virginia is safe."

"Just my keys and my money and my ID."

"Okay, hop in."

We drove her to the 630 W. Evergreen building in Cabrini Green, apartment number 1003. Rick and I headed towards the stairwell while she went to the elevator.

"Is you all gonna walk up?"

"You know the police always do that. We'll meet you up there."

By the time we got to the apartment, she still hadn't come up. The elevators in the Jets are slow, and people are constantly getting on and off all the floors in between, so this didn't surprise us.

I knocked on the door, and a young boy opened it.

"Hi, police." He was scared, and his little sister stood behind him with tears in her eyes.

"Police, is you gonna take my brother to jail?"

"No, honey, we're not going to do that. Step back and let us come in. What's your name, honey?"

"You already said it…Honey, and I'm eight years old."

"Oh, that's a nice name. How about you, big brother? What's your name?"

"I'm James. My birthday was yesterday, and I'm ten."

"Well, sorry we weren't here for your birthday, but happy birthday."

I made a habit of carrying a two-dollar bill on me at all times and handed it to him. "This is for you, but since I only have one, buy something with it that you can share with your sister, okay?"

The kids smiled and blurted out, "Yeah, like candy." They were much more at ease now.

We had made up our minds on who was going to jail, and it wasn't either one of the kids standing in front of us.

The apartment was no different from ninety-five percent of the units I've been in. The painted cinder block walls were covered in grime, the sofa was broken down, and a television stand was made of cinder blocks lifted from some construction site, I'm sure. The television had a small vise grip on it, acting like a knob to change channels. The floor was filthy, and the refrigerator, as well as the cabinets, had a chain laced through the handles, all padlocked just like the refrigerator.

This may seem strange to some readers, but in the "Jets," it's a common way of protecting your food source. However, that tactic should be employed when visitors come over, not for family members who live there.

The door swung open, and Momma came in. She was all high and mighty in her swaggering walk and attitude.

"Uh-huh, y'all was all so slick before I called the police, but now look at y'all whiney little scared ass faces. I told y'all little motherfucka's I would get the police on yo' ass. Well, here they is. Lock his ass up, officer, and I still ain't made my mind up about you, Honey, cuz you done ate the cake he stole out my motherfuckin' fridge too. You just as guilty as James is."

I asked #Belinda Walker where she kept the key to the refrigerator.

"I keep it on my house key ring right here."

"I see. So how did he get the key to open the refrigerator?"

"He didn't. When I went out to get me some Crown Royal, this little motherfucka….."

"First off, stop calling him that name. His name is James, as you well know, and you will call him James or son but stop using that term. Understand me?"

"Don't be tellin' me on how to talk to my childresses, but I hear you. Is you gonna take him to jail or not? Cuz if you ain't, I'll call some other damn police or your supervisor and make a complaint on y'all ass cuz he should already be in handcuffs."

"Don't worry about it. I'm definitely gonna be using handcuffs, but not at this point in our investigation."

I tried to open the refrigerator door, and it would only budge about an inch or so due to the chain. I could clearly see the birthday cake in question and noted that besides the cake, the only other visible consumable items were port wine, Schlitz malt liquor, a bottle of gin, and some tonic water. There were no food staples for the children.

"Here…see this? This is what the little mother…I mean, James used to get that cake out of there."

Belinda was holding a flat wide-bladed knife. It was taped to a wire clothes hanger straightened out into an extension handle. I looked at the homemade cake slicer and then at the opening and wondered how this kid could get two slices of cake out through such a narrow opening.

"Did you see him do it?"

"No. But when I came back, they had it on they faces, yellow and white frosting. That's when I asked him how he got it out, and he wouldn't tell me, so I whipped his ass good with my waffle cord."

"I see. James, show me where your momma whipped you." James shook his head no, but Honey wasn't so shy.

"It's on his back and on his legs." Honey lifted his tee-shirt from behind, and I could see six raised welts across his backside from the waistline to the shoulder blades.

"You shut the fuck up. Now you goin' to jail, little bitch."

"Yeah, you're right, Belinda, someone's definitely going to jail."

I winked at the kids and hoped they knew they were safe from arrest, but I didn't know. They were scared.

"James, show me how you got the cake out of the refrigerator."

James reluctantly took control of the instrument he had fashioned and looked at Honey.

"She has to help me do it, Mr. Police."

Without saying a word, Honey took off her shoe, and as James pulled as hard as he could on the door, Honey slipped her shoe in the opening heel first, and then James tapped it a few times to get the most out of the wedge.

The boy stuck his homemade slicer in through the narrow opening and sliced a one-inch wide piece of cake. He balanced it with a steady hand and pulled it out. I was amazed at how steady his hand was under the circumstances. It also helped that the refrigerator temperature was set on extra-low to keep the alcoholic beverages cold. That kept the cake from tipping and crumbling as he moved it.

I clapped my hands. "Beautiful, absolutely beautiful. Hey Mom, give me the keys to the refrigerator padlock. I'll tighten it up so they can't do that anymore."

Rick knew that was not what I had in mind at all. I opened the door all the way, and besides the items I previously mentioned, there was a half-used jar of Maraschino cherries on the inside door with mold growing in it. I pulled the cake out and passed it to my partner.

"Here, Rick."

Rick put the cake on the table and handed each child a spoon. "Eat up, kids."

"I'm reporting y'all. What's your name and badge number?"

It's disturbing to know that some folks really believe the police are at their beck and call to discipline their children for them. It's even more disturbing that they reproduce.

"Our name and badge numbers? Don't worry about it. They'll be on the bottom of your arrest report."

We placed her under arrest on several charges and had the children removed from the home and sent to the hospital to be checked out. I called an evidence technician to document the injuries to James's back. When it was over, we brought the kids to our station, where they finished off the cake and had some sandwiches and milk we picked up for them. It must have been a while since they had eaten because there wasn't a scrap of food left when it was time for them to go with the youth officers.

The kids were subsequently turned over to the Department of Children and Family Services, which is not always the best place but better than with their mother. I kept tabs on them for a while because I didn't want to see Momma get her hands on them again after the way she acted. Eventually, they ended up being moved into a house in Maywood, Illinois, with their grandmother.

Belinda spent three weeks in jail and made a plea of guilty on her first court appearance to time served plus one year of supervision. I hope she never had contact with her children again, but unfortunately, this is where our involvement ended. I wish we could have done more for every victim we crossed paths with as cops, but that's impossible.

We did the best we could under the circumstances, time constraints, and the legal process available at the time. I hope these kids lived better lives after our intervention, but I don't know. I only know that Rick and I made life better for them for a little while, and that's pretty much all any cop can do. Time to move on to the next case.

Chapter 24: Eaten Alive

"Hi…umm…are you guys the police?"

Sergeant Joe Kosala and I were working together as we often did whenever my partner was off in Public Housing Tac.

The young lady asking the question may have been confused by our appearance — long hair, heavily bearded, and construction worker-type clothing. But I was driving a run-of-the-mill though heavily damaged unmarked squad car, and that may be why she flagged us down.

"Yes, we are. What can we do for you?"

"Umm… well, I don't know if it's anything, but there's an older woman that lives in the ground floor apartment in that building over there, and I live next door. Every morning she raises her shade when I go to work, and she hasn't done it for the last three days."

"I see. How old is she?"

"Old…I'd say in her nineties at least."

Joe and I both knew what this meant. The woman was probably dead and most likely a stinker. We'd be able to tell as soon as we got close enough to the door if she was ripe enough.

"Franko, this ain't the projects, but you wanna check it out or call a beat car for a well-being?"

"Ahh, we're here now. Let's just do it and then call for someone to handle it if it's what we think it is. Maybe she went somewhere, and it's nothing."

"Yeah, right…wanna bet?"

"No."

We took turns knocking on all the windows and the front door but didn't get a response. We tried to see inside, but everything was locked up tight.

"I can't smell anything, can you, Franko?" Joe had never called me Frank in my lifetime of knowing him.

"No, but there's a pretty big gap under the front door. I'll get down there and take a whiff."

I got down on the ground and took a deep breath at the threshold, but there was no detectable odor other than the musty smell of an old frame building, which is what it was.

"I hear something, Joe."

I couldn't quite make it out, but it sounded like something was being moved, and I could hear something squeak and what sounded like a glass breaking on the floor.

Joe heard it too.

"I think she's hurt. Maybe that's her way of signaling for help."

Stand back, Franko. I'm gonna kick it in."

Joe blasted it open on his second try.

"Oh shit! Look at all the fuckin' rats on her. I'm gonna call a beat car to handle this one."

I was stunned. Most of the rats fled when we came in, but two of them took their sweet time and didn't jump off her until I got within a few feet of them, swinging my flashlight.

While Joe notified the dispatcher, I went to check on the dead woman.

She was a black woman, and when I say black, I mean she was the blackest woman I had ever seen. Her skin looked like the shrunken heads displayed at museums, leathery and well creased, and best described as looking mummified.

On the table next to her were an empty pitcher, some pill bottles, and a jar of coconut oil. A broken glass was on the floor. The rats had apparently knocked it off as they scurried about her body and on top of the small three-legged table.

I examined her body to see if there was any sign of foul play other than what the rats had eaten away. Her exposed ankles were eaten down to the bone on one side and about halfway through on the other ankle. Her fingertips had been gnawed on, and so had her lower lip.

I didn't know if a rat was moving under her loose sweater or if it was my imagination, but I thought I saw movement in her chest.

Joe talked to the complainant just outside the front door and waited for the beat car to arrive. That's when I picked up the dead woman's arm to see if she was in rigor. She was not. Her eyes opened and I jumped back.

"Whoa!"

Joe rushed in. "What's up, Franko?"

"Call for an ambulance. This woman's alive."

"She sure don't look it."

"Joe, she opened her eyes and looked right at me. She didn't say anything, but she looked at me."

"That might just be muscle contractions. They're closed now."

"She not only opened em', but she also looked directly at me. She's alive."

Paramedics arrived within minutes. After checking her vitals, they related the obvious. This poor woman was in really bad shape. I'm not an EMT, but I had already made that evaluation. The woman had suffered a recent stroke and was totally unresponsive both physically and mentally. Unfortunately, she passed away the following day.

Miss #Betty Hopkins was ninety-six years old. According to her niece, who was the only contact number we found for her, she was a retired schoolteacher who had never married and had lived in that apartment for more than fifty years.

No one deserves a death like that, especially a former grade schoolteacher. I can only surmise that the woman had used coconut oil as a moisturizer, which attracted the rats to start feasting on her ankles and fingertips.

Chapter 25: The Phone Order

I was dumped unceremoniously from the Public Housing Tactical Unit for the serious infraction of making inquiries about a transfer to the Organized Crime Division. I hadn't made a formal transfer request because it's not the kind of unit you can just be transferred to by making out the paperwork. You need clout. My clout was my friend and partner Bill Kieling. Bill was a black cop with just a few years on the job but a hell of a great street copper.

I was involved in conversations with guys who would speak on my behalf. If I got the okay, I'd make a formal request to leave my current assignment. Cops do it all the time.

Unfortunately for me, word leaked back to my boss in the housing unit, Lieutenant Bob Curry. I always liked Bob and had worked for him when he was a sergeant in 18. We always had a good working relationship, and he's the guy who asked me to come work for him on his public housing tac team while I was on the 15th District tac team. So I came and worked for him for two years and did a good job. I loved it there because not only was it busy, but the cops I worked with were all hell raisers and had stone balls. Ronnie Stieben and Rick DeFelice had come over with me from 15. Charlie Toussas, Scott Alberts, Robert Bradford, and Ken McNeil filled out the team.

When Lieutenant Curry heard about my organized crime aspirations without having first gotten his permission, which I didn't need, he blew his top.

He had me transferred to the 3rd District on midnights and did so in the most treacherous way he could. A "phone order." No one gets transferred out on a phone in the middle of the period.

For those who don't know how transfers work, it goes like this. You make out a request to be transferred from your current assignment to another unit. If it's approved, the order comes out once a month on a Thursday, and you check to see if you made it or not.

On the other hand, clout-heavy guys don't need to make a formal transfer request. They are just sent to the unit of their choosing via a phone call from a boss high up on the pecking order. These guys are known as "heavy" in cop lingo.

This is what happened the night I found out that a guy I liked jagged me around because his feelings got hurt.

My partner Bill Kieling and I had just finished up our last arrest of the night, and it was a good one. It was for the armed robbery of a game room on Division Street. We got the guy, the gun, and the proceeds. We were working the 3 p.m. to 11:30 p.m. shift at Cabrini. It was 11:22 p.m., and the detectives had taken our prisoner in for a lineup on other robberies in the area.

Bill and I were putting our gear into our lockers when Lieutenant Curry walked in with a smirk on his puss and handed me a hand-typed copy of a phone order.

"Looks like you're not going to organized crime, Goff."

Instead, I was to report to the midnight shift in the 3rd District as soon as I left Cabrini at 11:30 p.m. for the midnight to 8:30 a.m. shift. There was no way I'd make it in time, and he knew it.

There was also no way I'd be able to attend roll call at the district level the way I looked. I had long hair and a full heavy beard. In addition to that, I'd have to dig out the uniform I hadn't worn in years and hope it would fit me.

"What's this all about, lieutenant?"

"As you so eloquently say, 'Don't worry about it.' Just go."

"Lieutenant, can I get time due so I can get a haircut and shave?"

"No, you are no longer my concern. You are a 3rd District patrolman now and don't dare walk out that door before 2330 hours. Have a good night."

There was absolutely no reason for his infantile response. I always worked hard and did whatever he asked of me. Besides that, I wasn't sure I'd get into organized crime.

Oh well, I had a plan. I called the district and told them I'd be late because I had just gotten off work and had to go home to get my uniform. They got the okay from the midnight Watch Commander #William Frilly. I had heard a lot of negative things about him but had never had a personal interaction.

By the time I got to the district, it was one in the morning. I went directly to the watch commander's office. My uniform fit, but I had the same full beard and long hair.

"Who the fuck are you?"

"I'm Frank Goff coming directly to you from Public Housing Tac, sir."

"Sit down. Give me the story."

I laid it out to him and told him I could put in for time due so the public wouldn't see me like this, and I'd come back clean-shaven with a haircut the following night.

"Nah, you don't have to do that. I made a call before you got here, Goff. I wanted to know why I was getting a guy sent to me on a phone order. This ain't the place people get a phone call made to come to. OCD, yeah, but here, no way. By the way, you are on the transfer order to go to Organized Crime in eleven days. I made some calls myself to see why the fuck you were forced down my throat. Just be on time from now on and do the job while you're here, and you'll be okay. You can keep your look. I'm off tomorrow, but I'll let the watch commander know it's okay."

I was shocked. This guy was the boss I heard so many guys complain about. I'd never want to hear anybody say a negative thing about him from that day forward. If we had been long-time friends, I could see it, but we were strangers to each other, and he was an absolute gentleman.

I came to work, answered my calls, and worked with a different guy each night. All were good working coppers, but my partner called in sick on my last night in the district.

I said I didn't have a problem working alone, so I started heading out when my Sergeant #Leevon Wipps decided he'd hit the streets with me. His marked unit was down, so he pulled an unmarked tac car. Even though it was unmarked, every thug in Chicago, as well as virtually all the kids in the rougher neighborhoods, could recognize it as a squad car.

The sarge knew it was my last night in the district and had put my beat car down for the night. I was to be his driver during this wintery shift; he was giving me a farewell gift. I wouldn't get any calls for the night and would respond with the supervisor if one of the cops requested one. He knew what had happened and told me that is how he ended up in 3 from the 1st District, but it turned out he liked 3 and decided to stay.

The streets were quiet as they should be on a night like this. It was close to 2 a.m., and the snow was falling, but it wasn't a blizzard. I drove eastbound on 75th Street, where all the businesses that hadn't been extorted, robbed or burned out on an insurance claim had closed down for the evening. The only exception was a tavern that was still open but getting ready to shut down.

We observed a male black and a female black walking past the place and looking in. At first, it seemed they were just going to grab a drink or look for a friend as they turned and walked west back towards the door. I watched in the rearview mirror and could see that they changed direction and were walking east again. Something was up for sure. It was too cold to be so indecisive. Did they want a drink, or were they going to rob the place? That's when the female continued east, and the male walked a few more doors to the west and turned around. I knew that profile anywhere. I made a U-turn and headed back in his direction.

"Yeah, they're up to something. Hey Sarge, you wanna call for another car or…?"

"Let's just get out and talk to this guy and see what he's got to say."

"I think he's carrying under that coat."

As Sergeant Wipps and I got out, the target of our stop took off, running east and then south. I could see the female made it around the corner a little further east but would be paralleling our bad guy as he ran south. Either they were running to their crib or a getaway car. We didn't know.

Sarge and I took off on foot after the male, who made a quick turn east into the alley. We continued chasing him, and he made another southbound turn at the "T" in the alley. Sarge and I were running at full speed, and just as we came to the "T," a thunderous sound cracked the night air and echoed off the garages. We were running so fast that we couldn't stop, and both slid sideways on the ice into the telephone pole that just had a gash taken out of it by the blast. The dude had waited and came pretty close to hitting us.

"That motherfucka tried to kill us, Goff."

Instead of deterring us, we were more determined than ever to apprehend this guy. He was only about fifty feet in front of us now and hit a gangway heading towards the street his woman friend was on. He turned toward us again as we slammed the metal gate open. We each fired a single shot, and he went down just as he made it to the front porch area and rolled out of our sight.

Sargent Wipps called in shots fired over the air and requested backup. We cautiously approached the area where our guy had fallen. We had to be careful because we knew he had no fear of shooting at the police. I crept up the gangway, waiting for his next move and hoping there wouldn't be one. Sarge went through the adjoining gangway, hoping to come up behind him if he was waiting under the porch.

The sounds of a racing engine accompanied by the spinning wheels of a car on ice could be heard. Eventually, the tires caught dry pavement, and the vehicle was little more than tail lights by the time we ran into the street.

When we had converged on the porch, he was gone, but the sawed-off shotgun was on the ground along with a trail of blood and footprints from the front porch to the curb and disappeared at the curb line. There was no evidence of blood or footprints anywhere in the freshly fallen snow from that point on.

It was obvious that he made it to the car, and the woman we saw him with earlier had probably been the driver.

We returned to the office and made out our reports. I notified the area hospitals to let us or the detectives know if they received anyone with gunshot wounds from my sergeant's 9mm or my .357 magnum and to notify the police communications center.

Early the following morning, LaRabida Children's Hospital reported that a female, who did not identify herself, had brought a male black in his 30s to the emergency room at 5 a.m. He had no identification and sustained two through-and-through gunshot wounds to the torso. He was pronounced dead shortly after arrival.

The deceased man's palm print and a thumbprint matched the prints taken from the shotgun and one of the shotgun shells recovered from the sawed-off. He was wearing the same clothing as our offender. In addition, he was a convicted felon with a criminal history that included armed robbery. He was released on parole after serving eight years for armed robbery four days prior to this incident and was identified as the armed robber of a gas station the night before we got involved with him. His weapon of choice was a sawed-off shotgun in that case too. Sawed-off shotguns were quite popular in that era, just like the AR-15 is today.

The area's ERs were made aware of the fact that a male with one or two gunshot wounds may be seeking treatment shortly. Unfortunately, LaRabida Children's Hospital had been overlooked — something I learned and made sure to pass on to other officers in future violent encounters. The notification should also include local clinics.

I reflect on that night often and had it not been for a vengeful lieutenant, I would have never been put in a position to do what I was forced to do.

Chapter 26: Undercover Dangers

I walked into our little 10' x 10' office space in the Organized Crime Division and was met by the always smiling Julius Jones, or as I called him, Uncle Jules. Besides our sergeant, there were only four of us working tonight.

"Hey, fellas, here's my nephew now. We was just talkin' 'bout you, nephew. How ya doin', nephew Frank?"

I can't tell you how or why the family references came about, but even my wife and kids had grown to call him Uncle Jules.

"Uh-oh, this sounds like I'm being set up for something."

"Nah, nah, nothin' like that. You know your Uncle Jules wouldn't let anyone take advantage of you."

"Okay, so what's up?"

"Me and the guys were just discussing who we can trust to do a buy for us, and I said my nephew would be my first choice."

"Okay by me, but is there a reason one of you guys can't do it?"

"Well, yeah. Ya see, we got this Puerto Rican fella in the next room, and he's on probation. We busted him with some dope, and he doesn't want to get violated, so he's willing to work with us to take his supplier down."

"And?"

"Well, his supplier won't deal with any black guys, and me and Marvin, as you can see, kinda fit the description." Jules let out a belly laugh when he threw out terminology coppers routinely employ when they stop someone on the street. "You fit the description." However, most of the time, it's true.

Besides Julius and me, Marvin Pharr and Austin "Corky" Corcoran were partnered up for the night.

"Hey Jules, unless you guys know something about Corky that I don't, I always considered him to be a member of the Caucasoid race."

"Yeah, we thought about that, but Corky's too old. You look like a biker, so they ain't gonna think you're the police."

"All right, let's do it. Bring the guy in."

Big Marvin Pharr gave me a wink and navigated his large frame slowly around the cramped office. If not for being a cop, Marvin could be one of the linemen for the Chicago Bears. He was big and brawny with an infectious smile. Marvin brought the prisoner in to meet me and do some talking.

"Get comfortable, and don't be bull shitting our partner here. Tell this officer what you were telling us."

"Okay…umm…ya see, I know this dude…"

"Hold on. What's your name?"

"#Roberto Soto."

"What do they call you on the street?"

"Sapo. That means frog."

"You're starting off by lying to me already, and I don't like that."

"You know this guy, Frank?"

"No, I just met him, but I know Sapo means toad."

"Well, yeah, Sapo is kinda the same thing. I just didn't wanna say toad cuz that don't sound cool. That's why I said frog, but you're' right."

"Okay. Tell me what you told my partners."

"Okay, this dude I know, he's moving some big weight. Ounces, ki's, whatever you want, he can get. He just got outta Menard about two months ago. I've been dealing with him ever since. He's the one that set up that boxcar that got hit with all them guns on it about a month ago."

"What's his name?"

"They call the dude 'Gato' cuz he's like a cat, the way he can sneak up on you in the dark. That's why a lot of guys are scared to deal with him. He's a crazy motherfucker for sure."

"Do you know where those stolen guns are now?"

"Nah, man. They moved that shit out like the next day. I can set you up for a meet, though. The dude won't sell you nothing right away when I bring you to meet him. He's gotta feel you out, but at least you'll know who he is, and you two can make your own arrangements to buy something later on if he thinks you're cool."

"What are you talking about, coke or dope?"

"Cocaine man, he strictly deals in cola."

"And guns."

"Well, yeah, but his main thing is product."

"Does he carry a gun that you know of?"

"Man, he's always strapped. He carries a little ass .380."

"Is that from the boxcar burglary?"

"No, he's had that one for years. It's got notches in it for dudes he's killed."

"Has he ever been arrested for murder?"

"Nah, he's too slick. He was in Menard for something else."

"Who does he ride with?"

Sapo gave me the name of a Spanish gang in the area that Gato was part of, but Sapo claimed that he always dealt with him in a one-on-one setting.

After some name, background, vehicle, and address verification, we set out to the Humboldt Park area. So far, everything Sapo told us was verified. Gato was a bad guy and had done time for attempted murder while beating another murder case because the witness had disappeared.

I searched the informant before I let him sit next to me in the undercover vehicle. I never trusted informants. After all, they were telling on folks they had known for years and sometimes even snitching on family members if the deal was right for them.

Whenever I worked undercover, I knew I was dealing with bad guys. Bad guys are bad guys for a reason, and I never wanted to be at a disadvantage when driving my vehicle with them in the car. I also needed a built-in excuse to not let more than one thug in my car at a time. That way, no one was behind me and I could keep a pretty good eye on the guy sitting next to me.

To help ensure my safety, I moved the front passenger seat all the way forward and locked it in place using a bolt in the slide rail under the seat. That way, the passenger couldn't push the seat backward to get more legroom. In that position, he'd be jammed up against the dashboard. He wouldn't be as mobile as I was with my seat pushed back as far as it would go. If we got in a tussle in the car, I'd have a physical advantage as far as maneuverability.

The next thing I did was fill my backseat up with bags of old clothing, a cooler with beer, empty beer cans, a baby seat, and even a spare tire. I put anything back there I could to make it virtually impossible for someone to sit behind me. With everything in place, it gave me a built-in excuse not to have anyone else in the car, especially sitting behind me.

Once the car was set up, we were ready to go. Sapo directed me to the two-and-a-half-story frame building on Campbell. Gato used this address as a workhouse but didn't live there. He'd be meeting with us in an attic apartment accessible only by entering from the backdoor. Getting to it required going down a dark gangway to the rear of the building and then walking up three flights of stairs in an enclosed structure.

I didn't like the setup but had done similar undercover operations like this before, and they worked out. Still, this one gave me some concern. I can't tell you why; it was just a gut feeling.

Since I wasn't wired and had no way of communicating with my three backup guys once I left the undercover car, I was relying on their surveillance skills and instincts to help protect me if something went wrong. I also gave them a time limit of thirty minutes. If I wasn't out in thirty, there was a problem, and I needed help ASAP.

I walked down the dark gangway, and the path was made visible only by the light coming from the first-floor apartment. That was okay because I knew they'd be carrying flashlights if my guys came running. The only problem I saw was that these were old-timers. In other words, not the fastest-moving cops in the unit. But they had experience on their side, and that's a plus in police work.

We rounded the first set of stairs, with Sapo leading the way. Then we were on our way to the second floor and still no problems. As we started up the last few stairs to the attic apartment, Sapo broke it to me.

"Oh, hey, man. Listen, Gato might come off mad at me cuz I owe him some money, like sixty dollars, so be cool. I'm thinking with me bringing you in as someone that's gonna buy some weight, he'll write it off."

At that point, I realized my gut had been right. It was telling me to turn around now, but it was too late. They heard us coming, and one of the gangbanger's had opened the door. He put on a friendly face, but I wasn't buying it.

"Hey Sapo, wassup?"

They did the ghetto handshake accompanied by the frontal body slam.

"Hey Flaco, this here is John. It's the guy I was telling Gato about on the phone a while ago. He's expecting us. Is he here yet?"

"Oh, yeah, he's here, and he's waiting on you, bro."

When we walked into the apartment, I wasn't prepared for what awaited us. There were six guys in this two-room apartment, all in the kitchen, roughly a 10' x 12' room. The living room doubled as a bedroom about the same size directly in front of that.

Three guys flanked us on each side as we came in. Four of them had guns in their hands.

"Hey Gato, yo' boy is here, and he brought some company."

A shirtless Gato came out of the washroom, drying his hands with a pink towel. He had prison press going on and stood about five foot eight and weighed around one hundred sixty-five pounds. He was well ripped and had tattoos from his navel to his chin and down both arms. They were prison tats for sure.

He looked at Sapo and nodded to his boys.

"Take his ass."

It was obviously preplanned because the two guys who weren't sporting guns grabbed Sapo, one on each side. They held him by his wrists and one pulled him sideways while the other pulled him in the opposite direction. They each stood with one of their feet on his feet, so he was immobilized. His legs were spread apart. It looked like they were playing tug of war with a life-size Stretch Armstrong doll.

I knew I was in trouble. I was armed with my five-shot .44 Bulldog revolver in the small of my back. I could do some damage, but I wasn't going to win.

I put my hand behind my back and threw my left hand up, gesturing that I didn't want any trouble. Gato was sizing me up.

"Well, I hope you gonna be cool. Cuz we can fuck you up just like we gonna fuck up this piece a shit."

I glanced at the clock on the microwave. I had to last twenty-four more minutes before help would be on the way, and I had no way of warning them of the dangers they'd face when they came busting through the back door.

"So… you got his back?"

"Man, I don't know what you guys got goin' on with Sapo, but I just came here to arrange for some business. But this ain't looking like a business-friendly environment from what I'm seeing here. I'm done."

"Nah, nah, nah, bro. You ain't going nowhere till we get some shit straight here."

Sapo pleaded with Gato.

"Hey, man. This dude's got money. He wants to buy some weight. That's why I brought him to ya, bro. You know I ain't tryna get over on you, Gato."

"Yeah, Sapo, we straight. We so straight, you ripped me for sixty. That shit ain't gonna fly. You gotta be taught some respect, bro."

Then Gato looked at me. "Hey, you! Redneck lookin' mother-fucker! What's your name again?"

"John, and I ain't got all day to hang out here while you teach your boy some respect. How bout' we talk business then you can get on with his history lesson after I leave?"

Gato looked at his crew, then back at me. They all had a good laugh, and that was a bad sign.

"This whetto is fuckin' crazy. Hey John, watch this cuz you might just piss me off and be next."

Gato cracked his knuckles and stretched his arms out before he tore into Sapo. He wasn't bitch-slapping; he was working him like he was beating a heavy bag.

I figured that since this wasn't my beef, I should move off to the side and eventually work my way into the living room. Two guys kept a good eye on me, though occasionally glancing back to the ass-kicking in the kitchen.

I rested my hand on top of the television set and acted as a casual observer of the beating, making a point not to show any kind of emotion.

Unfortunately, when you're working undercover with an informant, they know you're the police, and for that and a number of other reasons, you're at their mercy. You don't know when they'll slip up or what they'll say, and that's exactly what happened here.

Sapo was hurting. I was surprised he hadn't passed out yet because the beating he was taking was vicious. It didn't look to me like Gato was going to stop anytime soon. He was enjoying it. The beating was as much for his crew's entertainment as it was a warning for me.

I guess Sapo was wondering why, as a cop, I hadn't announced my office and placed everyone under arrest. I didn't see it that way. He put me in a very dangerous situation and did so at the last minute. Had I known the full story, I would have made the meet in some public area where my guys could see me better.

That's when the hammer came down. Sapo couldn't take it any

longer, and I wasn't coming to his rescue. I couldn't even if I wanted to.

"Hey, Gato. Man, stop, please stop. I gotta tell you something, man, and you're gonna thank me, bro."

"Oh yeah? What you gonna tell me, bitch?"

"That guy with me is a fuckin' cop. He's a motherfuckin' cop that made me bring him up here."

I immediately threw the Lava lamp through the front window and hoped my backup saw or heard it as it crashed to the sidewalk below.

The two guys in the room grabbed me; the fight was on. I tried to fend them off long enough to pull my gun and start firing, but that was not to be. I grabbed one of them by the hair with one hand, had his right arm behind him, and twisted it upwards. I was using him as a shield for as long as it lasted, all of about a minute. It felt a lot longer. I was overpowered by the rest of the crew and fell to the floor. I expected to hear gunfire and be shot.

My gun was trapped under me. They were stomping and punching, and I could feel them feeling around for my gun. I was glad it was where it was because they couldn't get to it either. The thing that saved me was the fact that the little room was filled with furniture, and everyone was falling all over each other trying to get to me. It seemed that only two guys were getting clear shots at punching and stomping on me. When you're in situations like this, it seems like it takes forever for help to come, and that's what I mentally prepared myself for.

I was losing strength and wind. I had been fighting for a solid three minutes, maybe longer. That doesn't seem like a long time, but it feels like forever when you're using every ounce of strength you can muster. I didn't think I'd last much longer, but finally, I had my gun in my hand. But it was locked beneath me along with my arm. I struggled to arch my back to the point where I could pull it out and start blasting. If I was going to die today, people were coming with me.

I planned to empty my revolver into the two closest guys, figuring they'd fall on top of me. This would help shield me while I grabbed one of their guns and shot until it ended one way or another. I was able to raise my back enough to pull out my gun, but the hammer kept getting caught on my belt loop. Then I saw an iron and a toaster coming down. They were going to crash it down on my skull. I sure didn't want to go this way if it was going to be the end.

Then my gun was out, and just like that, I had breathing room. I had my hand on the trigger when I noticed that the hand holding that iron was black, and I recognized his ring. It was Marvin Pharr, one of my guys. I was gonna be okay. Jules, Corky, and Marvin came to my rescue. I don't have any idea how these "old guys" got up there so fast, but they were in full ass-kicking mode.

When the door crashed to the floor in the kitchen, it was because big Marvin Pharr ran through it like Superman. He hit it so hard that it came off the hinges and was lying on the floor. It was like a black tornado hit the cramped apartment.

They cleaned house. My attackers were in the prone position in less than fifteen seconds. All seven of them were brought down by a flurry of fists, feet, and elbows. It was over.

"You okay, Frankie boy?"

"Yeah, Corky."

"My nephew! These boys are lucky we got here in time to save their asses from you."

"Yeah, right, Jules. You guys are the best. I was worried you wouldn't get my signal."

Marvin was always a cool and quiet guy. He smiled and said, "That's the fastest I've moved in decades, Frank. I didn't think I still had it in me."

Sapo was hospitalized with internal injuries, a punctured lung, six broken ribs, and a torn liver.

Five of the seven people in the apartment required hospitalization as well.

Three of the thugs were convicted of aggravated battery on Sapo, and seven were convicted of aggravated battery on me. All seven were convicted of UUW charges. Gato was convicted of narcotics possession and possession of some stolen guns. Two of them had outstanding warrants. Two of them, one being Gato, also violated their parole. All involved received sentences ranging from eight years to twenty-six years. In all, four ounces of cocaine, a half-pound of marijuana, and thirty-seven guns were recovered from the apartment. Thirty-four of the guns came from the boxcar burglary.

Sapo was killed in a parking lot two years later during an armed robbery in which he was the offender.

I was lucky that my surveillance crew was on top of their game that night. I fault myself for not acting on what instinct was telling me. Humans are hard-wired for survival, so trust your instincts. They are a built-in warning signal that can save your life.

Chapter 27: When the Feds Try To Set Up Hardworking Cops

Papo was one of many drug informants I've dealt with over the years, and he supplied me with some major hits during the five months as my informant. He admitted to me that he used drugs, and every cop knows that's part of the equation when dealing with drug informants.

I can honestly say this, though — whenever I met with Papo, he was straight. What I didn't know was that Papo had decided to go into the business of selling drugs while he was my C.I. When you do that, your odds of getting busted by law enforcement go way up.

I noticed a pattern had developed with the last four cases Papo had given me. I recovered anywhere from two kilos to twenty-six kilos of cocaine in each of those cases. Word came through channels that I had interrupted an undercover federal drug investigation going on for eleven months by taking down their target. In that case, I recovered twenty-six kilos.

The feds came to our undercover office and demanded to know who my C.I. was. I wouldn't give them that information as I never gave up an informant. That's just part of the business and our agreement with them. The feds were not happy and found out who the C.I. was from our boss, who gave them full access to the C.I.'s file. Of course, the boss had no skin in the game and was not the type to rock the boat.

My view on the situation at hand was that if the federal agents' had a C.I. and he wasn't good enough to take down the guys I had taken down with the twenty-six kilos, then they should get themselves a better informant. I'd soon find out that's exactly what they did.

The feds set up my C.I. and caught him with two ounces of cocaine about three weeks later. He was with his wife and child, so they threatened him with the full weight of the federal government coming down on them if he chose not to become their informant. He and his wife would do federal time, and they'd lose their daughter. I can't blame him for switching sides, but he should have told me, and he didn't.

Papo called me one afternoon, and we met at the McDonalds at Armitage and Western Avenue in Chicago.

I knew the place, and fortunately, it was close to where I was conducting a narcotics surveillance. So I broke away and went to meet with him. I was surprised he was already there. Usually, when we were to meet up, he'd always show up fifteen to twenty minutes late. The conversation went like this:

"Hey Frankie, my man, I beat you this time."

"Yeah, that makes me think something's not right. Is everything okay?"

I noticed a change in his expression, which seemed odd. In retrospect, I think I hit a nerve. Something was up.

"Oh, yeah, man, everything's cool."

"All right, what do you got for me?"

"I got this dude that's moving big weight. He's from out of town, and he just comes in to do deals out of this motel in Stone Park."

"Okay. How do you know him, and what kind of weight are we talking about?"

"He's a good friend of a relative of mine that I gotta keep outta this whole thing. He's got about fifty or sixty kilos in the room right now and selling it like crazy, so you gotta move fast, or the only thing that'll be left is the money. You guys pay me by the kilo, so I want to make as much off the seizure as I can. So you need to move on this one. He leaves town tomorrow, man."

After I got all the information I could from the C.I., I went along with the rest of my team to set up on the location. We never knew who all was involved, so asking the desk clerk for information was out of the question.

Unlike a residence or business address where you can verify ownership or occupancy through the utility companies or other means, motel rooms are a different animal. We had to work with what we had.

I observed some activity going on both in and out of the room that the C.I. had told me about. There was a guy that fit the physical description of the target perfectly. He was even wearing the deep blue baseball cap backward like the C.I. said he would. But according to our C.I., this drug dealer never carried any guns. That was not my experience watching the comings and goings from this motel room on this warm summer night. Two of the people were clearly wearing holsters underneath their tee shirts as they returned with fast food.

I had an assistant state's attorney meet me near the location to approve the affidavit for a search warrant, and a local judge signed off on it. We were ready to make our move.

Once we were in position to hit the door of room 206, we knew from observing it for the past five hours that there were at least four occupants. But judging by the conversations going on inside, there were definitely more than four voices. One was of a female we had not seen during the surveillance.

Just before I was about to knock and announce my office, I heard one of the occupants say, "They're outside our door."

The only place that information could have come from was someone we had seen sitting in the van in the parking lot and facing the room. I sent two of the guys down to block it in with the undercover vehicle and to identify him. The room went quiet. I knocked and announced my office. There was no response. So I hit the door as hard as I could with the twelve-pound sledge. We were inside within a few seconds from the time I announced our intentions.

There it was in full display. FBI jackets lying on the bed and a monitor on the nightstand gave me a visual of the room next door with recording devices running. I opened up the door connecting the two rooms, and there was our alleged dope dealer. There were bundles of cash in an open canvas bag, a money counting machine, and three stacks of cash on the dresser right in front of the covert camera hooked to the monitor in the other room.

Were we or I being set up by the feds?

They were stunned.

"Hey boys, it looks like you guys are all disappointed that we didn't hit the room you guys tried to set us up in next door. It wouldn't have worked. We don't play that shit. Have a nice day."

We all started to walk out of the room and laughed at how inept their plan was.

The boss of the crew called me back in.

"Hey, you guys don't just get to walk out of here. You didn't have a search warrant for this room. It was for next door, and you just interfered in a federal investigation."

"I see that reading comprehension is not one of your strong points." When I said this, the female agent had already read the warrant and was trying to hand it to the boss before he looked any dumber. The warrant was for that room. Everything, including the two guys wearing guns under their tee shirts, was included in my affidavit with their full clothing description and logo on one of their shirts.

Our Sarge had been dumbfounded by this and was quiet the whole time but eventually snapped back to reality.

"We will be needing you to forward a copy to me of all of your reports when you complete them, but for now, I'm going to need a business card from each of you for our report."

I can't say for sure, but my guess was that the feds were hoping to nab someone in our crew doing something not by the book and come down on us to make a name for themselves and show us who the top cops were in Chicago. Their plan backfired. I don't know what kind of bogus reports they submitted because they never forwarded a copy to our sergeant, but I can guarantee there is false information in them. They had to cover their asses. Apparently, in all the confusion of my C.I. going in and out of room 206 when he was meeting with the agents, he gave me their room number instead of the one next door that had the cash.

In talking to my C.I. later and telling him I was dropping him as a C.I., he relayed to me that I treated him better and with far more respect than the federal agents did. The C.I. never went to federal prison and claimed he never did any more work for the feds, so I don't know what was worked out for him and his wife on that end of the agreement.

I often wonder…maybe my C.I. didn't make a mistake.

Chapter 28: Crook County Judges

I have literally testified thousands of times in courtrooms on the 2,688 cases I worked on. Most of them were in Cook County but also in Kane, Lake, and Will Counties during my law enforcement career and even after I retired. I have been before some outstanding judges; many of them are personal friends.

However, just like with bad cops, bad prosecutors, and bad bartenders, each profession has its share of bad apples.

After testifying in three hundred and nine consecutive felony trials, all ending up in guilty verdicts, I lost one. Not on the merits of the case, not based on case law, and not because a sympathetic jury let a felon walk because they bought some sob story. I lost the case because of a corrupt judge and a corrupt and later convicted attorney who went to prison for hiring a hitman to kill his wife. Fortunately, the woman survived the car bomb placed in her vehicle.

Class X cases in Illinois require a penitentiary sentence to be served for a period of at least six years and up to thirty years. Hand-to-hand deliveries of a Class X amount of controlled substance are no exception.

I appeared before Judge Lawrence Passarella (real name) to testify in the hand-to-hand delivery of the same and knew something was up the moment I walked into the courtroom, which was usually packed with people. Except for the judge, clerk, court reporter, prosecutor, and the defendant's attorney, there was no one else in the room. Not even the defendant.

The judge to hear the case was known to be an associate of some outfit guys in Chicago. I personally witnessed him having dinner with two mobsters at a supper club called Horwaths in Elmwood Park, Illinois. Somehow this didn't surprise me. The defendant in my case was family to a crew that had committed home invasions on the north shore of jewelers while pretending to be flower deliverymen. Once inside the home, they bound and threatened the wives and children and in at least one case, committed a sex act on a young girl. They threatened all kinds of dastardly things until the jeweler gave them what they came for.

With that said, we had to wait on the defendant. After about twenty minutes, #Guido Luigi strolled in looking like a homeless guy. He wore a long dirty wool overcoat, and his clothes were disheveled. On top of that, he was never asked to remove the black knit cap he wore. Ignoring this common practice was something I had never seen in my entire career.

His attorney, Richard Kagan, represented him, and the hearing was short. I testified in a bench trial, and when it was time for the defense to question me, he did not. He turned to his client and asked, "Did you do what the officer claims you did?"

His client answered, "No," and the judge quickly found him not guilty.

This is the same judge who found a guy not guilty of the attempted murder of a female police officer named Cathy Touhy. He was arrested while beating her face in with a steel bar. She suffered severe facial injuries.

Judge Passarella is not alone as far as being corrupt goes.

I will not use this judge's name because he still sits on the bench. But when he was a defense attorney handling a large number of drug cases, he approached me in the hallway at 26th and California and offered to give me four thousand in cash if I would testify in a manner that would let a drug dealer walk. This was his effort to make a path for himself into the Columbians I was dealing with at the time, which could have made him some big-time money. I didn't respond to the offer and entered the courtroom. When the case was called, I testified as honestly as I always did, and the drug dealer was found guilty.

Now I appeared before him years later. He was the judge on two Class X cases that involved the defendants' hand-to-hand delivery of cocaine to me. These open and shut cases that any other judge, except maybe Passarella, would have found guilty were tossed as my testimony "lacked credibility," in his words.

That's why we refer to it as "Crook County." It's not just judges. I had one prosecutor who had me wait in the jury room for my case to be called. After about two hours, I walked out into the empty courtroom with the exception of the clerk. I asked her if the judge took a break, and she told me no, they were done for the day. I asked her about my twenty-five-kilo case, and she told me that the prosecutor had the case called and because I wasn't there, they tossed it.

I found out later that the prosecutor was working with the feds, hoping to line himself up with a job with them. The feds needed my defendant to be out and about since the big money would stop flowing without him, and their cash seizures would come to a halt. I wasn't alone in this matter. A fellow officer had a similar experience with the same prosecutor. Reports were filed detailing this corruption, and as of today, no one has made any inquiries into the actions of this prosecutor.

Chapter 29: The Bikers Killed The Wrong Girl

Detectives #Ricky Blue and #Terry Sutcliffe were my backups when I went into a dive bar in Elgin, Illinois. I wasn't there to buy drugs. I went in for the sole purpose of accidentally on purpose running into a couple of the bikers I was going to be doing business with and was prepared to spend a few months on the investigation to take them down. I never liked to rush an investigation. When you do that, you make mistakes. And when you make the wrong mistake, the consequences could be fatal.

I hoped "SH" (Smiling Hillbilly) would show up and that his best friend "Blades" would make the introduction. SH would be more comfortable with me since we'd be meeting on his stomping grounds, and none of it was planned, at least on his end.

This group of bikers had planned on opening a chapter in Illinois but hadn't gotten the "blessing" they needed from the Dominate Club in Illinois. They were going to finance their chapter by selling drugs.

I went in alone because I didn't want my C.I. to be transactional in any future interactions I might have with this group. Since I already had met one of them, I didn't need another potential problem source on my back.

The guy I was hoping to see first was the crazy knife-wielder, Blades. He never had less than six razor-sharp knives on him at any given time and was the club's go-to knife sharpener.

When I first met Blades, he lived in a filthy, cramped basement apartment in the suburb. My C.I. made the introduction, so that was the easy part. To say Blades was not very friendly is an understatement. He was eyeballing me like no one else ever had in the many undercover operations I had been involved in. It was almost as if he could see right through me. But I maintained my composure and bad attitude so he wouldn't think I was a chump.

We had been making small talk for about ten minutes when his phone rang. He didn't say much. But every so often, he'd grunt and make it obvious that they were talking about me. I say this because he made a point to turn around and look directly at me with each acknowledgment of whatever was being said. I surmised that it was the "Smiling Hillbilly" on the other end of the line. Though I could only hear one side of it, I got the drift.

Blades ended the call with these words: "I don't know, but I'm damn sure gonna find out if he is."

That got my antenna up a bit because he was looking straight at me when he said it. Blades moved closer and sat down on a stool facing me, a foot from my face. I think SH asked him if he thought I was a cop.

Blades took an "Old Timer" lock-bladed knife from his pocket and then grabbed one of probably a half-dozen whetstones lying around the apartment. He didn't say anything. He just had that thousand-yard stare going on. Then he glanced at my belt and the buck knife I carried.

"When was the last time you had that buck sharpened?"

"It came sharp from the factory."

"Nah, a knife is never sharp enough unless I worked that sumbitch. Give me that thing. I'll put an edge on it for ya."

I had a feeling that this was his way of disarming me, or so he thought. I had my .44 caliber Bulldog cross-draw in my waistband and could easily access it with either hand if it came down to that. But I had to be on guard since I'd be handing him another knife.

"You know what, Blades? I was cutting some shit with it the other day, so it can probably use a tune-up."

I handed it to him, and he started working on it. After a minute or so, he asked me, "So, how long have you been a cop?"

"I'm coming up on my thirteenth anniversary in November. How bout' you?"

He smirked and then checked the sharpness of my blade by running it slowly through a piece of paper. It cut like a razor blade. I was impressed.

"Do I look like a fuckin' cop?"

"Yeah," I said, " you look kinda like a cop that busted me a few years ago back down in Chicago."

"Take out your wallet. I want to see some identification, so I know who you really are."

I held my wallet up but held on to it. I didn't give a crap about what he might find inside. It was my U/C wallet. The only things in it were an undercover driver's license, a cleaning ticket in my U/C name, some old lottery tickets with my U/C name on the back, and an old cash bond slip.

When he reached for it, I pulled back.

"Let's trade wallets."

He hesitated for about thirty seconds, trying to stare me down, but it didn't work.

"Fair enough." He unbuckled his wallet from the chain on his belt and handed it to me. The only thing in it was a driver's license, a lottery ticket, and some cash.

I was surprised he actually handed me his chain wallet. I memorized his name and birthdate for my supplementary report and quickly handed it back, pulling out one of the twenty-dollar bills it contained in a manner so obvious he couldn't' help but notice.

"What the fuck you rippin' my shit for?"

"I could use some beer money."

"Man…you could get your ass killed pullin' shit like that. That shit ain't funny. We ain't that cool yet."

"Yeah, either is going through all my shit. I thought you were cool to deal with, but I ain't interested in any of this third-degree bullshit."

I turned to my C.I.

"Let's go. I'll get that half "ki" from the Mexican."

"Hey man, we're ready to do business. I was just told to check you out before the hillbilly meets up with you. I'm gonna tell him you're okay."

I found that being combative worked better than being compliant. A mistake a lot of undercover cops make is going along to get along. Remember that you are dealing with some really bad guys, and when you do that, there is always some form of conflict. You are representing as a thug, so you have to act like a thug, or they'll make you.

"Yeah, well, while you're at it, let him know I'll buy the shit. But if he starts running me around from here to there and everywhere and playing that game or pulls any of that I-need-the-money-upfront bullshit, I'm done. I'll go back to doing business with the Mexican."

"I can't promise you how he'll do his thing. I just know he'll do it, and he's capable of more than you're asking for. But I'll tell him what you said."

"Cool."

Another thing I'd learned was to play it close to the belly. A lot of cops working undercover who are new to the game talk too much, and when they talk too much, they're lying. It's easy to remember the truth; lies not so much. You don't want to get caught up in one of your lies. The bad guys will remember something you said a week ago, and if you can't remember what it was, you're in trouble.

***

So I'm sitting at the bar when the guy next to me whips out a knife and starts cutting his long greasy hair. He must have had Blades put the edge on that thing because he was cutting thick handfuls off with ease. He dropped them into an ashtray before setting them ablaze. I don't know if you've ever smelled burning hair, but it has a horrible stench and makes a lot of smoke. I found an open seat at the other end of the bar, far away from that idiot. I sat one stool away from a blond woman of about twenty-five. It wasn't long before she started up a conversation. Though buzzed, she wasn't obnoxious. In fact, I ended up having a pretty pleasant conversation with her for about twenty minutes.

That's when a guy came in, and she motioned for him to come over. He waltzed over, doing a two-step dance and spinning around. He sported a wide-open mouth in a grotesque toothy smile full of black cavity infested teeth. It was like he had a mouthful of yellow dice.

"Hey, #Sheila baby, give old SH a big kiss."

"SH," I said, turning on my stool. "Are you the same SH who knows Blades?"

"Who the fuck is askin'?"

I introduced myself, and he turned around and walked out of sight. *I might have just blown it,* I thought, but a few minutes later, he walked up to me.

"How did you know I'd be here?"

"I didn't. I don't even know you. I just came back from the Casino needing a beer real bad, and this place looked cool. I lost four g's today, so I'm not in a good mood. Then I heard her call you SH and figured you must be Blade's bud, but if you ain't, that's cool with me too."

I'm not sure he was buying it. He turned his back on me and was talking to the girl when I ordered a shot of Jack Daniels and another beer and downed them as fast as I could. Without saying another word to SH, I waved at the girl and headed for the door.

That move worked.

"Hey man, where you going?"

"What's it to you… where I'm going?"

"Be cool, man. I just talked with Blades, and he said you were cool. I just gotta be careful, you know what I'm saying?"

"So are we gonna talk, or am I wasting my time?"

He shook my hand, and while downing Jack and Dos Equis for an hour, we agreed on a drug deal.

He chose the parking lot of Confetti's nightclub in Schaumburg, Illinois, the following night to sell me a couple of ounces of cocaine as a sample for a bigger deal later on. The deal that night in Confetti's lot went as planned. The cocaine was high quality, so I made a deal with him to purchase five kilos. This time, I set the location and chose the Oasis on I-90 near O'Hare Airport.

SH showed up with his bodyguard, Blades this time, which was good. It saved me from having to obtain an arrest warrant for him.

I gave SH $150,000 for the five kilos of cocaine and signaled for a bust once it was in my car. Terry Sutcliffe and Ricky Blue were on them before they knew what happened. Terry grabbed the gun SH attempted to pull out with one hand and slammed him to the ground with the other. Ricky tackled Blades as he ran away.

As Rick searched him, he started laughing. "Hey, you guys, see all the knives this guy has on him?" Rick recovered six of them hidden in different spots on his body, including up both sleeves. Both subjects were arrested and charged accordingly with Class X cases.

Sometime between the date of the arrest and the upcoming court date, arrangements were made to kill the C.I., but there was a problem. Somehow, SH got confused and thought the girl I was talking with at the bar was the informant. She wasn't. She was just a friendly woman who was well acquainted with SH and had known him for about five years.

A biker was hired to kill Sheila, chosen for the hit because they knew each other from the bar, and she trusted him. Sheila agreed to go with him to Wisconsin to pick up a car and drive it back one night. They left the bar at about 10 p.m. An hour into the drive, he forced her out of the car and into a farmer's field, where he ordered her to lay down and then shot her once in the back of the head with a .22 caliber pistol.

She lay motionless, feigning death, even after he gave her a good kick in the ribs to see if he needed to put another in her. When she was sure he was gone, Sheila made her way to a phone and called her trusted friend SH. The bullet meant to kill her hit a metal barrette in her hair and deflected. She was afraid to call anyone from the bar, so she told SH what had happened. He agreed to pick her up, and she was never seen alive again. SH made sure he had a solid alibi at the time of her murder.

Sheila's body was found in an Indiana cornfield the day after she confided in SH. A local thug with ties to SH and the community of Elgin, Illinois, was charged with the murder and convicted. He has since maintained his innocence and has not implicated anyone else in the matter.

SH was sentenced to twelve years, and Blades was sentenced to six years on plea deals before Judge Bailey. On a happy note, Blades was killed in a motorcycle accident two days after being released from prison. SH had terminal lung cancer and died at the age of forty-two one month after being released from prison. Maybe Karma was at play here…

Chapter 30: My Insurance Policy

I could write an entire book, maybe two, on the wild times I had working with Terry Sutcliffe and Ricky Blue. We were partners on a three-man team in the Organized Crime Division and were known as the Three Amigos. We were great friends both on and off duty, and that relationship is as strong today as it's ever been.

I never laughed harder working with anyone than I did working with these two characters. I trusted my life to these good solid cops in any undercover investigation we were involved in, like the one mentioned in the previous chapter. There would be many more to come.

This chapter is about a case that initially started as a narcotics investigation but ended up busting a massive "call girl" operation conducted at the highest levels in the City of Chicago and surrounding suburbs.

The initial information came in from one of our informants who knew a prominent defense attorney in Cook County. The attorney frequently used a prostitution service run by a madame in Chicago out of one of the many exclusive high-rise buildings located downtown.

The confidential informant relayed to us that this attorney also used cocaine on occasion and that the prostitutes from this call girl operation supplied the cocaine to him.

I asked if she knew which prostitute delivered the drugs to the client, and she relayed that it wasn't supplied by the girl herself but would be placed in the work apartment by the madame. I then inquired as to the name of the madame, and she gave that to me along with her full description, address, units involved, and other verified information.

A name check revealed that the madame was once an active prostitute herself but had now moved up, if you can call it that, to the pimping game. I won't use her real name, but for the benefit of her and her clients who may be wondering, her initials are "JH."

After we conducted hours of surveillance and verified all the information we needed in order to hit the operation, I wrote up a couple of search warrants. One was for the condo unit that JH lived in, and the other for the condo in the same building that JH also owned, and that her girls worked out of.

We had officers stationed just outside each of the two units and planned on making entry simultaneously, but there was a wrinkle even with all the planning and precautions we had taken.

Someone in the building saw us. I know it wasn't the desk clerk because we left one officer with him so that he couldn't make any calls. I suspect it was another defense attorney I knew from court. He was waiting on the elevator as we came in and said, "I hope you're not going to be hitting my place." He stepped back and let us have the elevator. As we rode up, I couldn't help but think that I should have had an officer stay with him.

These elevators moved faster than any I've ever been on, and we were on our floor within seconds. Positioned outside JH's door, we heard her phone ring and hoped to hear a deal go down. That's when we knew we had been made.

"Sledgehammers! I gotta go. Thanks, I owe you one." JH hung up and made a quick phone call. "You gotta get out of there right now. The cops are on the way."

Later, we learned that our guys at the other unit heard the phone ring, and the girl answered it. A young, very attractive woman came out of the unit and was intercepted by our team within a few seconds.

We knocked, and JH opened her door without even looking through the peephole. She knew we were there. I presented her with the search warrant, and she didn't seem surprised by any of the goings-on.

JH sat down and didn't say anything until I came across two Rolodex files packed so tight that I doubt if you could slip another file card into the holder.

"What are these for?"

"You're a smart man. I'm sure you can figure it out."

As I scrolled through the files, I was stunned by the amount of names I recognized. JH could have made a fortune in blackmail money or used it as a bargaining chip if she went down hard on our case. She had recorded everything possible about the men who had used her prostitution service. Not only were their names recorded, but so were the phone numbers they used, their business or profession, who recommended them to her business, and whom they recommended to her. She had other personal information on the men too. I'm sure they hadn't given it to her, but somehow it was in her files. I'm also confident that was why she didn't seem to be too worried, as you will see.

Some men used company checks and made them out to reflect a legitimate business expense such as "Temporary Clerk Services."

The guys at the other unit were inside searching when I came in. The girl that had come out was in handcuffs. A sizable amount of cocaine was recovered from that apartment, but this girl was scared, unlike JH, who took it in stride.

I introduced myself and asked her for her name. She told me it was #Tina Bridges, and so our conversation began.

"You are under arrest, Tina. I am going to read you your Miranda rights before any questioning because the cocaine was found in plain view in the apartment under your control just now."

She indicated that she understood her rights and agreed to talk to me.

"Where did the cocaine come from?"

"I don't know. It was just there, but I don't do drugs and didn't know what it was."

"Is this where you live?"

"No, I live in Boston."

"What are you doing here?"

"I'm an artist, and I came here to do some artwork for the owner of the apartment. It's how I'm paying my way through college."

"You came all the way from Boston to do artwork?"

"Yes, I get paid well for what I do." She opened her purse to reveal a large sum of cash. "Listen, can I talk to you alone, sir?"

"No. My partners and I don't have any secrets."

"I don't want to go to jail for something like this. My parents will be so disappointed in me. I'll do anything you guys want if you can let me go. You can have the money, or if there is something else you want, I'd be happy to oblige you…all of you. I don't want to go to jail. I just want to go home and be done with all of this stuff."

"Tina, people say things when they are scared and are willing to do just about anything. I understand the position you find yourself in, so I will use my discretion here and not charge you with attempting to bribe us. Is that all you have to say?"

"Yes, sir."

After all the required paperwork was completed and a court date set, the case went to a preliminary hearing and was mysteriously tossed. It was one of the very few cases I've lost. That's why I'm glad I had the foresight to keep an insurance policy. Yes, the statute of limitations and any repercussions from the Chicago Police Department have long passed. I kept one Rolodex and gave the other to a very trusted friend/attorney of mine. You see, I always thought that with the powerful and connected folks involved in this case, something might come back to haunt me in the future, à la Jeffrey Epstein. You will see a sampling of the file cards in the center pages of this book.

Here is a partial list of the types of clients who used the services provided by this high line prostitution ring. These men had various occupations during their lifetimes. I'm not saying when they had assumed these positions in life. Some were in that field at the time of this investigation, some had been in that position prior to us opening the case, and some came into prominence in that position after this case was closed but were listed as active clients at the time of the seizure.

They include a governor, two Aldermen, a high ranking member of the Archdiocese (referred to as "The Holy Ghost"), a billionaire, four Cook County judges, one Lake County judge, one Kane County judge, eleven criminal defense attorneys that I knew of or had cases with over the years, one radio personality, two TV personalities (one of which had a disgusting and mind-blowing fetish involving a dinner plate). So if one of these persons happens to be reading this, you know I have your reference card.

Also listed were the CEOs of seven major corporations, including one located in Japan. There were numerous stock traders from the Board of Trade in Chicago that had been recommended to the service by one of their own. A side note indicated that he had received a "freebie" for all those referrals. The owner of a chain of fast-food restaurants was in there, and the owner of a professional sports team. Each Rolodex has six hundred-plus names.

The two things her clients all seemed to have in common were that they liked prostitutes and were all willing to spend big bucks for the service provided. If a client wanted to have a line or two of cocaine waiting for him upon his arrival, that was extra, and his card would read: "Likes to ski."

The date, time, location, amount paid, and phone number they called from were listed on the card, which girl serviced the client and any special requests he wanted, and things and types of girls he did not want. The client's physical description, hygiene concerns, and personal traits were also noted. In some cases, the vehicle he drove with the license number was also listed, along with who referred him or how he came to know about the service. So you can see what I mean by the potential for blackmailing one of these guys if JH chose to do so.

It doesn't hurt to have an insurance policy. I still have the Rolodex files in a safe place.

Chapter 31: Dangerous Dude

I was working with a great street cop on this day in the 14th District. He wasn't my regular partner, but I would have been honored to have him as such.

Mario Ramirez and I were rolling down Division Street when I spotted a school bus through the open lot on an adjoining street. It was in a vacant lot next to a residence.

"Did you see that, Mario"

"That car with the gangbangers we just passed?"

"No, the school bus backed into the dark end of that lot on the next street."

"I already know what you're thinking. Let's check it out."

We came to a stop just out of sight of any occupants in the bus and approached on foot. They didn't see us until it was too late.

The door was open, and a woman was sitting on the steps of the bus while the male was hooking up a battery charger to an extension cord from her house. It turns out they are boyfriend and girlfriend. No children were being violated, but something still didn't seem right.

"Good evening, sir. We just wanted to check things out when we saw the school bus back here."

The bus had been turned into traveling living quarters, complete with cooking and sleeping arrangements in place.

"Well, now that you checked it out, you can leave."

"I'll decide when I leave, not you. What's your name?"

"#Joe Mays."

There was something about this guy I didn't like, and I could sense Mario felt the same way. While talking to him, my eyes roamed, looking for anything that might be out of the ordinary or that would give us probable cause to take this further. He had thrown a jacket on top of a five-gallon plastic bucket that sat behind the driver's seat as we came up to the door, and it looked like an attempt to conceal whatever was in there.

"Ya know you weren't quick enough. I saw what you were trying to hide in that bucket."

"I ain't tryin' to hide shit. Bullets ain't illegal."

I boarded the bus along with Mario and asked him to produce the required FOID card for the bullets. At the same time, I lifted the jacket and saw that the canister was full of various caliber rounds of military-type ammo, including the belt-fed rounds of the M-60 machine gun.

"I got one, but not with me."

"Well, you got the bullets with you, so you will be under arrest."

Mario cuffed him up, and when he did, the hate for us in our prisoner's eyes was obvious.

"As long as you're fuckin' with me, I need to lock up my bus before we go, so let's go now and get this bullshit over with."

"Hold on; we ain't going anywhere. I have to conduct an inventory search of the bus before we tow it. Do you have any valuables you'd like to claim, just so you don't say we stole it on you?"

"There ain't shit in here except my clothes."

"Okay, I'll check to make sure you didn't overlook or forget about something."

A curtain separated the front part of the bus from the rear. Stepping through the divider, I observed a .45 caliber model 1911 lying on the bed. A makeshift metal shop setup looked like he was making a silencer for the .45. A picture of him with his best friend posing with guns hung on the wall, and I recognized the POS as the guy who had shot his landlord as he came to confront him about rent due and other problems they were having. He left the bleeding man in the gangway and even shot him again as he lay on the ground, helpless.

Officer Richard Clark #13034 of the 19th District valiantly and without regard for his own life tried to rescue the dying man and in doing so, was shot and killed, leaving behind his loving wife and two children.

So now I knew the kind of guy we were dealing with. I found a few more guns, seven blasting caps, and a live hand grenade in his sleeping area.

"Mr. May, you are also under arrest for having explosives in your possession. I see you and the guy from Lill Street are buddies."

"Yeah, we are, and if you think he hates cops, I hate em' twice as much. Too bad he didn't kill more of you motherfuckers."

He was arrested and charged accordingly. Fortunately, we were able to take a pretty dangerous thug off the streets and relieve him of his weaponry. Who knows what he planned to do with that stuff.

Like I said before — it's better to be lucky than good. On this day, I believed it…we got lucky.

Chapter 32: Howling at the Moon

Akki and I were working Summer Mobile one year, and that's always a blast. The boss who runs it, Bob Guthrie, is hands-down best of breed. His supervisors are all top-of-the-line guys too. So it's a pleasure to work the lakefront and beaches for the summer, just for a break. The entire lakefront is your playground.

This night started out like all others. There were the usual complaints of loud music, teens drinking, etc. It was warm to the point of being uncomfortably sticky because of the high humidity. Of course, the fact was that no matter how warm, we always drove with the windows down so we could hear what we couldn't see. A scream, a call for help, or maybe a gunshot in the distance might be missed if we were wrapped up tight in our steel cocoon.

We were patrolling the lakefront at approximately 400 West Diversey when we observed a male white in his early forties. He was wearing a blue tee shirt, white shorts, and white gym shoes.

"Hey Ak, check this guy out over here."

"What the fuck? That asshole's pulling his pants down in front of those kids."

He was approximately two hundred feet from where we pulled over.

When the offender, #Clark Williamson, dropped his pants and exposed his erect penis to the boys, we could clearly make out the visual but not the audio of what was being said from that distance.

The boys were brothers ages seven and eight years old, and they took off running toward a male white in his late thirties.

"Now that nut job's saying something to some other kids by the tree. Let's sneak up on him and see what he's saying first."

"Looks like that other guy....maybe those kids' dad is coming after him."

By then, we were close enough to hear everything.

The flasher turned around on the father's approach, exposing his backside to Dad, and bent over simultaneously, placing his hands on his knees. Then he looked up towards the moon and started howling like a wolf. If that wasn't crazy enough, he wiggled his hips from side to side and panted like a dog.

That was enough for Dad. He turned around when he saw that we were now about fifty feet away. I think he was probably gonna kick some ass but seeing us led him to change his mind. Maybe we should have walked slower, but so far, Clark didn't see us coming up on him.

Suddenly, he took off running with his shorts in one hand and waved his arms over his head to draw even more attention. He was screaming as loud as his vocal cords would allow him.

"Will anyone give me a dollar to see my ass and big cock?"

Several people yelled for him to get out of the park area because children were present.

Akki and I were within ten feet of him now, and when he saw us, he immediately dropped down to his hands and knees and started barking like a dog while shaking his buttocks in an up-and-down motion like he was twerking.

We placed him under arrest, and Akki helped him put his shorts back on.

Apparently, Mr. Clark Williamson took a liking to Akki. I say this because when we were driving into the 23rd Police District, he wouldn't speak to me at all. He thought I was mean and had his eyes and heart set on Akki.

"Hey, hon, you with the nice hairdo." Akki was known for his male version of the bouffant hairstyle and always kept a can of hairspray at the ready. "Hey, hon… your boy's talking to you."

"The fuck you want, asshole? Don't be callin' me hon."

I said mockingly, "I think he's got hearts for you, Ak."

Akki turned around in the seat and looked at our prisoner for a minute. They locked eyes. It was looking like it was getting serious.

"Yeah, hon, you. You're the one I want to talk to. Your partner's too fucking cold."

"What do you want?"

"I'm nervous about being arrested, but at the same time, I'm sexually excited by it."

"Why are you telling me that and not my partner?"

"Because I have a special request, and you're not as intimidating as your partner."

"What's your request?"

"Can we stop somewhere and pick up some poppers so I can use them while I masturbate in the back seat of this police car? Then turn on the lights and siren for me while I'm doing it. That would really excite me."

"Hey Frank…can you believe this asshole?"

"I don't know, Ak. You and he seem to be pretty tight. Did you at least want to think about it?"

Akki was quiet for a few seconds, which is a rarity. So I thought I'd bust him out a little more.

"So, you are thinking about it…"

Akki got a great laugh and showed a full set of fronts. "You asshole, let's get him into the station before I get pissed off."

Bringing our prisoner into the 23rd District didn't stop him from hitting on Akki. Once we got back near the interview rooms, he motioned for Akki to come closer.

"Hey, hon, could you take me into one of these little rooms and watch me play with myself. I need someone to watch, or I just can't get excited."

"No, hon, I can't do that, but my sergeant will. He's a real nice guy. All you have to do is ask him. Would you like me to see if he's available to come in and watch you?"

"Oh my! A sergeant? They wear the white shirts, right?"

"Yes, they do."

"Oh yes, please call him in."

"I'll get him on the air now. 4232."

Dispatcher: "4232, go with your message."

"Can you see if 4230 is available to come into the 23rd District?"

The dispatcher didn't have to call 4230. Our Sergeant, Jimmy Hanson, always monitored the guys when they worked for him.

"4230. I heard it. I'm on the way. I'm about ten minutes out."

"10-4, 4230. Did you get that 4232?"

"10-4."

I took the handcuffs off of our prisoner, and that's when I took a good look at the watch he was wearing. It was a Rolex, going for about seven thousand dollars at the time. This was no knock-off.

"That's a mighty fine-looking watch you got there, Mr. Williamson."

"It should be. I paid over seven thousand dollars for it. I'll give it to you if you let me go."

"Are you serious? Because if you are, that would be a charge of bribery. Did you want to repeat that now?"

"Why are you so mean? I'm not talking to you anymore. Get hon in here. I'll deal with him. He's so much nicer than you are."

I typed up the arrest report, and part of that was asking for a prisoner's occupation.

"What do you do for a living?"

"I'm an executive with the Coca Cola company. That's why I can afford a watch like that."

"Hey Frank, Sergeant Hanson's coming in the front door."

"All right, Mr. Williamson, our sergeant will be coming in here in a few seconds. You can make your request to him."

"Ohhh...thank you sooo much!"

"Hey, Sarge...our prisoner isn't real happy with me, and he'd like to speak with you."

"Yes, sir. I'm Sergeant Hanson. What can I do for you?"

"Hello, sergeant. I wanted to ask you if you could watch me masturbate? Neither one of these officers will do that for me. Not even hon over there with the nice hair."

"I'm surprised that they wouldn't do that for you. No, thank you, and I'm outta here."

"Hey, Ak. I don't think Jimmy was too happy with that."

"I know, but did you see the look on Jimmy's face when he asked him?"

"Yeah... it didn't change one bit. I don't think there's anything that can shock him."

Clark Williamson was found guilty and received one day of time served and one year of supervision plus court costs. A slap on the wrist, as they say.

Chapter 33: The Swordsman

#Jimmy Zee and I were working summer mobile on our way back from lunch when we responded to a call for a backup at an apartment on Briar Street. It was only a block away, so we rolled on it. The call was for a possible violent mental.

We were the first officers to arrive at the third-floor apartment. The disturbance must have been going on for some time because residents directed us where to go during our travels. We had the apartment number, not that we needed it. The loud rantings of a male voice echoed through the hallways like a beacon.

The screaming stopped as soon as I knocked on the door. It was like someone hit the off button on a radio.

"Police. I need you to open the door for us."

Zee smiled and shook his head. "I can tell you right now this is gonna be good. Watch yourself."

I knocked and announced again.

"Just a minute." The voice behind the door sounded garbled, and we could hear spitting sounds.

"Are you okay?"

The door opened slowly, and a nude, skinny male white, about six feet tall and one hundred fifty pounds, stood before us. I don't know what the appeal of that is, but crazy people like to be naked for some reason. He had shoulder-length dark brown hair and blue eyes. His name was #Jeffrey Weiss.

Zee smiled. "I told you this was gonna be good."

Jeffrey was unfazed by the 30-inch long Civil War-era sword protruding from his abdomen. It was buried all the way up to the hilt and protruding from his back, roughly eighteen inches. Burying it in his body so deeply might have worked in his favor because it prevented the blood groove in the blade from doing its job externally. Jeffrey's abdomen had swelled around the entrance wound, choking off a path for the blood to flow out. I examined his backside, noting there was slightly more blood oozing from it, but it helped control the amount of leakage since the blade was angled upwards.

"Who the fuck called you here? I wanna know who the fuck said you could come to my home without my permission?"

"Hey Zee, get fire moving on this."

Anytime you encounter a person who's not acting rationally, it's a good idea to notify the EMTs. They're better equipped to handle possible pharmaceutical-related issues than we are. It's even more important when you have someone with a sword running through the midsection of his body.

Jeffrey had a white plastic plate in his hand when he answered the door, and though I could see there was blood on it, I hadn't taken a good look at what else was on there.

"You need to sit down, Jeffrey. It looks like you're bleeding internally from that stab wound and might choke on your own blood."

"I don't give a fuck, copper!"

"Just relax. Help's on the way."

"Hey, cop, look in that plate and tell me what you see."

Zee looked at it and calmly said, "There's just a few teeth."

"Yeah, and ya know how they got there? Like this!"

He grabbed the flat head screwdriver off the counter and plunged it into his mouth, working the gap created by one of his missing teeth. He was using it as a pry tool and was nearly successful in getting the tooth extracted.

"Hey, cop, there's pliers on my bed. Will you get it so I can pull the rest of this tooth out?"

"I'm gonna handcuff this guy, Zee, until the beat guys get here."

The ambulance and the paper car arrived at the same time.

"Holy fuck, what did you guys do to this guy?"

"We found him like this. Hey buddy, you may wanna cuff this guy up after I take mine off. He has a penchant for hurting himself."

"Don't you guys want to handle it?"

"He's all yours."

Chapter 34: Police Impersonator

When I say police impersonator in this chapter, I'm not referring to the folks who jump to a desk job at the first chance and hide in the safety and comfort of the station house. Those folks are what we call "house cats," not impersonators.

I'm talking about the civilians who play dress-up and hit the streets conducting street stops both on foot and in vehicular traffic, sometimes outfitting their cars to look like police vehicles.

They're usually males, although I did have one female who played the role. They present themselves as plainclothes tactical, narcotics, or vice officers to their prey. Sometimes they even step it up to impersonate detectives. This gives them a built-in excuse for not being in uniform, and to the average person on the street, the cop who's not in uniform is psychologically more intimidating.

Most of these wannabes are in it to play a tough guy role. Others, so they can shake down people and businesses for cash or other items of value. Then there are the deviates — they're in it for sex. During my investigations, I've found that many of these morons tried to become cops and, fortunately, didn't make the grade. Though with the standards dropping as they have been lately…enough said.

It's remarkable how well some of these guys are at plying their trade and fooling so many people, even other cops. I'm going to tell you the story of one such fake cop, #Alberto Garcia, and how he had been fooling folks for years and making a living doing it.

Akki Mares and I had been out hunting for bad guys one night when suddenly one appeared right in front of my face. The only problem was, I didn't realize it.

Akki had a nose for police impersonators like no one I had ever worked with. We arrested a half dozen of them, and most were Akki's call. For brevity, I'll just go into one case and demonstrate how important it is to take these folks off the street.

We were driving south on Kimball when a white unmarked Ford coming north turned into the alley going east. I didn't think much of it. The car bore all the typical earmarks of an unmarked squad car. It had the spotlight on the driver's side, black wall tires, and no hubcaps like most of our units did.

"Did you see that, Frank?"

"What, Ak?" I was thinking something just went down on the street, and I missed it. In fact, I did.

"That asshole that just turned into the alley there is playing police."

"Well, he's pretty good at it cuz I thought it was the police."

"Make a U-turn. We gotta stop this jag-off."

I turned around as quickly as I could. If Akki was right (and I knew based on past experience that was more likely to be the case than not), this guy might slip away on us. I hit the alley just as our target was pulling into his garage. I lit him up with the spotlight and expected that he'd get out of his squad with the swagger only real cops would display under these circumstances.

"Hey, guys. What's going on?"

"Don't give me that 'what's going on' bullshit," said Akki. "You know what's going on."

In case I hadn't mentioned it, Akki can be blunt at times, especially when he thinks people are trying to play him.

"I don't know what you mean," said the impersonator. "I'm a cop just like you're a cop. We all play for the same team, and I'm tired. I just had a long shift because we've been working on some gang homicides for the last couple of weeks."

"Bullshit. Let's see some police I.D., a badge, and your driver's license."

"Okay, man, I don't get where you're coming from, but that's cool. I know working the streets out here, you can't be too careful."

I was there as Akki's backup and let him do all the talking. I'm embarrassed to admit it, but until a good solid minute or two had gone by, I thought the guy was the police. I knew he wasn't the Chicago police but thought maybe he worked for the county or one of the political investigatory arms. As a precaution, I did take the time to relieve him of his weapon.

"All right, all right, shit's getting real here. Let me show you guys something before this goes any further. Cuz I ain't in the mood for no accidents in the alley here."

He pulled up on the chain he wore around his neck, and there was a Cook County Sheriffs badge on the end of it, just like we would wear our stars when working in plain clothes.

"That's bullshit. I don't know where you got that badge, but you ain't the fuckin' police."

It was a real Cook County Sheriff's badge, but I had to go with my partner's gut on this one. Akki had been right every time before.

"Let me look at your bullshit I.D. now."

The guy handed Akki his driver's license and a Cook County Sheriff I.D., and another identification piece that indicated he was a gang crimes investigator. The names and photo's matched. Everything looked real but not to Akki's sharp eye.

"Look at this, Frank. Ya see this right here? That's not on the real Sheriff I.D. cards."

If Akki hadn't told me that, I would have never known. I've never taken the time to study a Sheriff's identification card, and I'll bet most cops would have thought it to be the real thing too.

"Let's get someone to drive this asshole's car to the station."

We placed him under arrest and transported him into our office. Once there, the lieutenant came in to check on what we were doing with our arrest.

"What do you guys have him in here for?"

"He's playing like he's the police. Akki is calling the Cook County Sheriff's IAD to have them come in here on this."

The lieutenant looked over everything before speaking up.

"I don't know, Frank; all his stuff looks real."

"I know, but Akki is really good at this, so we'll wait to see what IAD says."

"Hey, lieutenant, tell your boys to let me go. You can call the commander over at Area Seven. I've been working on a gang homicide with them for weeks. As a matter of fact, I had just come from there when your guys stopped me. Call the commander; he'll tell you. There's no reason to be putting me through all this bullshit. I think your guys are just doing this bullshit to me because I'm Puerto Rican."

"You say you are working with Commander #Fournier?"

"Yes, I am. Check it out yourself."

The lieutenant had me step out of the interview room.

"Hey Frankster, Commander Fournier is a very good friend of mine. Are you guys sure about this guy?"

"Absolutely."

"All right, I'm gonna give him a call. I have his cell number in my phone."

Akki came back into the room and said, "IAD is on the way. What did the boss want?"

"He just wanted to know what we busted this guy for, and he's calling up Commander Fournier to find out if what this guy is saying is true."

"If what's true?"

He told the lieutenant he'd been working closely on a gang homicide and that Commander Fournier knew him and was actively keeping up with the team's progress.

"Hey Frank and Akki, step out here for a minute. I just got off the phone with Commander Fournier at Area Seven. He says this guy is from the county and has been helping them on a homicide case they've been working on. He says the guy comes in and is part of their briefings. He's given them updates on where the offender might be laying his head and what he's been driving lately. No license plates yet but a description of the wanted car."

Akki is not one to mince words. "Then the commander's been duped by this asshole too."

"I don't think so, Akki; the commander's a real sharp guy."

"I have to go with my partner on this one, lieutenant. I know the commander, and he is sharp, but sometimes things happen."

"All right, but let me know as soon as you know for sure because the commander's gonna be hot."

The guys from IAD showed up. They verified that the badge was a replica, the IDs were phony, and it turned out that they were actively looking for this guy for impersonating a police officer in the Mexican community. He had been shaking his victims down for cash and sex. They had six open cases on him, but I'm sure there were many more. I say that because it's been my experience that the Mexicans are pretty stand-up people and rarely make complaints against the police as a group. So Alberto must have been doing a number on the community.

That left me wondering just how much intel this impersonator was able to glean during these strategy sessions in Area Seven. Did he pass information to folks who were involved in the homicide? Was he cashing in on that information? Or was he feeding them a line of crap and sending them off on wild goose chases?

If not for Akki's sharp eye, how long and how many cases would this guy have been involved in, and to what extent? I wonder if he would have ever been exposed for the fraud he was.

The investigation was turned over to the county, and the commander was informed. Appropriate measures were put in place to ensure this never happened again.

Chapter 35: The Godfather of Trap Cars, Walter Smith

Hands down, Walter Smith is the best "trap" guy in the country.

I'll explain for readers who don't know what a trap car is. It's a vehicle that has had some portion of it modified for storage purposes, usually in the interior and an integrated part of the normal makeup of the vehicle. The difference is that the modification is done on a part of the vehicle not designed for such use.

The newly created storage compartment is what we call a "trap," designed to conceal contraband from law enforcement. Most are done so cleverly that the average cop on a street stop overlooks them and misses the gun or contraband it may house. That's what makes them inherently dangerous.

They are set up to be operated in a number of ways. However, the three most common methods of releasing their locking mechanisms are by pushing a hidden button that is nothing more than a trunk release and the accompanying locking hardware. Once this button is pressed, the trap will pop open. It makes the same sound you would hear when hitting your trunk release.

The button will almost always be hidden where the driver has immediate access to it, within arm's reach.

I've seen where criminals concealed the button underneath the carpet on the rocker panel wall and then made a cigarette burn mark to see where it's at if they need to get it open quickly. Other times, it's concealed in an area of the car that you can't see. It may require that you take a thin object like a straightened out paper clip and push that through a small hole somewhere in the dash or console. It might even be in the windscreen pillars where one tiny screw is missing.

Another way to release the trap is by using a magnet. All that is needed to open a trap with this method is to know where the magnetic relay is located in the car and then pass a magnet over that area. Contact does not have to be made. Just being close enough will cause the compartment to open.

The third is operated by a series of maneuvers that, when done in a particular order, trigger the relay switches they are connected to and allow the trap to open up. These open slowly rather than popping open. The reason being is that instead of trunk lock type hardware, they use power window motors or linear actuators that people mistakenly refer to as hydraulic motors.

Most cops have never opened a trap, I can tell you from experience. They pose a deadly threat to law enforcement, and that's why Walter Smith and I got together to write and have a law passed making them illegal to manufacture or have without a legitimate purpose. The law was in place for years until the courts struck it down.

Very few officers are trained as to the inherent dangers these pose to cops on the street, and that's why, at Wally's urging, I joined him in teaching classes on our own time and expense to cops wherever and whenever we could set up a one-day program. We taught six days a week at every district and all of the detective areas, including side classes for those who were day off or on a shift we missed. We also taught this class in Quantico to the FBI and DEA as they did not have their own people at the time. Wally and I were called out on numerous occasions to open traps for the federal agencies, and often, it was done on our own time.

You may wonder about the catalyst for wanting to train law enforcement. I'll give you a prime example of what could have ended up very bad for the cops involved and why we started the program in 1997.

Detective Walter Smith and I were on duty and driving near a long and lonely dark stretch of road called Torrence Avenue near 128th Street when we saw two gang crimes guys who had just searched a car and a couple of bad guys. The cops felt comfortable because they had already conducted a thorough search and found no weapons. So now they would run a name check and release these guys if no warrants came back on them.

We stopped to offer assistance, but they told us they had everything under control, and it looked like they did. However, we wanted to check out things a bit more closely in case these cops weren't up on traps.

Wally walked up to the passenger side and blocked the thug about to get back into the car and sit where the officers had told him to go while they checked them for outstanding warrants. Wally reached in through the open car window and simply tapped the airbag on the dash.

His knowledge and sense of touch were spot on.

"Hey Frank, I think everything's okay here."

That was a code we agreed to use to alert one another to danger.

The thugs would have already been in the vehicle if we had not stopped.

The cops, on the other hand, presumed the bangers couldn't go anywhere since the cops had his car keys and the engine wasn't running. But they were wrong.

Wally had just signaled me with that statement that something was not okay. With that, we drew our weapons and ordered the one thug who was almost all the way in the driver's seat out of the car and the second one closest to Wally down to the ground.

The gang guys came running back to the car.

"What's going on, guys?"

"Cuff these guys up first."

They clicked the bracelets on.

"Did you check the trap?"

"What do you mean?"

"The airbag is trapped out."

It was obvious they didn't realize what we were talking about, and these were good street cops. They had some serious bad guys here. If experienced cops like this could miss a trap, any cop could.

"Should I get my jumpers or try to figure it out using the relays?"

"I don't know, Wally it's starting to rain. Why don't you just jump it?"

Wally retrieved his homemade jumper wires, which look like car jumper cables, except they were made from 25 feet of lamp cord with two alligator clips at each end. He attached the jumper wires to the battery just like he was jumping a car. He looked under the dashboard and found what he was looking for. That being two after-market wires that were not running through a wiring harness or loom. Wally pressed the alligator clips hard into each wire, making metal-to-metal contact, and the trap started grinding open. It was on two linear actuators.

The cops could have been in serious trouble if the killer in the front passenger seat decided to act. The bad guy had two murder warrants out for him from the State of Florida, a second set of car keys for the vehicle, and a fully automatic Mac 10 inside the hidden compartment.

As we drove in, I had to tell Wally that he was "badass" in the way he was able to detect that trap by simply a touch. I had to get in and pound and pry on things before my sense of feel came into play.

That's when Wally came up with the idea that we should start a program and teach cops about traps, so we spent years doing it. In fact, as of this writing, Wally still conducts classes when called upon.

Many trips were made to the impound yard, and a lot of videos were made of numerous concealed compartments for teaching purposes, along with confiscated traps from the seized vehicles that we would bring to our training programs.

Very few bosses recognized the importance of teaching trap detection to officers but two of those who highly recommended the program were my former partner, Captain Edward Griffin, and Deputy Chief Jimmy Maurer. In fact, Deputy Maurer ordered his troops to attend our classes on a regular basis. He's also a man who, in my personal opinion, should have been promoted to superintendent, but his balls were too big. The politicians couldn't have handled him.

Some people have asked me how I learned about traps since the Department didn't have a program, and it's not taught in any academy that I know of.

In truth, I didn't find my first one through skills or knowledge from some senior officer enlightening me. My first one was by accident. As a matter of fact, I wouldn't have found it if I weren't doing something I'd get suspended or maybe fired for today. But since I'm retired, here goes.

My partner Bill Kieling and I had stopped a carload of thugs on Western Avenue not far from Little Italy. As we were going through these guys, a shiny black Cadillac came off a one-way street the wrong way, moving west. We weren't big on traffic violations, so I just glanced at the car to see who was driving it while I searched one of the guys we had stopped.

The driver and I made eye contact, and he gave me a waving hand gesture like mind your own business.

I didn't take kindly to this and figured he only did it because my partner and I looked like young guys. Maybe he thought we were "rookies."

"Hey Bill, let's stop that guy."

It took us a few blocks to catch up to him; he kept driving for another two blocks, looking at us every now and then through his rearview mirror. He finally pulled over and jumped out like a boss.

"Do you know who the fuck I am? I'm asking you again (with forced emphasis), Do you know who the fuck I am?"

"Sorry, I can't help you with that. Don't you know who the fuck you are?"

"Ohh…smart guy, huh? So you wanna play games with me? Okay, let's play, punk!"

"Punk?"

"That's right, you heard me. I didn't stutter."

I had already sized this guy up. He was a forty-something Italian and trying to come off as a member of the Chicago outfit. The top four buttons of his shirt were open, revealing just as many gold chains. I'm sure if you asked him, he'd tell you that the Pope had blessed one of them.

"Let's go. Do whatever you're gonna do. You wanna write me a ticket or look for a quick sawbuck?"

"He seems to be in a hurry, Bill. Let's take our time and run his name. I'll pat him down, then put him in the backseat."

"Oh, searching me now without my consent, huh?"

"You're free to try and stop me."

"I ain't fuckin' stupid. Betcha you'd love that."

"Put him in the car, Bill."

I started going through his car, hoping to find anything illegal; if not that, maybe he'd come up dirty on the name check, but he didn't. Instead, his name came up with a message that we should make an information report and forward it to the Organized Crime Divisions Intelligence Unit. I didn't know this until I got back in the car with Bill.

In the meantime, I had found what I thought was a hockey puck in the glove box. It turned out to be a heavy-duty magnet. I had an idea. I always heard that you needed to keep magnets away from tapes because they would erase the data on them.

This would be a good time to put that to the test. Frank Sinatra was playing on his eight-track stereo, so I pulled it halfway out and rubbed the magnet around on top of it. Then I pushed it back in and hit play. What I heard about magnets and tapes was true. It just made hissing noises.

The guy had been so obnoxious I thought I'd leave him a present before we left. There was a small eight-track carrier that held about fifteen tapes on the back seat, so with the magnet in hand, I reached over it to place the magnet inside the carrier. I heard a popping sound and thought I had broken the seat because the front seat's backrest opened up from the top. Somehow this magnet tripped a release mechanism that held the back of the front seat in place. I had never seen anything like this before, so I spread it open a little more and could see the contents attached to a piece of plywood that was secured in place.

There was a silencer for a handgun but no gun, a sawed-off shotgun, a hairdryer, an ice pick, a hunting knife, leather gloves, rubber gloves, a straight razor, electrical tape, and wire.

It turned out he really was an outfit guy and a driver for one of the mob bosses in Chicago. We called the Intelligence unit, and they came out and took the pinch. I had to ask what the hairdryer would be hidden for, and the copper from intelligence told me that they would strap a guy in a chair and spread his eyelids to heat up his eyeballs as a form of persuasion.

For the next few months, every time I saw an Italian-looking guy in a Cadillac, I checked it for a trap like that. I never found another one until I started doing the same with gang bangers' cars.

Finding traps became more and more commonplace as time went by. I wondered how many guns I missed on street stops before this encounter and how lucky I was not to have been put in a bad situation because of my lack of knowledge in dealing with them. I'm sure most cops have missed guns in the same way, and hopefully, because of Wally's classes, they are safer today.

If I hadn't done something wrong, I would probably be as oblivious as most cops are when it comes to finding traps in a vehicle. Like I said before, it's better to be lucky than good sometimes.

Chapter 36: Dumped to Uniform for Doing Police Work

Yes, it's true. Joe citizens might not believe it, but many good working coppers have gotten jammed up by a boss for doing police work. It's usually because that boss spent most of his career as a "house-cat" and not as a street copper. In fact, those bosses are always more politicians than cops and are always on the lookout for their next career move up the ladder.

We were assigned to the School Patrol Unit. The six of us had been hand-picked by the unit's original commander, Bob Guthrie. He was the type of boss anyone who wanted to do real police work would love to work for. He had the balls and the experiences to go along with harrowing stories of some deadly encounters he had to deal with on the streets of Chicago while a member of the Gang Crimes Unit. He is not the typical politician in uniform. Bob Guthrie was a cop's cop.

Commander Guthrie had chosen us for this plum assignment based on our arrest activity when he commanded the Summer Mobile Force.

At the time of this incident, our undercover team was made up of my partner Bob Fischer, a great guy, and the team marksman Andy Marquez, a very knowledgeable and quick-witted street cop. Because of his youthful appearance despite his age, Andy could get up close and personal at any high school scene before the bad guys knew what was happening.

Rick Erbacci, Andy's partner, was like the enforcement arm of the team. He was an accomplished bodybuilder and a no-nonsense street cop. Scott Freeman and Darren Washington were black officers, and both were hands down ballsy street cops who knew the city's hot spots and were able to easily blend into the communities we were trying to clean up. I trusted all of these guys in any situation, and that trust would be put to the test late one night on the far south side of the city.

I'm not sure how the term Ninja came about as it related to us, but I have a feeling that my former partner Carey Orr, who was now our sergeant, came up with it. It wasn't long before all of the supervisors and office personnel started referring to us as the Ninjas. We worked in plain clothes and would often ride six deep in an undercover Chevy Suburban with blacked-out windows. Maybe that had something to do with our team nickname. The acronym for our team was Sputac. It stood for School Patrol Unit Tac. AKA "The Sputac Posse."

Whenever we did a jump out, there was always enough manpower to handle anything that came our way. Most bad guys don't expect a six-man jump coming down on them from a single vehicle.

We did the job as passionately as we could. The kids who actually went to school and wanted to better themselves by getting an education needed protection, and we were determined to see that they got it.

During one particular week, there had been an unusually high number of shootings around the schools. We were deployed to that area to find the punk who had just murdered an honestly good student by shooting him in the chest. We learned later that this shooting had all been a part of a gang initiation. Pull the trigger, and you're accepted into the gang life.

It took a couple of days of shaking up the streets until we identified the killer. #Leon Hammer was seventeen and had been registered as a student at the school. But he hadn't attended classes in months, which is not unusual in some parts of the city.

We were lucky enough to find him sitting on a porch not far from our victim's school and took this thug into custody without incident. We got a lot of credit for what was really a pretty easy pinch. He was formally charged with that murder and, after losing all the motions to suppress, pled guilty and was sentenced as an adult to twenty-five years.

While working that case, as in all others, we were constantly developing new information on other crimes. At times the information was solid and complete, and other times, it trickled in bit by bit. We were getting intelligence from our informants and street stops that led us to house more bad guys. The information just kept snowballing. It was like a giant jigsaw puzzle, so to speak. We had a lot of pieces and just needed to find out how and where they fit to complete the picture. We continued developing as many leads as possible into gang-related shootings and drug dealing as it related to the schools. We were on the right track and made a number of high-profile arrests. Any good street cop will tell you that you don't stop rolling at the end of your shift when the leads are hot. Everything can change tomorrow.

One of the leads we developed down the line was that a high-ranking gang member had recently been released from prison after serving seventeen years of a fifty-year sentence for murder. I will refer to him as Big Mutt.

He wasn't just any murderer. I knew who this guy was because of his involvement in the murder of an off-duty Chicago policeman on December 23, 1974, in the parking lot of a discount store located at 5601 South Cicero Avenue. The victim, along with his son, who was eight years old at the time, was doing some last-minute Christmas shopping when four thugs approached them. One was armed with a .22 caliber handgun. During the course of the armed robbery, Big Mutt found out that Harl was a cop and immediately opened fire on him.

Harl Meister went down but not without a fight. He was able to get off seven rounds. Unfortunately, none of those rounds hit the intended target.

Big Mutt murdered Officer Harl Meister #10054 on that day while Officer Meister's son, who was only eight years old, sustained a gunshot wound to the jaw, neck, and shoulder. Fortunately, his son survived the attack.

As soon as we heard that Big Mutt was out on parole, we went to work gathering all the information that we could on him. We wanted to see how this big-time banger supported himself now that he was a free man. The only occupation I knew him to have, was that of a stickup man and murderer. I believed he was still a danger to society and needed to be dealt with swiftly.

We learned through a lot of hard work, surveillance, and tips from our street sources that he was selling dope within a thousand feet of a school. As school unit personnel, we needed to follow up on this information. So that's what we did. Eventually, it led to the execution of a search warrant on his basement apartment.

We put his residence under surveillance for hours and waited for him to return home before we executed the warrant. We wanted to catch him in possession of the goods and see how he'd react to our arrival.To our surprise, he gave up without a fight. During the search, we recovered narcotics and several guns. That would certainly violate his parole, plus we had these additional charges for which he would stand trial. After two days of testimony, he was convicted on all charges.

When Big Mutt left the penitentiary earlier than he should have, I'm sure he thought he'd never go back and was looking forward to lifelong freedom. Big Mutt's freedom was short-lived. It lasted all of ten months. Little did he know we were working on him for a good chunk of that time. It's how the Ninjas operated.

Big Mutt was violated and sent back to prison. He was given an additional twelve years on our case to serve consecutively to the VOP. But unfortunately for Big Mutt, he was unable to successfully complete his bit. He died in prison while serving time on our case.

From that point on, we knew we had a couple of good informants and shortly thereafter developed some strong leads on where the gang bangers operating near the public schools were keeping their guns and how they were financing the purchases of those firearms. As you can probably guess, it was through drug dealing, extortion, and armed robbery.

During the course of our investigations, we learned of a group of gang bangers who were operating a drug dealing safe house on the west side of the city for a major street operation. It was directly across the street from a school. In addition to that, they had an arsenal of weapons. From time to time, they were known to rent out guns to street thugs for cash or a portion of the robbery proceeds.

We sat on one of several locations in our undercover Suburban and watched hundreds of transactions go down. We wanted to see who picked up the money and who dropped off the new supply of dope so we could follow them back to the safe houses. In addition to that, and for our own safety, we wanted to figure out who was the armed street security for the dope operation.

After a few days of surveillance, we were ready to make our move. After identifying most of the players, we moved in on them late in the afternoon and started making arrests. By 4 p.m., the six of us had recovered eleven guns and a large quantity of crack cocaine bagged up for sale on the street.

Unfortunately, we lost two members of our team with prior commitments. So the four of us continued our investigation "past school hours" with the blessing of our supervisor and current commander.

The investigation led us to 110th and Wentworth. The information we developed was that a beige Dodge Shadow would be dropping off a kilo of crack cocaine bagged up in quarter kilo packages and that it would be hidden in the trapped-out area behind the back passenger's seat.

Our C.I. gave us an address on 110th street and said to be careful because the guy dropping off the drugs (I will refer to him as Popeye) always got out of his car with a gun in his hand. This was his common practice when dropping off product and picking up money from the safe house on that block.

My partners and I set up. Scottie Freeman was driving the U/C Suburban. We were lucky to get a spot a couple of doors from the target's house. Darren Washington got out on foot and hid in the vestibule undetected by the occupants. That was some stone balls as Darren wasn't a known gang member in that hood and could have had a violent outcome if confronted. This was extremely dangerous but a necessary move.

Bob Fischer and I stayed in the rear seat of the Suburban where, as white guys, we wouldn't draw attention to ourselves but could clearly see everything on the street and facing the building that Darren went into.

When the bad guy showed up, we would have him covered on two sides, and if any of the occupants from the safe house came out shooting, Darren was on point to deal with it and would.

The C.I. called us to say that Popeye was on the way with the dope and had at least one gun on him. Unfortunately for us, the C.I. didn't know that Popeye had switched out trap cars after the C.I. left him because the beige car we expected to pull up had an electrical short. Popeye transferred the dope, guns, and money to another trap car.

We were sure that the drug dealer would pull into the empty parking spot ahead of us, and we could take him by surprise.

Scotty was in the driver's seat when a car approached.

"I see headlights. This might be our guy. Oh, never mind, this guy's in a Blue Honda. Aw shit, he's taking the parking spot we need. We gotta get him out of there before the other car gets here. Hopefully, he's a legit neighbor. I'm gonna tell him to move."

Scotty got out with his Chicago Police Star hanging around his neck on a chain and approached while showing his star to the driver with one hand raising it. The driver was opening the door to step out of the vehicle. He looked like a food delivery guy because he had a white plastic bag that could have contained carry-out food in one hand and a tan cardboard box that resembled something used to transport pizza in the other.

Bob said he was going to get out with Scotty just so the guy saw that there were two officers.

As they approached and announced their office, the driver opened fire on Scotty with what sounded like a fully automatic weapon. It had been concealed in the box, and he shot through it.

Scottie was shot in the collarbone area and was bleeding but managed to return fire. The offender, who had never shut his engine off, was firing wildly at Bob, who was next in line, while the gang-banger gunned his vehicle from the parking spot. Bob moved alongside him. Knowing I wasn't wearing a protective vest like he was, Bob shielded me with his body as I stepped from the back seat to join the gunfight. Bob was lucky that he wasn't hit; our vehicle took several of the rounds meant for him. Hearing the barrage of gunfire and seeing that his partner was shot, Darren started firing at the fleeing Honda as I ran down the street after it.

The offender's vehicle continued west on 110th while Darren and Bob immediately went to Scott's aid. They called in the shots fired and direction of flight, asking for backup units.

I continued after the vehicle on foot, hoping I could catch up to him at the corner. He tossed a .38 caliber revolver from the driver's side window. I guess that was to make me think he was no longer an armed threat. I knew this wasn't the gun he had been firing but scooped it up and continued running. I was hoping cross traffic would jam him up at Wentworth.

Without regard for traffic, he didn't let anything stop his getaway. The Honda roared across both lanes to the opposite side of the street and crashed into the parked cars as he tried to turn north.

His vehicle looked like it was disabled at that point, and he appeared to be unconscious. His head was lying on the steering wheel, and his face turned toward me. I had him now, and he was in my sights. I was almost up to the passenger's side window, maybe ten feet away. Suddenly, two young boys, approximately ten years old, ran up to the car window on the driver's side. The vehicle was facing north in the southbound lane of Wentworth.

"Get out of the way! Move, Go home!" I waved my free hand at them.

"Hey, police..."

They didn't move.

"Get out of the way!"

"Hey, police, he needs an ambulance. He's hurt!"

"Move away!"

I couldn't take the shot if this guy came back to his senses and started shooting at me with them standing in the landscape of the driver's window. That worried me. I already saw what he did and didn't know Scott's condition or if anyone else was hurt on the street with all the gunfire exchanged. I certainly didn't want to add two kids to the mix.

They froze.

As I neared the passenger door, it happened. Popeye was faking like he was out of it. He saw that I was the only one coming after him, and while holding the gun low but tilted upwards, he fired three times. I felt a burning sensation on the left side of my neck. It was like someone was holding a lit cigarette there. Blood ran down into my collar as I threw my free hand up to cover my face and was hit by a second round at the inside of my forearm. That felt like I got hit with a fast pitch.

That round had come through the door handle and, fortunately, helped slow the bullet down; the hot projectile welded itself into the leather sleeve of my bomber jacket. The kids stood there in shock. I had no place to go but forward and hoped at some point they'd move. If I could get close enough, I'd take the shot. I would just shoot low. His last round was when he pulled away shooting, and it struck my top right epaulet and passed through the top of the shoulder area, leaving only a graze wound.

The guys were taking care of Scotty, I jumped in the Suburban and took off after the shooter. A blue compact car made a right turn at 107th street, but when I caught up to it was a woman and the wrong make of vehicle. Our shooter was nowhere to be found. I started looking on the street for a fluid leak; maybe one of the police rounds hit something that would leave a trail for me to follow but no such luck.

Back at the scene, plenty of help had arrived, along with CFD paramedics who were treating Scotty. My injuries were minor. When we were in the ambulance, a call came out of a man shot in the head approximately a mile from our location. We knew it had to be our guy.

A woman had made the call to 911. Fortunately for us, it was Popeye's girlfriend. He had called her as he raced to her house and told her he was on the way and had been shot in the head. He didn't give her specifics but wanted her to make sure the door was open, and all the extra security locks were open, so he didn't waste time getting to safety. He didn't know how badly he was injured but knew he was bleeding pretty good. Popeye didn't tell her to call for an ambulance but lucky for us, that's what she did.

Plainclothes officers knew of our shooting and figured it was connected, so they immediately responded to the address.

Before going inside the residence, they took a few minutes to check the immediate area and located the bullet-riddled Blue Honda. Next to the door where the driver would have gotten out of the vehicle were several of the rounds fired by Bob and Scott. The bullets had been slowed down after passing through the sheet metal and glass of the car. When they hit Popeye, they lost a lot of their impact and stuck to his thick outerwear and embedded in his clothing. Apparently, Popeye had been wearing a protective vest. Those expended rounds became our silent witnesses when they fell to the ground.

Popeye was transported to the hospital for treatment by paramedics for his head wound and identified by all of us as the shooter.

The car was towed after this incident to a secure location and stored because it had been involved in a police shooting. My partners and I went to that garage a few days later. I knew it was trapped and knew how to release the trap. We also knew that drugs, guns, and money had not been recovered from the vehicle or from Popeye at the location of his arrest.

I talked to the impound officer because I wanted to get in the car for an inventory search of its contents. He told us that no one was allowed to go in the vehicle per the deputy superintendent. The deputy superintendent was wrong on this call. We wanted to go through it on the night of the shooting and were told to back off.

It seems we were on the deputy superintendent's shit list. He couldn't understand why the School Unit was operating that late at night and wrongly assumed we were up to something nefarious. In addition, he questioned why a guy who was allegedly a member of a politically connected church would shoot it out with the police. In his mind, that was so far removed from the reality of the streets, we must be doing something wrong.

Apparently, he never read the case reports and all the work we put into what we did. He just made an assumption and rolled with it.

With the exception of the Blue Star Awards that come automatically when injured by gunfire, the only recognition we got for getting a cop killer off the streets, seizing a total of twelve guns along with a large quantity of crack cocaine, locking up a bunch of gangbangers, and almost getting killed in a shootout, was being dumped back to uniform. Even Rick Erbacci and Andy Marquez, who had nothing to do with the shootout, got dumped. That pissed me off. If you're going to dump people, dump the guys who were there.

To show you what a big-time bad guy this shooter was and how high up in the gang hierarchy he is, he had a ledger in his car that I reviewed. It showed that he had collected a total of $362,000 from seven locations on the day of the shootout. That was the two-day take in this multi-million dollar street operation.

It wasn't until a few weeks later, when the impounded vehicle was moved to the open impound yard, that suspicions were raised about the contents of the vehicle.

Several times unknown persons had been caught attempting to gain entry to the vehicle by climbing over the fence. They were spotted and scared off by the impound guys.

A gang unit was made aware of this, and from the word on the street that police had not recovered any dope, guns, or money from Popeye, they must have missed it while searching the vehicle because the car was trapped out. So it must still be in the car and the gang wanted it back.

The gang officers went to the impound yard and searched the vehicle. They came up empty, so they had a drug dog come out. The dog did a narcotics alert at the backrest of the back seat.

The gang guys didn't know how to release the trap, and I doubt if they even knew it was trapped by the way they tore up the upholstery. If they had called me, I would have come out to open it. If I wasn't working, I could have told them how to release it over the phone. Either way, common courtesy dictates that the original officers be notified, especially since they were shot and shot at in the process.

The trap was one of the simplest of all to open. It operated via the push of a button on the driver's side near the rocker panel. It utilized the trunk lock mechanism I spoke of earlier. It had even been marked for convenience with a cigarette burn in the carpet where it covered the button.

The officers tore the car apart. They started by shredding the back seat upholstery to ribbons. After not finding the dope hidden inside the cushion, they pried open the backseat from both the trunk side and the inside of the car with a Chicago bar. Once that was opened, they found the trap, and it contained another gun, thousands of dollars in cash, and twenty-eight quarter kilos of cocaine in the form of crack. The street value was a quarter of a million dollars.

Popeye was convicted of all the charges that we had put him on but was not charged with what was seized from the trap car as there was a chain of custody issue thanks to the deputy superintendent.

We never received an acknowledgment or a pat on the back from the deputy superintendent or a reprieve allowing us to go back into plain clothes. So we all moved on to other assignments.

During our time there, we made hundreds of arrests with a near one hundred percent conviction rate. The Ninja squad was dead in the water; we all ended up leaving.

Bob Fischer, Rick Erbacci, and Scott Freeman were promoted to sergeant. Andy Marquez went to work with a federal task force, and Darren Washington went to the K-9 unit and soon after left the job. I went back to Organized Crime.

There is a saying in the Department. It seems like most of the bosses think this way too. It goes like this:

Big Dope = Big Problems
Little Dope = Little Problems
No Dope = No Problems

It's drugs and gangs that are killing so many young people and ruining so many lives, and destroying families. So I still see it as a major problem. In fact, it's the number one crime problem in the country, especially in Chicago. Virtually every murder that takes place here can be traced back to gangs and drugs. That's why Chicago will always have a drug, gang, and murder problem. Cops aren't allowed to do what they know how to do. The leash is kept very short on long-term investigations.

Unfortunately for the working copper and the good citizens of Chicago, most of the brass in the Chicago Police Department has become as useless as the politicians they bow to.

I'm lucky to have come on the job when I did and experience a time when incompetence wasn't so prevalent. It was there but nowhere near what it is today.

Chapter 37: My Buddy, Sergeant Jimmy Hanson

It was freezing out that night, and the strong January winds made the subzero temperatures feel like a polar vortex. Not a great night for anyone or anything to be cruising the streets of Chicago, but that's what cops do.

In a way, it's a good thing because it keeps a large percentage of the criminal population off of the streets. Most of the night is spent rolling up and down our beat, trying to stay warm, and hoping that we're not going to be called out to direct traffic around some horrendous accident, or worse, a fire. The fires are bad because depending on where you have to stand, you're likely to get sprayed with a healthy dose of water that instantly turns everything it touches to ice, including your mustache and eyebrows.

But this is Chicago, and the city doesn't sleep. There's always something to keep the coppers busy, and this night would be no different.

Dispatcher: "1313."

"1313…ready to copy."

"1313, see the landlady at 999 N. Western on a well-being check. She will be waiting on the second floor."

"1313…10-4."

Beat 1313 arrived in a matter of minutes, and the landlady in this predominately Lithuanian area greeted them just outside of her apartment door in the enclosed hallway.

"In here, officers," she said, pointing to the open door.

"Okay, ma'am, what did you call us for, exactly?"

"In there, they're in there."

"Okay, just tell us what's in there before we walk inside. It's something we need to know."

"My tenants, they haven't paid the rent in a while, and they always pay on time ever since they've lived here. So when they didn't pay, I knocked on the door and didn't get any answer."

"Okay, so is that when you opened the door?"

"Oh no. I thought maybe they went to visit their grandchildren out of the country and would be back because they have done that in the past. But they usually pay me before they go, even if it's a few weeks early. I thought maybe they would pay when they come back."

"Okay, so when was the last time you saw your tenants?"

"About a month ago."

"A month ago, huh?" The beat guy sniffs the air by the open door. "Well, I don't smell anything. So then what happened?"

"So, this time I opened the door with my key, and I went inside and saw them. One of them, the wife is on the floor and …the other one, he is her husband he is in the bed."

"Were they moving? Breathing?"

"I don't think so. I called out their name, but they didn't answer."

"All right. You stay here, and we'll check it out. How old are they, do you know?"

"Mid-eighties, both of them. They're from the old country."

The officers went in but stopped at the bedroom door. The male was lying face up with a blanket pulled up to his chin. His open mouth and ashen face were enough for any experienced cop to recognize that he was dead.

The female was lying on the floor and obviously dead.

"It's colder in here than it is outside. Hey landlady, do you control the heat in your tenants' apartment?"

"No, they pay for their heat."

"I'm surprised the pipes ain't busted yet."

"Officers, I just checked my calendar. It was twenty-six days ago. I saw the wife but not him."

"Well, it's possible that they could have been dead for twenty-six days since it's been below freezing almost every day. I'm betting they froze to death in here. The only thing that stands out to me is that he looks like he's been dead longer than her."

"I can't remember the last time I saw him, officer. Maybe two months ago."

"Well, they're pretty well preserved. We're gonna call our supervisor."

"1313."

"1313, go with your message."

"1313, we need a supervisor over here. We have two DOAs in the apartment."

"10-4, 1313."

Sergeant Jimmy Hanson responded."1320, I'm about a block away. I'll take it."

"10-4, Sarge. Beat 1313, did you copy that? 1320 is en route."

"1313 copied."

Sergeant Hanson met the two officers in the hallway. It was cold, and they were trying to soak up some of the residual heat escaping from the landlady's apartment. The emanating heat rolled out like the opening of an oven on Thanksgiving Day.

"What are ya's doing out here? Ya got some stinkers inside?"

"No, Sarge. It's warmer out here, believe it or not. You could hang meat in that apartment. It's fuckin' freezing in there."

"All right, let's see what ya got."

The beat guys led the way. "Look at him, Sarge. I'll bet the old-timer froze to death with that thin-ass blanket on him."

"What about her? Did you guys check for any signs of violence?"

"Yeah, nothing that we could see that was obvious. It kind of looks like she had a heart attack or something while making dinner because there's a plate and knife that fell next to her when she collapsed."

"All right, I'll call the Dicks, and they can talk to the medical examiner. I'll see if they want to come out on this now. Then get the wagon guys to remove the bodies if you get the all-clear."

"Okay, Sarge."

"Did you look around for any identification or phone numbers for next of kin?"

"No, this is as far as we went, and then we called you."

The sergeant sauntered into the kitchen, only a few steps from the deceased couple's bedroom.

"Yeah, I think you're right. The woman still has an apron on, and there's a pot on the stove with some meat that looks like it's being boiled. It's all whitish, but there's no water, not even frozen water in the pot, so she had to have gas to cook with at some point. We'll have to let the Dicks know. They can check to see when the gas was cut off; at least that will give us some kind of timeline. There's nothing to go with the meat, though. No vegetables…nothing."

Sergeant Hanson opened up the refrigerator door to check for other food items.

"Look around this apartment; there's nothing in here but the two beds in that room, the stove, and this refrigerator."

"Yeah, it was pretty easy to do a recon on this joint."

"There's nothing to eat in the fridge either. The only thing they got is an open box of baking soda."

"That might be for odors. I know my wife keeps one in ours."

"Let me see what's in the freezer."

Sergeant Hanson pulled open the freezer door and saw a few cuts of meat wrapped in newspaper.

"What kind of butcher uses newspaper?"

"Maybe they buy their meat from some garage butcher. You know how some of these old immigrants are."

"Yeah, well, I'm out of here. We can't find any phone numbers or next of kin stuff lying around, so once you get the approval to have the bodies moved to the medical examiner's office, get a wagon crew up here."

A short time later, permission was granted to remove the bodies.

"Beat #1371."

"1371, your wagon crew is at your service."

"1371. You have two DOA's 999 No. Western 2nd floor. Beat 1313 on the scene. Permission granted for removal to the M.E.'s office."

"10-4."

The wagon crew arrived about fifteen minutes later and brought their field gurney up.

"Hey Charley, let's take the woman down first; she's in the way."

The beat guys stood back as all good wagon men know how to handle a DOA. The beat guys are sharp enough to know they don't want to be sprayed with any bodily fluids, though in all probability, they'd be frozen solid.

"She's lighter than she looks but stiff as a board."

"Good! No smell and no leaking for a change."

They loaded her up and came back for the male.

"Hey Charley, ya wanna leave the blanket on him or wrap him in it?"

"Nah, the blanket's all soiled. Let me see if he's got pants on." With a quick yank, his question was answered.

"Holy shit. Do you see what I see? This fuckin' guys been deboned."

"1372."

"1372, come in with your message."

"We need 1320 back at this location."

"1320…I heard the wagon crew, and I'm on my way."

Sergeant Hanson, who had just picked up a cup of coffee, carries it up with him. It would freeze in a few minutes if he left it in the squad car at these temperatures.

The smiling faces of the wagon men greet Hanson. The original beat officers who don't say a word are nudging each other as he comes up.

"I can tell I'm in for some bullshit now just by the looks on your faces. So what changed since I left ten minutes ago? Did you guys find a million dollars in here, or what?"

One of the wagon guys motioned for him to step into the bedroom. He stood next to the bed, holding the blanket at the two opposite ends like a magician pulling a tablecloth off of a fully-set table.

"Gentleman in the audience and Sergeant Hanson, watch and be amazed by what you are about to see firsthand. The speed and skills that I employ while removing this blanket will not only amaze you but transfix you on a sight you have never seen or experienced before." He pulled the blanket completely off the man's body.

Jimmy Hanson was not one to be shocked, impressed, or amazed by much. I've never seen him excitedly respond to anything.

"Well, it looks like we'll have to call the Dicks back. I don't think they're gonna be too happy. I'm gonna finish my coffee now, but I did appreciate the show." He left.

The man had died of natural causes. Apparently, the wife didn't want to leave her husband after sixty-five years of marriage and had no one to turn to in her time of need. She was also penniless, starving, and probably had some mental disorder.

After eating what little food they had and having no one to help her out, the poor woman started cannibalizing her husband's remains into roasts. His entire upper thigh had been removed and partially eaten. She, too, died of natural causes. An autopsy showed that the contents of her stomach contained human flesh.

An autopsy of her husband showed he had died of cardiac arrest at least a month before his wife had passed. The contents of his stomach showed that he had consumed newspaper.

This is a sad commentary on life and desperation that you wouldn't expect in a great city like Chicago. There are good and very generous people, churches, and organizations that are always willing to lend a helping hand. It's a shame that someone's last moments in life would end in this manner.

My message to everyone is to check on your elderly or house-bound family, friends, and neighbors when you haven't seen or heard from them for a few days. No one should ever have to face what this lonely elderly widow did in the golden years of her life. I can't even imagine the thought process she had to go through before considering cannibalism to be her only option. The fact that this couple may have been too proud to ask for help is mind-blowing, and if it wasn't that, maybe it was a mental disorder.

Whatever the case, no one should starve or freeze to death in this country. This is a rare but not isolated example of desperation.

Chapter 38: Mike Mondane, the Fastest Cop in Chicago

I had to put this short story in here because it demonstrates the fact that no matter how long or how well you think you know someone, everyone has secrets. Mike Mondane kept a big one not only from me but everyone who worked with him.

I met Mike while going through basic training at Fort Jackson, South Carolina. We became fast friends with something in common; we both had ambitions of becoming Chicago police officers. That became a reality in the early 1970s.

I worked on the South Side, and he worked on the North Side, so our paths rarely crossed. I was more likely to run into Mike in one of the bars cops frequent after work than in a courtroom. Mike was not a ball of fire when it came to making arrests but was always there when you needed him in a tough situation…as long as you agreed to handle the case in court.

When I ended up working North, I'd occasionally respond to calls that Mike was assigned to, often beating him to the scene. I'd be taking notes to document the case facts when Mike would pull up. If the victim or witnesses were female, young or old, Black, White, Asian, or Hispanic, it didn't make a difference. All attention turned to Mike.

To be honest, it was for good reason. Besides being tall with dark-featured movie star good looks, Mike was physically fit and always had a smile and good words for the ladies on the scene. Even though it was Mike's job, I kept asking questions and writing while he charmed the women. So I think you get the idea of how Mike operated. That's why what happened one day shocked me, but in retrospect, it was right in front of me for years. I just hadn't realized it.

I had spent two days looking for #Ziggy Morris. He was wanted on a Bond Forfeiture for Armed Robbery. As I drove around Cabrini in my unmarked car, I was pulled over by Mike Mondane, who was in uniform and a marked squad car.

"Hey, Frankie Goff! I thought that was you. What are you doing over here?"

"What am I doing here? What are you doing over here?"

"Good question. I'm heading back to Rush Street ASAP."

"I'm just poaching over here looking for Ziggy Morris. Do you know him?"

I flashed a mug shot of Morris to Mike, but he didn't recognize him. We continued bantering when Ziggy came around the corner. We saw each other at the same time, and he took off running.

"Oh shit, that's him."

Morris took off through the open field and across the blacktop covered in broken glass. I wasn't going to take a chance on getting a flat tire, and there was no way in my forties that I'd catch this nineteen-year-old on foot, let alone with him having a twenty-five-yard head start. Mike watched as Morris fled.

"Do you really want that guy?"

"Yeah, but he's gone now."

"I'll get him, but you got the arrest."

This guy was literally seventy-five yards away when Mike took off. I jumped in his squad as it was still running and took off to circle to the front of the closest building, hoping he hadn't made it inside yet.

When I came around the corner, my attention was drawn to the crowd near the parked cars. They were about a block and a half from where the chase began. *There's no way they could have run that far in that time period,* I thought, but I thought wrong. Mike had him pinned to the ground with his hands behind his back.

"Throw me your cuffs, Frank."

Time for some ball-busting.

"Why Mike? It's your arrest."

Mike laughed, but even though he was laughing, he was serious when he looked up at me.

"I'll let him go right now. I swear, Frankie…"

I cuffed him up and put Mike down as the assisting officer, even though he should have had full credit.

I was amazed at how fast Mike ran, and until his death in May of 2014, I never knew why. I learned these facts after he was laid to rest, unfortunately. Records at the University of Iowa reflect that Mike was a three-time All-American and a six-time Big Ten Champion for the Iowa Hawkeyes. Mike had set a 45.20 in the 400 meter in 1967 and had been inducted into the National Iowa Varsity Club Athletics Hall of Fame. Keep in mind, the fastest time ever recorded in the 400 was 43.03!

He was an Olympic contender who was hit by a personal setback on the eve of his Olympic trial and hadn't slept all night. But even with that weight on his shoulders and being dead tired, he came in just shy of making the team. Had it not been for that, Mike Mondane could also list among his accomplishments that he was an Olympic Champion... but I doubt he'd do that; Mike was too humble for the accolades.

I will always remember your smile, how glowingly you spoke about your daughters, and your big heart, my friend. RIP, Michael Mondane, May 19, 2014.

Chapter 39: Crazy White Boy

The call came out at about 1 a.m. on this wintery early morning, a testament to the fact that crime in Chicago never takes a rest. It's a 24/7 proposition, and every street cop knows it.

"Attention all units in the 20th District and units on the city-wide frequency, we have a man with a gun, a man with a gun in the hallway at 4898 N. Marine Dr. He's a white male wearing a police vest, and he's described as being about five foot ten to six feet tall with blond hair. He is armed with a large caliber handgun. Use caution."

I was fortunate enough to be working alongside two well-seasoned homicide detectives, Tommy Johnson and Phil Mannion. We responded to the call just to conduct the follow-up investigation, but not to make an arrest, that had already been taken care of.

One man was dead, and the other was clinging to life. Both had been transported to the hospital before our arrival.

The arrest of the violent culprit was made by the district watch commander, believe it or not. That is a rarity in the command structure of the Chicago police department. When most cops become watch commanders, they pretty much meld into the background of the station, safe behind their desks, and venture out only if absolutely necessary. Fortunately, Tom Whalen wasn't that kind of man. Throughout all of his career he was a hard-working copper and wasn't going to stop just because of his rank and current assignment.

We met with Lieutenant Whalen in the vestibule of the building, and he relayed to us that he had turned the offender over to two beat officers for transport into the detective division where we would conduct our investigation.

"Where's his gun, boss?"

"Fortunately, it came apart somehow and is lying on the floor by the victim's door over there."

"What else?"

"There was one guy shot in the head. He was in bed when this all went down, apparently sleeping, but he got popped in the forehead when he sat up. I found another one in the closet whom I initially thought was dead, but he was breathing faintly, so I had them both rushed to the hospital just in case there was any possibility of saving them."

"Good…anything else you can tell us?"

"A couple of my officers found two bullet holes in the wall. That's about it. No one else in the building is injured, at least that we know of at this time, and there are two witnesses in apartment 1010. They know the guy I found in the closet. Here's their information. They made the original call of a man with a gun."

"Okay, we'll take it from here."

The scene was a mess. There was blood in the hallway leading up to the door of the ground floor apartment and on the door itself.

Inside the living room, blood had spattered in several directions, but it wasn't the high-velocity pattern that would reflect coming from a gunshot wound. This stemmed from a beating, courtesy of a military-issued .45-caliber semi-automatic pistol model 1911, which came apart during the ferocious attack on the first victim.

The second victim and resident of the apartment was a young Nigerian male in his early twenties, studying to be a doctor. He was shot once between the eyes when he sat up in bed to see who had just burst through his door at 1 a.m. Fortunately, his brother, also studying to be a doctor, escaped death when the offender's gun came apart.

Phil Mannion mockingly pointed to the two bullet holes in the wall. "Wow, this guy was a hell of a shot. Look how he placed two rounds right through the center of those tiny circles."

It turns out the "Chalk Fairy" was here. The two rookie cops must have thought we needed the bullet holes circled for some reason. I've seen young cops make a chalk outline around dead bodies too. I don't know why. It must be something they pick up from TV because seasoned cops don't do it, and it's not taught in the police academy.

The medical student's bed, headboard and the wall behind it, showed what a .45 caliber bullet moving at 830 feet per second can do to the skull. I'm no doctor, but it was apparent to me that the medical student could not have survived a cranial invasion of this magnitude.

Once we processed our end of the crime scene, we went to Illinois

Masonic to examine the deceased man's wound and document what our supplemental case report required.

This non-stop investigation carried over, into, and through Super Bowl Sunday. The surviving Nigerian brother was in a state of shock and added little to the investigation, but enough to give us a good picture as to what happened once "the crazy white boy" burst into the apartment.

We interviewed the male and female who were with the surviving victim, and their story added a dimension that we were unaware of up to this point.

As it turned out, the three had returned from an evening out for drinks and had stopped to pick up some carry-out food to share in the apartment. One of the men lived in the apartment, and the other, the beating victim, was on a blind date with the female witness and was simply visiting his friend.

They were waiting for the elevator when a man wearing a protective vest with police markings and carrying a walkie-talkie, handcuffs, and a loaded .45 caliber handgun approached them and identified himself as a Chicago policeman. He proceeded to search them while giving them verbal commands. They initially cooperated with him, but at some point, the victim said that he did not believe that this guy was a cop as his garments did not look like CPD, and he looked too young.

About that time, the elevator doors opened and the trio walked away and ignored his commands to halt. The victim planned to report this encounter to the real police once they got to their destination. Apparently, this enraged the wannabe cop, and he proceeded to drag the victim off at gunpoint. His friends let the door close and proceeded to the apartment to notify the police.

The offender, whom I will refer to as #Biff Golden, then struck the victim in the face and about the head with the pistol until he was unconscious. Then he dragged him to the medical student's apartment door and put him in a sitting position against it. He removed the victim's belt, which had a large buckle, and then beat the unconscious man back and forth across the face and head. Splattering blood in several directions. The noise alerted the apartment occupants, and one of the brothers opened the door to see what the commotion was about. When he did, Biff identified himself as a policeman, dragged the beating victim into the apartment, and locked the door.

Once inside, he started beating the victim again. That's when the second brother sat up in bed and told him to stop. Biff fired several rounds at him, striking him once between the eyes. The second Nigerian medical student opened the door to flee, but Biff stopped him and threatened him with the gun, telling him to lay face down on the floor or he would be next.

Then Biff went back to beating the man with the pistol, causing the slide, spring, and barrel to fly off the ramping and into the open hallway. In a panic, Biff fled from the apartment and into the arms of Lieutenant Tom Whalen, who had quickly responded to the residents' call for police.

Meanwhile, the Nigerian brother, who knew the fate of his own brother, went to the aid of the beating victim, who was near death, and dragged him to a closet for safety in case Biff returned to finish the job. That was a hell of a thing to do for a complete stranger and showed a great deal of compassion in light of the circumstances.

We returned to the detective division, and Mannion started the paperwork, phone calls, and notifications. Johnson and I took turns with Biff. I spent most of the time with Biff and was trying to determine if he was actually a mental case or playing one so he could beat the murder and attempted murder raps. I had a plan.

"Hey Biff, I'm Detective Goff. My partners are Detective Mannion and Johnson. You'll be dealing with Johnson and me for now. Any questions?"

"No, I'm just wondering how long you plan on holding me here."

"Don't worry about it."

Biff was white, six feet tall with an athletic build, well-groomed, blond-haired, and blue-eyed with a clear complexion. He was a very young-looking twenty-year-old and could have easily been a male model. He had the look of someone that comes from money. I don't know what it was, but it was just a feeling.

"First of all, let me give you your Miranda rights because you are under arrest for murder and attempted murder. In case you need to be reminded of them or want to review them at any time during my interrogation of you, they are printed on the wall above your head. Look at them now, so I know you understand what I'm telling you."

He looked up at the poster. "I know Miranda by heart, detective."

"Fine, but I'm going to read them to you." I proceeded to read his Miranda rights from the printed poster on the wall. "Before I ask you any specific questions, do you understand each and every right as I've explained them to you?"

"Of course I do. I'm not stupid."

He then proceeded to recite Miranda back to me. "Detective, do you understand the Miranda rights as I just recited them to you?"

"Great, now tell me what happened tonight at the building on Marine Drive."

"I could tell you, but don't you want to hear what happened before I got there?"

"Sure, I get paid for listening and don't leave anything out. Go into as much detail as you want."

I had no idea what I was in for.

"Okay, it started out after me and my friend went to the Park West for some entertainment. We met some girls there, and they were hitting on us, but I already have a girlfriend. Her name is GiGi, so we blew them off. They were pretty hot, so I was wondering why my friend didn't go with one of them. So I asked him, and he said he rather go to his apartment and play some video games, so that's what we did."

"Keep goin'."

"Well, in a way, I thought that was a little weird, and I started thinking that I remember him asking me if I had ever tried gay sex. That was like a week earlier."

"What did you tell him?"

"I told him hell no. I asked if he thought I was gay, and he told me yeah. He told me he had tried gay sex with a guy and enjoyed it but that he wasn't gay either."

"Then what?"

"Well, I started thinking that if he thought I was gay, maybe I was and just didn't realize it yet. So I didn't want to have sex with a guy yet because if I wasn't gay, it would be awkward."

"So, what did you do?"

"Oh, let me tell you. Do you have any idea how hard it is to find a toilet plunger with a plastic handle that doesn't have a seam in it?"

"No, but why would that be part of this conversation?"

"Because I planned on testing myself to see if I was gay or not. I went to at least a half-dozen stores until I found one, and it turned out to be perfect. It had a pink plastic handle and was void of any visible seam, and it was short like you would use in a sink as opposed to a toilet."

"What happened after you located this prized plunger?"

"I went home and filled the bathtub with the hottest water I could stand and used this shampoo that makes a lot of suds, and I soaked in the tub for about ten minutes. Then I put shampoo on the handle and coated it real heavy. That's why I didn't want a seam cuz that could tear my insides if it was, you know sharp how it is when you rub your finger on a raised plastic seam?"

"Then what did you do?"

"I positioned myself over it and, in a sitting position, stuck it by my anus and gently sat down as far as it would go in me. After a few seconds, I started, like, riding it up and down and up and down."

"Okay. Did you come to a conclusion as to whether you were gay or not, based on this experiment?"

"No, I didn't ejaculate. So I figured maybe I'm not gay."

"How does any of that play into why you did what you did tonight?"

"Because I went to my same friend's house to drink and play video games, and while we were on the couch, he leaned over and kissed me on the mouth."

"Then what happened?"

"Well, he asked me if I like it, and I told him no, I wasn't gay. So he did it again, and while he was doing that, he reached down and grabbed my penis through my pants and started to unzip my fly. I jumped up and said, 'Hey man, I told you I wasn't gay,' and I left the apartment."

"Then what did you do?"

"I was gonna prove to myself that I was not gay! So I went to my car and got a police vest that I had picked up from a suburban department, put my walkie-talkie in one of the vest pockets so it hung out and looked official. Strapped on my grandfather's .45, and by the way, he was a famous general (we confirmed this), slung some handcuffs over my belt, and went out to get some action."

"How would that prove you weren't gay? We have a lot of gay cops."

"Because I was gonna do some shit gay guys are afraid to do cuz they're pussies. Only guys like me and you and maybe your partners can do shit like that."

"Meaning?"

"I was gonna kick the shit out of some fags!"

"How did you end up on Marine Drive?"

"I saw two guys and a girl walking down the street, and I immediately knew the one guy was gay. They were headed to a building, so I got up on them as fast as I could. The one guy gave me some lip, so I busted him up real fuckin' good. The other guy must have been gay too, cuz he scampered up the elevator with the girl instead of jumping on me. I was prepared to kick his ass too."

"How did you get into the apartment where the man was shot?"

"The idiot opened up the door."

"Why did you shoot the man in the bed who was no threat to you?"

"I didn't shoot anyone. I had my grandfather's war souvenir, but it wasn't loaded. The gun was for show. I've never even shot a gun. Someone else must have killed that guy, and they're trying to blame me."

"You're telling me that in your entire life, you have never shot a gun?"

"Exactly, never. Detective, did you know I can hear things in your head right now?"

"Really? What do you hear?"

"I'm hearing that you think I'm lying. There's one other thing too. When you talk, I can see the words coming out of your mouth in colors."

He knew we got him, and I thought he was angling for an insanity defense, so I thought I'd set him up and show that he was sane enough to try to cover up his crime and that he did know right from wrong.

"Okay, Biff, since you've never shot a gun, I'm gonna arrange for a special test that we conduct to see if you have ever shot a gun. I'll be back in a little while."

I left the room for a few minutes and relayed the crazy story to Johnson and Mannion. Then came back into the interrogation room as if it was an afterthought.

"Hey Biff, I forgot to ask you something, and I know this is gonna sound crazy. I'm gonna give you a special magnetic gas particle and resonance resistance test by placing your hands and head into the reader. It will show if you fired a weapon tonight. But before I do, I have to ask, have you gotten any piss on your hands and rubbed it in?"

"No, why?"

"Because no matter how many times you washed your hands, face, eyebrows, or hair, the trace particles can be detected for up to a month. They imbed themselves in the hair follicles. The only thing that erases them totally is urine. I know it sounds stupid cuz no one's gonna be bathing in urine, but it's something by law we are required to ask. By the way, do you need to use the restroom? I'll take you, but I'm required to watch you for both of our safety."

"No, detective, I'm good, but I'll let you know later if I need to."

I left the room. If he were really insane, he would not try to conceal his crime because he believed he did nothing wrong. On the other hand…

I waited about fifteen minutes and told detective Johnson that I'd had it with this guy. Maybe he should take a shot in the interrogation room.

Johnson opened the door and immediately started yelling at Biff.

"Did you piss on my floor? Why the hell did you piss on the floor? All you had to do was let us know you needed to use the restroom, asshole. Now, clean it up."

"What happened, Johnson?"

"He pissed all over the floor."

"No way."

"Go look."

When I opened the door, Biff was using his jacket to clean the floor and trying to conceal the fact that he was rubbing the urine-soaked garment on his hands and wrist while doing so. I could also see that his hair was slightly damp, and his eyebrows looked rather moist.

"Hey, Biff. We gotta get you into the restroom and wash up. You got piss all over yourself."

I brought him in to get cleaned up, and he scrubbed up pretty well, using plenty of soap and water. He even dunked his head under the faucet to wash his hair and face. Once he was done, I led him back to the interrogation room that the janitor had just sanitized.

"Hey, Biff. That crazy act ain't gonna work with me. You just tried to cover up evidence by pissing all over yourself."

"Yeah… well, who's smarter, me or you? That piss destroyed any evidence you thought you'd get with your special machine."

"Listen carefully, Biff…there ain't no machine."

It didn't take long before we learned that Biff came from power and money. This was the first time in twenty-eight years that I had a murder case go before a judge and have it decided on a plea deal all on the same day! No motions, no arguments, just a deal. I spent less than six hours in court on this case. He had been given a mental examination, charges were reduced, he pleaded guilty and got twelve years, which meant he might do up to six but could get out earlier!

The Nigerian family went along with the sentencing agreement and expressed their wishes to me that they hoped Biff would get the help he needed to get his head right. They were probably the most compassionate people I've ever dealt with as a cop. I could never see myself responding in that manner.

Chapter 40: Once a Predator, Always a Predator

He was like an animal incapable of generating his own body heat. This low-life thug required an outside stimulus to perform sexually, and in that department, he came up short again and again.

Charges: Multiple Counts of Home Invasion / Armed Robbery / Deviate Sexual Assault / Rape / Unlawful Restraint.

This was a follow-up investigation assigned to the Area Three Violent Crimes Detective Division. The case was initially assigned to another team of detectives who had doubts about its veracity, and I can see why.

On its face, it seemed to be too far-fetched and may have ended up in the suspended file with little time and effort devoted to the investigation. It did sound quite bizarre and seemed as though it may have been scripted by the victim's fiancé for any number of reasons, if one was to speculate. But as it turned out, the facts of the case were the facts of the case.

In a nutshell, a man and his fiancée were getting ready to leave their apartment for a night out. While still inside the apartment, the female heard a noise at the unlocked front door. When she checked on it, she was immediately set upon by a ski-masked thug with a gun in one hand and a hunting knife in the other. She took off screaming and ran to the rear of the apartment where her fiancé was. But he was caught off guard, and the thug had him at gunpoint.

He ordered them into a bedroom and tied up the man. He ordered the woman to disrobe and put on bikini bottoms and dance for him. While she was doing this, he had specific phrases he demanded she repeat. Once he was sexually aroused, he forced the woman to orally copulate him in front of her fiancé, after which he ordered the woman to mount her fiancé and have sexual intercourse with him. After his voyeuristic pleasures were met, he robbed the woman of her very expensive engagement ring and a large amount of money and took cash from her fiancé before fleeing.

Once the home invader was gone, they called an off-duty cop they knew who was a friend. He told them they needed to report the crime to the on-duty police.

I can see why the original detectives were skeptical. That whole scenario just sounded fishy. But it wasn't, and I knew it.

Unfortunately for the home invader (and this is why cops need to put in detail the exact language an offender uses), he used a particular phrase, word for word, during multiple home invasions where he had raped, robbed, and sodomized his victims twenty years earlier.

In those prior attacks, one of the things he was known to order his victims to repeat was the phrase: "Fuck me, Daddy. Fuck me" over and over before and during his sexual assaults.

I asked my sergeant, Frank Kajari, if I might be able to take over the case and do the follow-up, as I had a hunch. When he asked me if there was any reason I wanted to add to my workload, I explained that I "believed" the victims and remembered the culprit — a guy with a very short last name of four letters. He had been convicted of home invasions in the past. He lived in the Northwest suburbs at the time, and his name sounded like Mope (so that's the name I will use for him in this chapter). Sergeant Kajari agreed to give me the case, and the former detectives who had a boatload of other cases to investigate were happy to lighten their load a bit.

I was fortunate enough to be paired with one of the premier detectives in Area Three at the time. Detective Bobby "Downtown" Browne was a thirty-plus-year veteran who had worked a number of high-profile cases that all ended with a lot of really bad guys being put away for extended periods of time. Bob was closing in on retirement but always eager to work a good case, no matter how much legwork was involved. I was confident that with his guidance and the perseverance he had shown in seeing investigations through, we could put this case to rest.

Bob was sitting at the computer and closing out a recent arrest when I walked into the office that evening.

"Hey Bob, we got that weird home invasion case."

"Oh yeah...how'd we get that, I wonder?"

Unknown to me, Sergeant Kajari had already clued Bobby in on the reassignment.

Bobby had that all-knowing smirk that I'd seen a hundred times. He was waiting for me to make up some bullshit story on how it ended up in our lap, but instead, I told him the truth.

"I asked for it."

"All right. Let's do it, buddy."

With that nod from Bobby, the investigation was on. We looked for every possible way of identifying this thug by perusing the files in our office of previous arrestees and by talking to other cops who might have remembered the home invasions from twenty years earlier.

It wasn't good police work on our part that led us to come up with the bad guy's name. That information came from a district sergeant named Gene Richmond, who supplied it to us. Gene remembered the description of the guy and his M.O. from twenty years earlier. The name he gave us was Tim Mope.

Tim Mope was the offender who had brutally raped the girlfriend of a guy Gene went to high school with. As soon as I heard that name, I knew we were on the right track. Without Sergeant Richmond's timely input, this case would have been stalled, and the rapist would have certainly claimed more victims before we brought him to justice.

There are an untold number of potential victims in the city of Chicago who don't even know the debt of gratitude they owe to Sergeant Richmond for helping to bring this case to a successful conclusion.

To give you some background on this predator, we have to go back to the 1980s. During that time period, motels gave their guests a brass key to unlock and enter their rented rooms. If a guest failed to turn the key in when they left, they were billed five dollars extra. Most guests turned the keys in, but some with evil in their hearts did not. Tim Mope was one of them. The locks were never changed when keys went missing. Instead, the motel just made up a new key for the same old lock and gave it to unsuspecting guests. Apparently, guest security didn't seem to be a high priority.

One of the first reported attacks by Tim Mope at a motel happened after out-of-town visitors — a couple and their three daughters and a son — checked into room #204. The girls were aged sixteen, ten, and two, and the boy was five. The father put the chain lock on the door before they retired simply as an added safety measure.

At about 2:30 a.m., Tim Mope used his stolen key to unlock the door and then, using a homemade device, was able to circumvent the chain lock and gain entry to the room. He wore what would become his trademark rapist outfit — all-black clothing and a black knit ski mask. He was armed with both a hunting knife and a pistol. These would become his go-to weapons of forced compliance.

He gained entry to the room undetected. Once the door closed behind him, he'd announce his presence to the startled occupants.

"Get out of the bed now and keep your hands where I can see them."

The mother woke first and gasped. Her husband jumped out of bed and moved quickly toward the assailant until he saw the gun pointed at his face.

"Don't be a hero. No one will get hurt if you cooperate with me. I'm just here for the money."

The father told him where his cash was in his pants pocket, and the mother pointed to her purse. Tim Mope relieved them of their cash and the mother's jewelry. Little did they know they were all in for a nightmare that would last for several hours.

Mope woke up the girls. As you can imagine, they were shocked and confused by what they were seeing and hearing. A masked man with a big hunting knife and a gun was ordering their dad around, and their mother was crying.

"All right, I want to make sure no one calls the police or tries anything stupid, so I'm going to have to handcuff you."

Mope handcuffed the father, wrapped duct tape around his ankles, and ordered him and the ten and two-year-old daughters to sit in the bathtub.

Mope dropped his pants to the floor and ordered the mother of four to orally copulate him in front of the family.

"Suck my dick."

The father spoke up, demanding that Mope leave the room and leave his wife alone.

"Shut up, big man. You had your chance before I cuffed you up. Open your mouth again, and I'm gonna stab someone you love."

In fear for the safety of her loved ones, his wife complied with Mope's demand.

"Now I got to have some of that pussy and make it good for me."

After raping the woman vaginally, he attempted to have anal intercourse, but the victim was able to dissuade him.

Mope then moved on to the sixteen-year-old and had her put on a negligee and model it for him.

"Do not touch my daughter," came shouts from both the mother and father.

"That's it. I'm cutting someone's throat now."

The daughter pleaded with her parents to be quiet. She didn't want to see them hurt and said she would do it.

"Listen to your daughter. She's smarter than both of you. No one will get hurt if I get what I came for. Now, honey, I want you to dance for me and make it sexy."

He fondled every part of her body as the terrified teen moved on his command. Mope enjoyed seeing the fear in her eyes. She was embarrassed beyond words as her helpless family looked on.

"That's good. You like when I touch you, don't you? Now say, 'Fuck me, Daddy, fuck me."

"Mom, can I swear?"

Her mom nodded.

The teen complied with his perverted request, and then he vaginally raped her.

He fled the room after putting this family through three hours of hell. Fortunately, the little boy slept through all of it.

Mope wasn't done. On another night, a young couple checked into a different room. Apparently, Mope had stayed in this room too and kept the key. His M.O. was the same. He raped the female and robbed the two of cash and jewelry.

The couple was sound asleep in the king-sized bed when he crept in. They only woke up when he turned on the lights and yelled "Surprise" while pointing his gun with one hand and holding the knife in the other. He was wearing his rape outfit and ready for action.

"No one will get hurt if you give me enough money."

The male spoke first. "All my money is in my pocket over there."

"That's a good start, but I'm going to need more than that, or someone's going to die in here tonight. How about you, honey?"

"I've got two dollars in my purse and some change in that sweater pocket on the chair."

"Change? Fuckin' change?"

"I'm sorry, but it's all I got. I didn't know we were gonna be robbed tonight."

"Oh, that's cute, that's real cute. Put some underwear on, and then tell your boyfriend to turn on his stomach. I want you to put these handcuffs on him behind his back and do it tight, or I'll do it, and it won't be fuckin' pretty."

The woman did as she was ordered.

"Okay, now it's my turn to have some fun with you." Mope put the man in the bathroom. "What's your name, boyfriend?"

"Kevin."

"Okay, Kevin. Is it okay if your girlfriend sucks me off a little bit while you watch?"

"Hey man, you got our money. Just go. We won't tell the cops or anyone. Just let us be."

"Who the fuck do you think is in charge here, Kevin? This is my power trip."

"You're in charge. I'm just asking if you could go and leave us alone."

"Sure. When I'm done. You, what's your name, honey?"

"Nancy."

"Okay, Nancy, start dancing for me, and I want to see some sexy moves. Act like your dancing for Kevin, who's laying over there like a big pussy and didn't defend you like I would have if you were my girl and some asshole came in on us."

Nancy did her best to comply with the demands her attacker made. Mope was really getting into it.

"Now say, 'Fuck me, Daddy, fuck me,' and keep saying it until I'm all the way inside of you."

The woman screamed in pain, and Mope loved hearing her cry. He spent the next three hours raping and assaulting the young woman in every deviate way imaginable.

"All right, I'm leaving you, so don't report this to the cops, or I will find out and come back and kill you. I have your driver's licenses, and I know where you both live."

Tim Mope fled.

Mope struck again a few nights later at another motel where he had stolen another key. He watched the young couple when they crossed the street and went to the motel. *How good can this be?* he thought. He had the key to that very room. He took a seat by the window to see if the room would be occupied or not.

They had been drinking in the same bar as he was. Mope set eyes on her even before he learned that they would be his next victims. She was attractive and definitely well built. The guy he sized up as an average Joe who would crumble at the sight of the armed masked man bursting into the room uninvited.

Mope had a few more drinks and waited for the lights in the room to go off. He'd give it another hour or so and then hit them.

When the bar closed down for the night, he made his move. It was safe to assume they were in bed. Only this time, Mope would be surprised. He encountered a real man this time, who was not about to be a victim or allow his woman to be hurt.

It was 2:20 a.m. when the female heard the door open. She quickly alerted her boyfriend, who jumped out of bed. Tim Mope had already gotten into the room, and even though he had his gun and knife in hand, the man fought valiantly. He beat Mope about the face and head and knocked him out of the room with the aid of his girlfriend, who had opened the door. Mope fled like the coward he is.

The motel caper must have put a scare into Mope, so he changed his M.O. a bit. Now he chose to hit a house rather than a motel room.

A woman and her daughter sat in the kitchen by the rear door and waited for the father to return from work. It was almost midnight when they heard Dad coming up the steps, and the daughter opened the door to greet him.

It wasn't Dad. It was Tim Mope in a ski mask, armed as usual with a gun and a large hunting knife. He quickly tied up the mother and had her watch as he ordered her seventeen-year-old daughter to orally copulate him. She also had to repeat the phrases that were his trademark.

He took cash and jewelry from the home and was about to rape the girl when he heard someone coming to the door. It was Dad, but Dad was too late. Mope took off. Dad ran out the front door looking for him, but Mope disappeared into the night.

Tim Mope was involved in several other robberies and sexual assaults, and you get the idea of how he operated. He was eventually caught and made a plea deal for thirty years in the penitentiary. Of course, in Illinois, that never means you're actually going to do thirty years. Mope did nineteen before being paroled; it didn't take long for him to resume his old ways. His biggest mistake was…"Fuck me, Daddy, fuck me."

The current home invasion rape robberies that Bobby and I were working on were in full swing. A rape robbery crime pattern had been distributed to all police officers in the affected area.

Our case started on a bitterly cold and snowy night in January at about 6:30 p.m., perfect for this type of crime. Few people were out and about, so witnesses were not in abundance; therefore, suspicious person calls were at a minimum. Everyone was hunkered down inside warm homes with shades drawn and not paying much, if any, attention to the outside world.

This was an ideal time for our predator to roam through the neighborhood in his beat-up brown Thunderbird. He was looking for any signs of life.

Tim Mope was an experienced hunter of the innocent and was looking for a tell-tale sign that would give him pause. He liked to pounce on his victims at vulnerable moments.

Remember, it was bitterly cold outside. Most people who braved this kind of weather would run out and start their cars but make the mistake of not locking their front doors, knowing they were going to run right back inside and wait until their car warmed up. At least, that was my way of thinking if I were looking to home invade someone. As it turned out, Mope and I thought alike as our investigation would disclose.

The first couple did exactly that. Stan started his car and was waiting until it was warm before he and Basia left. This young Polish couple was engaged to be married in June. They both had good jobs and looked forward to a great future together.

Stan spent a small fortune on the brilliant diamond stone set in a platinum setting and was proud that he was in a position to lavish his sweetheart with such a beautiful engagement ring. He spent nearly twenty thousand dollars on this piece of jewelry.

As the couple got ready to leave, Stan went to retrieve his jacket and was back by the rear bedroom closet. Basia was already dressed and ready to go. She was waiting at the unlocked front door when she heard a rattling sound. That's when she looked down to see the doorknob turning. She opened the door to see who was there.

It was Tim Mope in a black ski mask, pointing a gun at her. She screamed and took off running back to her fiancé. But it was too late. Before her fiancé could make a move, Tim Mope had joined them. Threatening Stan with his pistol in one hand and swinging the hunting knife at them with the other, he let them know he meant business.

"Both of you get down on the bed, face down! I'm not afraid to use these if I have to. I've killed before."

In his rush to get inside the residence, Mope forgot to bring his handcuffs and tape, so he rummaged around looking for something to tie them up with.

"What are your names?"

"I'm Stan, and this is my fiancée Basia."

"Okay, I'm gonna tie you up, so don't do anything stupid, Stan, and no one will get hurt. I'm just looking for money."

He tied Stan's hands behind his back with a shoelace and then proceeded to blindfold Basia with a long black sock and tied her hands behind her back with a bra. He pulled Stan's pants down around his ankles while on the bed to immobilize his legs.

"Where's the money, and don't lie to me. If I find any money you didn't tell me about, I'll kill ya's."

"I have a bag with some money in the sock drawer and some more under the bar."

Mope found the cash quickly, and it was a substantial amount.

"Not bad, not bad ...how much is here, Stan?"

"Twenty-five hundred bucks."

"Yeah, good, but I'm gonna need more than that."

"I have a Rolex, and she's got a Cartier watch. They're worth about six thousand, and there's some other jewelry worth about a thousand up on the dresser behind the picture frame."

"Okay, things are looking better for you two, but I want to look around, so you two have to keep busy, so I know you're not gonna try anything stupid."

"We won't try anything. Just take the money and jewelry and go."

"That's not the way I operate, Stan! This is my fuckin' power trip, not yours."

Basia started to say something but was cut off...

"Shut up, Basia. I'm in charge here. Now I'm gonna untie your hands and take your gag off. Don't scream and don't try anything stupid, or I'll ram this blade through you... got it?"

"Yes."

Once he freed her bindings and gag, he ordered her to pull Stan's underwear down and roll him over so that he was face up.

"Now get naked, Basia, and while you're at it, give me that ring on your finger."

Basia hesitated and looked at Stan. That's when Mope gave her a hard slap across the face.

"Now!"

She slipped the ring off her finger and handed it to Mope, who put it inside the coin pocket of his black jeans.

"Now, get naked and do everything I say if you want to live through the night."

Basia was nearly out of her head with fear and disbelief when he gave his next command.

"I want you to get on top of Stan and start fucking him while I watch."

"What???"

"Get on top of him and face me while you fuck him!"

Basia mounted Stan and tried to have intercourse as ordered, but the high-stress situation made the act impossible for Stan to participate.

"You're not fucking him good enough. Besides that, Stan's got a small dick, doesn't he? Look at my dick. I have a big one, don't I?"

"Yes."

"That's cuz it's fourteen inches long." It in fact was that long in a flaccid state, and was a corroborating piece of evidence in his arrest.

Mope rummaged around in her dresser drawers before he came across the victim's bikini bottoms.

"Here, put these on, and I want you to dance for me and make sure you do a sexy dance."

Basia, in fear of her life and that of her her fiancé did as she was instructed.

"That's good. Now say, 'Fuck me, Daddy, fuck me' while you dance."

Basia complied with his orders.

"Hey, Stan. You don't mind if your girl sucks me a little, do ya?"

"You have the gun. Just please leave us. We gave you all we got to give. Leave her alone, man."

"I told you, I give the fuckin' orders here! Now, come here, Basia. Suck my dick and squeeze my balls real hard. While you do it, tell me how much you love doing it."

Basia complied but stopped after about five minutes.

"What did you stop for bitch?"

"I'm sorry, but my mouth is dry. I'm gonna have a panic attack. I need to get some water."

"All right, let's go in the kitchen."

That was probably the best move of the night. When Basia got the water, she had a plan. Hopefully, she could get him to take a drink, too, and see more of his face.

"You must be thirsty too." She poured him a glass of water and handed it to him. It worked —he lifted his mask and took a big gulp. Basia memorized everything she could about the exposed part of his face, especially the big gap between his front teeth.

"Kiss me, Basia, and don't kiss me like I'm your brother. Kiss me like I'm your lover."

Basia complied, and he groped her everywhere and then some. He inserted a leather gloved hand into her vagina several times, and it was terribly painful, but she refused to show weakness to this pervert.

"Okay, I'm done here. Don't call anyone for five minutes after I leave. If you do, I'll send my brother in, and he's not as nice as me. He's killed four people."

Tim Mope left the apartment, and Basia and Stan remained motionless in the bedroom. They were doing exactly what Mope ordered them to do.

They watched the clock, and when three minutes had passed, the front door flew open again, and Mope ran into the bedroom with the gun in hand.

"Very good. That was a test, and you listened, so you will live tonight."

Tim Mope fled for real this time.

***

Bobby was busy at the computer again when I came in. He held up one hand to stop me from walking past him while he continued typing with the other hand. Apparently, he had some good news to share, and I was eager to hear it. He stopped a few seconds later and swiveled toward me in his chair.

"Hey Frank, I just checked out our guy, Mope. He's out on parole."

"Did we find out who his parole officer is?"

Bobby gave me his standard-issue sly smile. "Absolutely, buddy. I have an address on this asshole too."

But before we could get out the door, Sergeant Kajari handed me a second home invasion in the same neighborhood.

"Here, Goff, this looks like it could be our boy. But this time, he invaded a guy that lives alone."

"He buggered a dude?"

"Well, if it's our guy, he did do nineteen years in the pen, so that wouldn't be unusual. But to answer your question, no, he just robbed him. He's a young guy, so Mope might have thought there was a woman to be had in the apartment."

Bob and I poured over the report and came to the same conclusion. This was our guy, and he wasn't going to stop on his own. He enjoyed what he did and needed to be caught. We hoped we could catch him in the act of home invading someone while dressed in his rape outfit and armed with his weapons of choice. But that was not to be.

The facts of the case involving this latest home invasion didn't turn out the way, so many others had in the past. However, it did start the same way. This time, the victim was a male who had gone out to warm up his car and was in the process of entering his apartment. Unbeknownst to him, he had company coming up right behind him. When the victim pushed the rear door of his ground-level unit open, there was Mope, wearing his standard-issue home invasion outfit and pointing a gun in the victim's face.

This victim would react a little bit differently than most of the others. #Tony Woods was a fighter and immediately grabbed for the gun, but Mope pulled it back just in time.

"You motherfucker, don't try that again, or I'll kill you. I'm an addict with nothing to lose. I just want money for drugs."

"Okay, I've got some money in my pocket. Take it."

"Not until I'm sure you won't try to fight me again. Lay down on the floor."

Tony laid down, and Mope duct-taped his hands behind him and bound his feet. Personally, I can never understand complying with that demand, but most victims do.

Mope pillaged the apartment, taking more cash and even emptying a change jar into his black canvas bag. Then he pressed the hunting knife to Tony's throat.

"Okay, that looks like everything. Now, where are your porno tapes? Don't lie to me cuz I know you have some."

"I do. They're in the box in the closet."

Mope stuffed them into his canvas bag. The problem was, Mope never just wanted to rob folks. He was always looking for some sexual action and tonight was no different.

"Who lives upstairs?"

"Two women."

"I know you have their phone number, so call them. Get them down here."

He cut the tape from Tony's hands and gave him back his cell phone.

Tony made the call and let it ring until it went to voice mail.

"No answer. They probably went out."

"No good, Tony. Try them again, and you better hope they answer cuz I need an audience, and I'm horny."

Tony redialed the number, and fortunately for the intended victims, it went to voicemail a second time.

"Well, I'm gonna cut you a break. At least you tried to get the bitches down here. Since I'm not gonna kill you, don't call the police because if you do, I'll know about it and come back to kill you. My girlfriend's brother is a police dispatcher, and I listen to him every night on the scanner I have in my car."

Tim Mope fled into the darkness, porno tapes in tow.

It was a big break for us and a testament to what cops can do working together. Cops have a lot of data from past cases and experiences stored up in their heads. Gene Richmond is an example of that and was able to provide us with the name we needed. From there, Bob and I could connect the dots.

We set out to snatch him up before he could victimize any more innocents. We went to the apartment building at 869 Buena and up to the fifth floor. His name was on a piece of tape on the door, so that made verification easy.

Convicted sexual predators are not supposed to be in possession of pornographic materials, and I could see the flickering of the television accompanied by what sounded like porn. I laid on the floor to hear better from the opening at the bottom of his door. After about fifteen minutes, I heard the phrase "Fuck me, Daddy, fuck me" several times. I knew we had the right guy. It must have been the part of the tape that he fantasized about because he rewound it and played it back at least six times.

I wrote up an affidavit for two search warrants for Mope's apartment and his Thunderbird. It's good to have connections. Lieutenant

Nick Nickeas had a judge he knew sign off on the warrant at 3 a.m., and I had a state's attorney who approved the warrants without any changes. Along with our team of detectives, we hit the apartment.

Mope's unit was wallpapered with porno. Everywhere you looked, it was evident. Prominently laid out in the order of size were three penis pumps. I guess that explains his fourteen-inch trouser mouse.

We were able to recover almost all of the victim's property in both of the latest home invasions, and it was identified by all of them and returned.

The main item we were looking for was not there. That was the $20,000 engagement ring.

I searched Mope's vehicle and came up with the weapons used to commit the crimes. They were pretty well concealed in the trunk and not something officers would find on a normal search of the car. Mope was placed under arrest and transported into Area Three Detective Division for processing.

Lieutenant Nick Nickeas was our boss in the violent crimes unit at the time. Besides being a dapper dresser, he was a well-seasoned, smart, and tenacious detective in his own right. So we were in good hands as we worked our way through the investigation. In other words, Nickeas didn't pull any punches and let his guys do their jobs but was hands-on along the way to make sure that everything went by the book.

Once I had Mope in the interrogation room, it was clear to him that we got him. He wasn't going anywhere, and we both knew it. So I started working him. It's always been a mystery to me when I hear people say that a hardened criminal will never cooperate, especially if they've done some serious hard time. That's bullshit. Everyone will talk if they "think" it's in their best interest. Mope was no different; it just took me a little extra time.

I laid some things out that I knew or suspected he had done and how and why he did it that way.

He smirked and shook his head. "You don't know shit, detective. You're just guessing."

"You're right. I am guessing, but I'm guessing right. Now it's time we dig into your sins."

Without going into all the details, he finally broke.

"Hey, Detective Goff…if I tell you where the ring is, that's like admitting guilt."

"So? We both know you're guilty, so what's the big deal? You're going down for these crimes, and nothing is gonna change that. I think what would be nice, that is if you've got a spark of decency in you, and I think you do, is to at least give the girl back her engagement ring setting. I know you probably pawned or sold the stone, but the setting was an heirloom from her great-grandmother to her grandmother to her mom, and now to her (I made that up). She wants to keep it in the family and pass it on to her daughter someday. It's not all that valuable, so what do you say? Can you make that happen for her after all you put her through? She doesn't even care about the stone; she just wants the setting."

I knew we'd get the stone because we recovered some indicators as to where it might have gone. The setting was just another nail in the coffin.

"Let me think about it."

A lineup was held, and all the victims positively identified Mope. I was a bit worried when I first saw the volunteers for the lineup. One guy looked like he could be our guy's twin brother and the others were almost as close.

Once I led Mope back to the interrogation room, he asked what every guilty party asks.

"How did the lineup go?"

"Real good, real good… I mean for us. Real bad for you. Everyone identified you."

"How could that be? I was wearing a mask."

Bingo! Another nail in the coffin and soon to be included in my report. Sometimes I'm shocked at how easy it is to get guys to walk into the trap we set for them, and he just did.

"Not only did they identify you, they all corroborated it with voice identification. You are our guy, and you will be charged."

"I'm fucked…they'll probably give me another thirty years."

"I don't know about that, but what I do know is that it would be a gracious thing on your part if you would tell us where the lady's setting is so we can get it back to her. In fact, if you do that little thing for her, I'm willing to tell her that you're very remorseful and even broken-hearted for the evil shit you did to her. I'll even go one step further and tell her it was your idea to get it back in her hands again, not mine. Does that sound good to you?"

"I've been thinking about it, Goff. Get your boss in here with the prosecutor."

Lieutenant Nickeas and the prosecutor met with Mope in the interrogation room. He relayed to all involved and in my presence that the stone had been sold and that the setting was in the coin pocket of his jeans, rolled up in the dirty clothes hamper in his apartment. He signed a consent to search, and the ring was recovered by two of our best detectives, Magnine and #Bronko.

Thanks to the tenacious follow-up investigation conducted by Detective Cheryl Bronko, the expensive diamond that had been removed from the setting was located in New York City, where the current owner of the stone had paid thousands of dollars for it. Detective Bronko not only convinced the new owner of the diamond to return it to the victim but to do it at no cost to the victim. On top of that, she had it overnighted back to Chicago and into the hands of our victim, where the victim positively identified the stone. Bronko is one helluva detective.

Thankfully for all involved, with the exception of the guilty party, the case was handed over to Cook County's top prosecutor, #Angelique Peroni. Miss Peroni had come to interview me and asked if I'd be willing to testify in this matter even though I had been retired for a couple of years. The answer was an easy yes. There was no way in the world that I was not going to see justice done for the victims.

First off, I knew it would be a well-orchestrated prosecution under her tutelage, as ASA Peroni knew the facts of the case better than I did. Not a single detail was overlooked, and she spent considerable time prepping me for what was to become a battle of wits and legalese peppered with motions to suppress and defense attorney shenanigans. In the end, all motions were denied, and the case went to trial.

Enter Judge Kenneth Wadas. He would hear the case at a jury trial and ultimately sentence Tim Mope when he was found guilty as charged in the indictments.

It's always an honor to appear before this judge. Unlike some of the others I've mentioned, his courtroom was run like a well-oiled machine, which probably stemmed from his military background during the war in Vietnam. Judge Wadas is a former Captain in the Marine Corps who served honorably from 1968 to1972. While serving, he was a rifle platoon commander and weapons platoon commander with the 1st Marine Division and an intelligence officer 1st MP Bn Danang. In other words, he was no weak-in-the-knees judge when it came to the battlefield or the courtroom. Putting bad guys away when the facts called for it is an awesome responsibility, and he was at the top of the food chain when it came to that. If more judges were like Ken Wadas, the streets of Chicago would be a lot safer. The repeat offenders who run wild, shedding blood and leaving a path of destruction, would cease to exist.

Tim Mope was found guilty, and Judge Wadas sentenced him to three life terms to be served consecutively plus sixty years. In other words, Mope will die where he belongs, in prison.

Side Note: Mope was on home monitoring when these attacks occurred but had requested personal time away from his residence. That facilitated his ability to go out and commit these violent acts. Even though he was granted the time away from home and violated his curfew on each of these assaults, no action was taken to address the violation. If it had, maybe the victims would have been spared the trauma forced upon them by a career criminal.

Though Bob Browne and I received most of the credit for bringing this case to a successful conclusion, we didn't do it alone. There were other detectives involved in the execution of the search warrant, the consent to search, and the lineup that followed. Some did not want their names used, and others preferred an alias, as in the case of Cheryl Bronko. I have been unable to get ahold of the now-retired detectives to obtain permission to use their names in this chapter. I am thankful for all that they contributed to this investigation. You guys know who you are.

Chapter 41: Blue Man

I'm sure many of you have heard of the "Blue Man Group," a very well put together, long-running live theater show. It's been a highly rated show by thousands of folks who have attended one of its sold-out performances.

That's not what I'm referring to in this recollection of the events at one of the outdoor fests held in Chicago.

Due to the massive numbers of people who frequent these types of venues, restrooms are at a premium, and therefore port-a-potties are set up to accommodate the folks.

On this particular summer day, a young lady entered one to use the facility and noticed movement below. Upon closer inspection, she realized this wasn't part of the normal toilet functioning process. It was, in fact, "Blue Man," a very small-framed guy known for climbing into the well of these toilets at busy events and enjoying the many views, smells, and sensation of being covered in blue disinfectant, among other toxic creations.

Fortunately, we were not tasked with removing him from the toilet, and neither were the first officers she ran to. That was a job we all thought was perfectly suited for the Chicago Fire Department, who, upon arrival, said, "Not this asshole again." They readied a fire hose to blast him, and that they did with extreme pleasure, I can assure you. He was arrested and charged accordingly. It was his third reported violation.

Chapter 42: Profiling

You always hear about cops "profiling" and how it's discriminatory, evil, and just plain wrong. The problem is that those who complain about it haven't shared the life experiences of a cop on the street.

Let me give you an example of one of my many profile cases and demonstrate how it is an effective approach to combatting crime in the real world. Yes, I profiled and I think after you read this chapter you will see why it can be an effective tool for the street cop.

On a cool Chicago afternoon, I thought I'd take the scenic route to get to a witness's place of employment not far from Grant Park. A light rain had settled over the city and kept most people from enjoying the serenity of the park, but there were still those who were undeterred here and there. That's when I noticed the man outside the women's public restroom, perhaps waiting for his significant other or maybe his daughter.

I don't know why, but thoughts of the murderous fiend from the 70s flashed through my mind, and I thought of the five women he raped, murdered, and cannibalized after getting hyped up watching porn at the local peep shows.

I decided to circle back and watch this guy for a while and did so for about twenty-five minutes. *Maybe he's a 'flasher'* was my first thought, as he was wearing a knee-length tan trench coat, which seemed to be the uniform of the day for those perverts so inclined. Here I am, engaging in a prohibited behavior. I was profiling … "gender profiling" this man.

During the timeframe, I mentioned I hadn't observed any women go in or out of the restroom, and it was time to move on before my witness left work for the day. But before I left, I needed to satisfy my curiosity, so I conducted a street stop on this suspicious male. It went like this.

"Good afternoon, sir. I'm detective Goff. I saw you standing here in the rain and was wondering if everything's all right?"

"I'm just waiting on my wife. She's in the restroom."

"Just for my safety while we're talking, remove your hands from your pockets."

He did so without question. In his right coat pocket, I saw the point of an inverted steak knife. I removed it for my own protection, and his demeanor went from cooperative to that "fight or flight" stance I've experienced so many times during my career.

"Turn around, face the wall and put your hands on top of your head."

There was slight resistance that ended when I flattened him against the wall rather abruptly and cuffed him. A further pat-down revealed a .380 in his pants pocket.

I banged on the restroom door and asked him his wife's name. He remained mute. I walked my prisoner into the restroom after calling out several times. We were the only two in there.

The question of "Where's your wife?" was met with silence. A quick name check revealed he had a warrant out for a criminal sexual assault case in Chicago, and another one was for a bond forfeiture for another criminal sexual assault from Kane County Illinois.

When I went to court, I testified to the events that led up to the arrest, and the thug was convicted for the weapons violations and went on to stand trial for the sex cases.

Fortunately, the offender in this case was as white as I am. Otherwise, I'm absolutely positive that race, as it relates to profiling, would have made its way into the conversation even though race had no bearing on why I made the stop. But "profiling" did play a major role, and I fully admit to it. Had I observed a female standing outside the restroom, I wouldn't have given it a second thought. I would have never thought back to the brave man holding his baby boy while his wife used that restroom and hearing a horrific scream before a man bolted from the restroom with a bloody knife in the 70s. The victim's husband tackled and held the culprit for the police, not knowing his own wife had been murdered. Thanks to his bravery and quick action, a thug responsible for at least five murders was removed from the streets.

Good cops criminally profile, and it's based on years of experience. Can race play a role? You tell me.

If I had been a cop on patrol in the racially charged South and saw a white man place a box under the steps of a black church in Birmingham, Alabama, and walk away, I would have immediately stopped him and conducted an investigation. That form of profiling would have been based on race and saved the lives of four little black girls who were later blown up by the bomb in that box. By the same token, if I saw a black man do it, I honestly wouldn't have thought much of it. I would have probably thought he was leaving a package for one of the congregants, and I would have kept rolling.

In today's world, when I see white folks lining up in an alleyway in a black neighborhood, I know without a doubt they are there to buy drugs. So profiling can play a role if it's based on your years of experience as a cop on the streets.

Do all cops profile? No! But experience tells me the ones who do, take more criminals off the streets and save more lives than those who don't. End of story.

ACKNOWLEDGMENTS

First to my wife, Sharon Rose, and my family who have been with me through the best of times and the worst of times and always stood tall. My youngest son Leif is carrying my Detective Star now and, as of this writing, works homicide in Chicago. I'm hoping none of my six grandsons or my granddaughter embark on a career path in police work. I will do everything in the world to discourage that. Police work can be very rewarding, and you can really impact the lives of people and save some lives in the course of your employment. Still, the non-stop BS cops face today makes me wonder why anyone would jeopardize their life and financial stability pursuing a career that has so little support from those who need it most.

I salute the cops who are still doing the job and wish them and their families all the best. Remember to always "watch their hands."

ABOUT THE AUTHOR

Frank Goff began working with the Chicago Police Department in 1970 at the age of eighteen and retired in 2002. He also worked for the Highwood, Illinois Police Department under a great Chief named Dave Wentz. Following that, he worked corporate security and private investigations for CSI in Roselle Illinois. In 2011, he authored The Guardian, his first true-crime novel, followed by Chicago Crime Story in 2022. Currently, he is a trainer for the highly successful "Street Crimes Program" created by retired Gang Crimes Specialist Pat McCarthy.

Made in the USA
Middletown, DE
26 February 2025